WHITE-HOT HACK

A Kate and Ian novel #2

TRACEY GARVIS GRAVES

"My primary goal of hacking was the intellectual curiosity, the seduction of adventure." Kevin Mitnick

"We love because it's the only true adventure." Nikki Giovanni

PROLOGUE

THE MAN IN THE BUSINESS suit looked up from his phone when the tall blonde pushed through the glass doors of the office building, the rapid clicking of her high heels reverberating through the lobby as she hurried toward the receptionist.

She hoisted her shoulder bag a little higher and set a cup of coffee and sheet of paper on the counter. "I have a ten o'clock interview with Christopher Hill. I'm so sorry I'm late. There was an accident on the Beltway." She sounded panicked and slightly out of breath.

He watched her with interest from his seat directly across from the reception desk. Arriving thirty minutes early for his appointment had left him with a severe case of boredom, and he welcomed the distraction.

"Please have a seat. I'll let Mr. Hill know you're here," the receptionist said.

As the woman turned to go, her elbow hit the coffee cup. Though they both reacted, neither she nor the receptionist moved fast enough to catch it before it spilled. There wasn't enough coffee left in the cup to make a truly embarrassing mess, but it was enough to ruin the piece of paper lying on the counter.

"You have *got* to be kidding me," the woman said, her voice carrying more than a trace of hopeless exasperation. She pulled a tissue out of her bag and dabbed at the liquid, then held up the stained document. "That was my last copy."

"Résumé?" the receptionist asked. She looked old enough to be the woman's mother, and her expression was kind and empathetic.

The woman blew out a breath and raised her fingers to her temple as if she felt the beginning of a headache. "Yes."

He couldn't help but feel sorry for her.

"Hold on a minute," the woman said, sounding hopeful. She rooted around in her bag again, and when she withdrew her hand, she waved a USB drive triumphantly in the air. "I have the document saved on this. Could you please print me another copy? I hate not having my employment information at my fingertips, and I really need to nail this interview, especially since I'm late."

The receptionist hesitated as if she seemed a bit uncomfortable with the request. But before she could protest, the woman leaned over the counter and pressed the USB drive into her palm. Then she pointed to a picture on the desk. "Whose baby is that? I've never seen such a beautiful child. He could model for baby-food ads." She picked up the silver frame and took a closer look.

A look of pride spread across the receptionist's face. "That's my grandson. My daughter-in-law entered that picture in a contest. We haven't heard anything yet."

The woman leaned against the counter but did not make eye contact, keeping her focus on the picture instead. "He's a shoo-in to win. Those dimples are to die for." She sighed and mustered a faint smile. "It's amazing how a picture of a baby can brighten your day, especially when it's going so badly."

The receptionist waited, the USB drive held awkwardly in her hand, but finally she inserted it into her computer, and moments later the printer whirred to life and spit out a piece of paper.

"You're a lifesaver," the woman said, holding out her hand for the résumé and tucking the USB drive safely back into her bag.

"It's no problem. If you'll take a seat, I'll let Mr. Hill know you're here."

"Thank you."

The woman sat down next to him, giving him a nod and a smile. She held the résumé loosely, careful not to crease it, and waited patiently.

The receptionist looked worried when she hung up the phone. "Miss? I'm sorry. Mr. Hill is not actually in the office today."

The woman rose and walked toward the reception desk. "I don't understand." She sounded utterly defeated.

"His secretary said he took the day off. There aren't any appointments on his calendar."

She seemed to deflate. "Well, I guess I don't have to be embarrassed about showing up late. The only thing more embarrassing than showing up late is showing up on the wrong day. I'll double-check my notes. I must have written it down wrong. Thank you. You've been more than kind. I hope your grandson wins the contest."

He caught a glimpse of the woman's pink cheeks as she turned to go, and she left the building as quickly as she'd entered it.

He put away his phone and approached the desk, giving the receptionist a thousand-watt smile. "I'm sorry. I've been called away unexpectedly and won't be able to stay for my meeting with Mr. Matthews."

She smiled back at him. "Would you like me to deliver a message?"

He handed her a white card with the word SUCCEDO on the front in raised black lettering. "Please see that he receives this as soon as possible, and tell him I'll be available by phone after two p.m. He has my number."

The man left the building and headed for the parking garage to his left. The temperature was still in the high fifties and quite mild for early November, but the colder weather he loathed would arrive all too soon.

The woman who was having a colossally bad day was up ahead, walking a little slower now. He followed her into the garage and quickened his stride, catching up to her on the landing of the stairwell that connected the first and second levels. When he was close enough to reach out and touch her, she turned around and they slapped their palms together in a victorious high five. Ian pulled Kate into his arms and squeezed her tight.

"Too smooth," she said, smiling and running the back of her hand along his clean-shaven cheek. He lowered his mouth to hers, and her bag slipped off her shoulder and landed on the concrete floor.

"I thought we weren't going to break cover until we were in the car," she said between kisses.

"I couldn't wait that long, sweetness," he murmured against her mouth. "You know delayed gratification isn't really my thing."

She pulled back and looked up at him, her expression hopeful. "How did I do?"

"You were incredible. I'm so proud of you."

"Something came over me when the receptionist stuck that flash drive into her computer."

"That something was the thrill of penetration. You'll be chasing it from now on."

"I felt like such a—"

"Bad girl?"

"I was going to say hacker."

"I like bad girl better."

"I bet you do. No wonder you like manipulating people so much. It's just so…"

"The word you're looking for is arousing."

"Yes. That's it exactly."

She kissed him and ran her fingers through his hair, which he hadn't cut since the wedding. Why bother? Kate liked it long. He hooked her leg around his hip, causing the skirt of her business suit to ride up, and deepened the kiss because there were few things he enjoyed more than kissing his wife. When he finally pulled away, he reached for her hand and led her up the stairs.

"There are so many explicit thoughts running through my head about what I'd like to do to you in this stairwell, but we should probably be going. I've found that after infecting a network with that much malware, it's never a bad idea to be on your way."

The Escalade had been swapped out for a white Lincoln Navigator on their way back from Roanoke Island, and Ian unlocked the car and opened Kate's door.

"Now what?" she asked as he slid behind the wheel and headed for the exit.

He yanked on his tie to loosen it. "Now comes the part when I get to explain to the client that the reason the IT department is losing its mind is because my partner did, in fact, successfully breach the network." He glanced over at Kate and grinned. "This is the part of penetration testing I really enjoy."

She laughed. "I bet you do."

"I'd love to tell him the beautiful woman in the lobby was my wife and that it was her very first assignment, but I'll refrain from bragging." As proud as he was of Kate, the last thing he wanted to do was draw attention to her, and he certainly didn't need word getting around about a husband-and-wife hacking team.

"Did the client think we wouldn't be able to do it?"

"He was confident their computer systems were secure, and they are. Not secure enough to keep *me* out, but fairly difficult for others. When I write my report, I'll point out their vulnerabilities and show him what I'm going to do to fix them. But what so many business owners fail to recognize is that one of the biggest threats to their cybersecurity is not their technology. It's their employees. Humans are incredibly susceptible to manipulation. There's a reason hackers consider the USB ruse an oldie but goodie: it almost always works. That receptionist didn't really want to stick your flash drive into her computer, but she wanted to help *you,* so she talked herself out of saying no. She probably rationalized that someone as nice as you, someone who was having a bad day but who'd still taken the time to compliment her grandchild, couldn't possibly be there to do any harm."

"How bad was the malware?"

"It's the real thing—I designed it myself. A penetration test isn't going to be as effective if it doesn't mirror an attack on the network. Using live malware will send them scrambling, but it's nothing their IT department can't handle. It's good practice for them because if it actually happens someday, they'll know what to do."

"The receptionist won't lose her job or anything, will she? She was so nice to me."

"No, we're not trying to get anyone in trouble. The reason the client hired us is so we can show them the ways in which a malicious hacker might take advantage of their employees so they can better prepare them. That receptionist will be the most secure person in the whole organization after this."

"That's true. No one is ever getting past her again."

Ian looked over at Kate and grinned. "Was the baby really that cute?"

"Supercute. He probably *will* win."

"Good for him."

"I got lucky today. That was pretty much the ideal scenario."

"Don't sell yourself short. You're much better at this than I was when I started, and you seem to enjoy it more than I ever did."

"I loved it, but I know it won't always be that easy."

"That's why we practice." He and Kate had rehearsed dozens of possible scenarios so she'd be prepared no matter what obstacles she encountered.

She reached over the console and laid her hand on his inner thigh. "When we get home, I am going to climb you like a *tree*. You know that, right?"

He pressed down slightly on the gas pedal and smiled. "Sweetness, there was a reason I told the client I wouldn't be available until after two. And even then, I'm not totally sure we'll be done."

CHAPTER ONE

Two months earlier

THE HOUSE WAS EASILY TEN thousand square feet. Two winding staircases flanked the entryway on either side, and beyond them was a dining room with a table large enough to seat twelve and a formal living room that was three times larger than Ian's entire apartment in Minneapolis.

"Isn't it beautiful?" their Realtor, Linda, asked as she led them on a tour of the first floor. The ceilings were so high her voice echoed.

"It's something," Ian said.

When they reached the cavernous kitchen, Kate's eyes widened. She opened her mouth as if she were about to speak and then closed it.

"Look at her," Linda said, gushing. "She's speechless."

"Yeah, about that," Ian said. "I specifically remember listening to my wife tell you what we wanted to see in a house. This isn't remotely it."

Linda gave him a conspiratorial smile and leaned in, enveloping him in the cloying scent of her perfume. "I've found that it helps to start with something a bit nicer. Sometimes when a husband sees the look on his wife's face, he finds a little more room in the budget."

Ian cocked his head toward Kate's shell-shocked expression. "Is that the look you usually see?"

Linda's smile faded. "Well, no. Not exactly."

"The budget is not a concern, because we can afford whatever my wife wants. The specifications we gave you reflect what Kate felt comfortable with."

"Well, perhaps she'd like to make some adjustments."

"I would," Kate said cheerfully but firmly. "I'd like to adjust them downward, in price and square footage. The number of bedrooms should be in the single digits. It's just the two of us, and we're going to be sharing one."

Linda pulled an iPad out of her bag and began typing. "Let me check my list again. I'm sure I can find something that's a better fit."

Once Linda stopped trying to upsell them, they toured several homes that were more in line with their requirements, all of them located in secure, gated communities. But a gated community meant neighbors who might want to socialize, and that had never really been his style. The logistics of staying under the radar, especially with a wife in tow, were slightly more complicated than he'd anticipated.

"Do you have anything more private?" Ian asked during their second week of house hunting. "Maybe a little farther out?"

"A new listing just came on the market in Middleburg. I know you wanted to avoid small towns, but the home is on the outskirts and quite secluded. Of course, it's *much* more square footage than you wanted," Linda said pointedly," but it might be just what you're looking for. I can show it to you if you'd like."

In the past when choosing a place to live, he'd always gravitated toward bigger cities. He could blend in, get lost. With over six million people in metropolitan DC and the surrounding area, the odds of randomly bumping into whoever had doxed him and hacked Kate were extremely low. But since they planned to stay for a while, maybe the size of the town wasn't as important as finding a secluded property where they could keep the rest of the world out.

"Sure," he said. "Let's go check it out."

As they crossed the state line, they passed a sign that said Welcome to Virginia and underneath that, Virginia Is for Lovers. Ian glanced at Kate, and they shared a secret smile. Traffic thinned out and the view shifted from suburban freeway to lush, open pastures and rolling hills.

"This is horse and wine country," Linda said from the backseat as they entered the Middleburg city limits, which explained the abundance of horse fences and the two wineries they'd just passed.

"My wife *loves* wine," Ian said, laughing.

Kate smiled, turning around to address Linda. "He's right. I really do."

"Then you'll love it here. There are five wineries in Middleburg alone, and at least fifteen more in the surrounding areas."

"Sold," Kate said.

The GPS guided Ian down a narrow road off the highway, and they followed it for nearly ten miles before they reached their destination. The home remained hidden from view behind a tall stacked-stone fence. Ian typed the five numbers Linda gave him into a keypad mounted on a stone pillar, and a gate with a sign that read SOUTHFIELDS FARM swung open.

"This is a custom-built French colonial on seventy-five acres," Linda said. "It doesn't get much more private than this."

The house came into view as they drove up the long, winding gravel driveway. Linda hadn't been exaggerating about the size. Words like "country estate" and "chateau" came to mind, and he wasn't sure Kate would go for it. But the stone exterior gave the home a solid, impenetrable feel that he liked, and if it didn't already have one, he could arm it with a state-of-the-art security system for an added layer of protection.

"I can't wait for you to see the inside," Linda said, keying in the code for the lockbox that hung on the door.

On the main level, the rooms were spacious and plentiful. A floor-to-ceiling stone fireplace served as a focal point in the family room.

"The fireplace is two-sided so you can also enjoy it when you're in the kitchen," Linda said.

Adjacent to the family room was a large den that would work well for a home office. Linda showed them the formal dining room and living room and a smaller sitting room that could have a number of uses. The previous owners had been partial to pastel wall colors and floral wallpaper, which wasn't Kate's style at all. But that would be an easy fix.

"Isn't this amazing?" Linda asked when she led them into the eat-in kitchen, which managed to be both large and cozy. She pointed out the Viking range, double oven, large-capacity refrigerator, and eighteen-bottle wine cooler. The fireplace Linda mentioned had room in front of it for a loveseat or a couple of chairs.

"It really is," Kate said trailing her hand along the granite countertop of the large center island.

"Do you spend a lot of time in the kitchen?" Linda asked.

"No," Kate said. "We eat out quite a bit."

Linda's smile faltered as if she couldn't comprehend the thought of a young woman who didn't cook, but she recovered quickly. "Well, Middleburg has some wonderful restaurants that are less than twenty minutes away."

There were five bedrooms and three full baths upstairs. "The basement level has an additional two bedrooms, two full baths, and a separate kitchen that would make an ideal guest suite," Linda said. "There's also a wine cellar, theater room, and home gym."

They walked outside. The garage could hold up to four cars, and the backyard featured an outdoor fireplace, stone terrace, pool, and a giant barn. A stable with eight stalls sat adjacent to a large paddock enclosed by a wooden fence.

"This property is ideal if you think you'll be keeping horses."

"Yeah, we probably won't be doing that," Ian said.

"What do you think?" Linda asked when they finished the tour.

"It's a beautiful home," Kate said.

"Gorgeous," Linda said.

"How many square feet is it?" Kate asked.

"About six thousand."

Kate winced.

"The lower level would be great for when your family comes," Ian said. Because Kate was so close to her parents and brother, he'd urged her to let them know they were always welcome to visit. "I know the paint and wallpaper aren't your style, but you can change anything you want."

"I know an interior decorator," Linda said. "I'd be happy to make introductions."

Before they headed home, Linda showed them the Middleburg Historic District. The downtown area spanned six blocks and was comprised of stately Federalist homes and quaint storefronts located along brick sidewalks. The foothills of the Blue Ridge Mountains could be seen in the distance.

"This is such a lovely place," Linda said. "Wide-open spaces with small-town charm. Wonderful for raising a family. The leaves will be changing any day now, and the fall colors are truly a sight to behold."

As they drove down Washington Street, Linda pointed out restaurants, coffee shops, and other small businesses. "Bring anything to mind?" he asked Kate, lowering his voice so only she could hear him.

He caught the wistful sound in her response when she smiled and said, "It reminds me of St. Anthony Main."

That night they ate dinner up in the main house with Phillip—head of the FBI task force and the closest thing Ian had to a father since his dad died—and his wife Susan who treated Ian like the son she never had, lavishing far more attention on him than Ian's own mother did. Afterward, he and Kate returned to the guesthouse and Ian poured them a drink.

Though these four walls had been the closest thing he'd had to a home base for many years, he was ready to move on. Kate was as fond of the guesthouse as she'd been of their summer cottage, but she'd readily agreed they needed more space if they ever hoped to retrieve their belongings from storage, and a friend of Susan's had recommended Linda shortly after their return from Roanoke Island.

"I think we should buy the Middleburg house," Kate said after they settled on the couch.

He smiled. "Was I that obvious?"

She reached for his hand and gave it a squeeze. "Yes, but I can understand why the property is appealing to you."

"But do you like it enough for it to be our home?" Kate had given up a lot of things to be with him, and he wanted her to be happy.

"Sure. It's a great house. I might need to leave a trail of breadcrumbs so I can find my way from the wine cellar in the basement back to the wine fridge in the kitchen."

"We can go a little more high tech than that. I'll put a homing-beacon app on your phone and program it to start beeping when you get close."

Kate laughed and took a sip of her wine. "Problem solved."

"We'll probably be there awhile." He was looking forward to that because he was tired of moving, tired of never spending more than six months to a year in the same place.

"That's a good thing."

"You can do anything you want to the house. Redo every single room until it's exactly the way you like it."

"Oh, I plan to. I'm going to start at the top floor and work my way down. That French colonial might not look so traditional when I'm done with it. I'll be the talk of the town."

"Try not to create too big a scandal. We're still on the down low."

That was a bit of an understatement. Before Kate's parents left Roanoke Island, Steve had pulled Ian aside and asked lots of questions, namely how he planned to keep his and Kate's identity hidden. Phillip had helped to reassure Steve that it wasn't the first time they'd dealt with an issue like this, and they would follow the protocol designed to ensure they left no trail, digital or otherwise. Ian knew if Steve wasn't satisfied with the plan, he'd rally hard to keep his daughter from being part of such a risky endeavor, and he understood. Someday he might have a daughter of his own, and the thought of her being in Kate's shoes gave him all the perspective he needed. Though he and Phillip felt the odds of someone nosing around Kate's parents or brother were fairly low, they'd spent a considerable amount of time discussing how the Watts family should respond should they be approached by anyone looking for Kate.

"What about the commute? Are you sure the drive in to headquarters won't bother you?"

"Phillip's been commuting roughly the same distance from Frederick for almost the entire length of his career. I won't be going in every day, so it's not a big deal to me."

"I'm going to miss Susan."

"She'll be less than an hour away."

Ian had done the preliminary work on the pentesting he was doing for Phillip from his laptop while sitting on the couch, which wasn't ideal and gave him no room to spread out. Kate hadn't wanted to disturb him, so she'd spent most of her time with Susan while he was working, either up at the main house or visiting the many tourist sites DC had to offer. It made him happy to see the two women getting along so well, but he'd felt guilty about displacing his wife.

"Who would have thought we'd end up on a horse farm in northern Virginia?" Kate said.

"Virginia *is* for lovers, sweetness." He pulled her onto his lap, slipped his hands under her jaw, and gave her a number six kiss.

She kissed him back, letting her lips linger. "Clearly it was meant to be. But come on, Ian. We both know Linda had me at wine."

The cash sale went through quickly, and after the closing they drove to the house to wait for the movers. Ian turned off the car, but before they got out, Kate said, "What are we going to do with a barn and stable?"

He shook his head. "I have no idea."

They walked up to the front door, and after Ian unlocked it, he reached for Kate's wrist to stop her from taking a step inside. He looked into her eyes and said, "This is it, Kate. This is where we begin." Then he swung her up in his arms and carried her over the threshold.

CHAPTER TWO

KATE WAS IN THE MASTER bedroom unpacking the last few boxes. She'd finally located her pajamas, but when she carried an armful to the dresser and opened the drawer, a stack of them— brand-new, in a rainbow of colors—were waiting there for her to discover.

Ian was in his office hooking up computer cables. He was wearing jeans and a worn, faded T-shirt that said HACK NAKED. "Hey, sweetness."

She hopped up on the desk. "Nice shirt."

"I found it in a box I hadn't opened in years. It's a souvenir from a hacking convention I attended a long, long time ago. You wouldn't believe how much I've mellowed since then."

"I can barely wrangle you now. I can't imagine keeping you in line back in the day."

"I'll admit I was a bit of a handful."

"I've almost finished unpacking. It seems as though the pajama fairy has already paid me a visit. Can I just tell you how much I love that? I can't wait to wear them."

He winked, and her heart did a little flip because no one looked sexier when they winked than her husband.

He reached into an envelope sitting on the desk. "I have something else for you."

Kate examined the Virginia driver's license with her picture and the name Diane Smith. "Strange. I do not recall making a visit to the DMV. Where did you get this?"

"I made it." He looked so proud.

"Is it fake?"

"It's legit…ish. I hacked my way in, created our IDs, and had them mailed to our new PO box. It wasn't that hard. Your mom could probably do it."

"Please do not tell her that. Let me see yours."

He reached into his wallet and withdrew his license. He'd used a photo she'd taken of him a few weeks before the wedding in which he was darkly tanned and shaggy-haired. A blond surfer. The name on his was Will Smith. They'd decided their middle names would be a good compromise: familiar enough that they'd respond to them, but common and therefore quite anonymous. Kate's biggest fear while house hunting was that she'd accidentally call Ian by his real name in front of Linda, but luckily that hadn't happened.

Kate handed the license back to him. "This is all very Mr. and Mrs. Smith. If I find out you're really an assassin, you will be in *so* much trouble."

"I promise I'm not an assassin. And legally you are Katherine Diane Bradshaw and I have the documents to prove it. They're just hidden safely away. The online records are, unfortunately, missing. Shame about that."

Their home had been purchased by the LLC they'd created for Ian's new company and neither of their names—real or otherwise—appeared anywhere on the title.

Ian fed a cord through an opening in the desktop and crawled underneath the desk. "What's on your agenda today?"

"I've got a few more boxes to unpack, and then the decorator is stopping by. She called this morning."

Between them, they barely had enough furniture to make a dent in filling the rooms of the large home. Linda had given their names to the decorator she'd mentioned, and Kate had received a call from a woman named Jade Lynn.

"She called me too. I gave her your number and told her you were in charge." He came out from underneath the desk and powered on the computer and both monitors.

"What time are you meeting Phillip?" Kate asked.

"Noon. He said he has a lot for us to go over, so I probably won't be home until dinnertime."

"That's okay. Jade has no idea what she's gotten herself into. I have a feeling we'll be tied up all day."

Jade Lynn arrived with an armful of design books and an enormous bag hanging from her shoulder. She shifted them and held out her hand. "Diane? I'm Jade Lynn."

"Come in," Kate said, shaking her hand and opening the door wide. "It's great to meet you."

"Likewise."

"Here, let me take those."

"That would be fabulous," Jade said, handing the books to her.

"Let's go into the kitchen," Kate said. "We can spread everything out on the table."

Kate guessed Jade's age as midthirties. She wore her blond hair in a long braid that lay over her shoulder, and her clothing was as bright and colorful as the fabric swatches and paint chips she pulled from her enormous bag.

"How much of the existing décor do you plan to keep?" Jade asked.

"None of it. My style is a little funkier. A little less…"

"Horse and fox hunt?"

Kate smiled. "Exactly."

"Let's get an idea of the colors and textures you like. Before I leave, I'll take pictures of every room, and then I'll go back to the store and choose things I think you'll like. We'll bring them out and you can see how they look."

"That sounds great, but I don't want to spend a lot."

Jade laughed.

"What's so funny?"

"Your husband told me you would say that."

Ian picked up a pizza on his way home. They brought their plates into the family room and sat down on the sectional that used to be in his apartment in Minneapolis. Kate's couch was now in the master bedroom along with Ian's king-size bed, and Jade had promised that any new pieces she selected would match the ones they wanted to keep.

"How was your meeting?" Kate asked. "Are the hacktivists still giving Phillip trouble?"

"I think they're worrying him a lot. He's expanded the list of systems he wants locked down tight."

"Did you ask him about it?"

"A little. We didn't really discuss the details."

"Why? Is he not allowed to?"

"He can. I still have clearance. I just don't need to hear a lot about it if I'm not going to be working with everyone."

Kate could see the longing on his face and knew he hated not being part of the action.

"Are you sure?"

"Positive." The speed with which he assured her it didn't matter told Kate that it absolutely did. "Phillip will get along just fine without me. He's still got Charlie."

"Who is Charlie?"

"Someone who's been involved with the task force almost as long as I have."

"Is he as good as you?"

"No one is as good as me."

Kate grinned. "Is he at least a bit more humble?"

He reached for another piece of pizza. "Maybe a little."

"So you're really okay with not being on the task force?"

"Between getting this new company going and all the pentesting that's piling up, I wouldn't have time for it anyway."

Somehow Kate didn't totally believe him.

He took a drink of his beer. "How was your meeting with Jade?"

"Productive. I really liked her." Kate explained Jade's process and how she'd taken pictures of each room and would be returning with several different options.

"Sounds like quite a project."

"It'll definitely keep me busy." Kate had never imagined spending her days with nothing more pressing than choosing which color to paint every room and whether she wanted leather or upholstered furniture. Equally unfathomable was Ian's assurance that he didn't mind not being a member of the task force.

Kate tried not to dwell on the fact that despite their assurances to the contrary, neither one of them could possibly be one hundred percent satisfied by their choices.

CHAPTER THREE

KATE WAS SITTING AT THE kitchen island on one of the new stools Jade had delivered. Almost every day she and her deliverymen would buzz the gate, and Kate would check the video monitor connected to the surveillance camera to confirm their identity before she opened it. They would pull up in front of the house, park their van, and unload artwork and rugs and furniture. Jade had given Kate the name of a contractor, and several workmen had descended upon the top floor and were busy stripping wallpaper. As soon as they were done, the painters and carpet layers would complete the next step of the transformation.

She opened her laptop to send an e-mail to the food pantry. She'd reached out to Helena as soon as they'd returned from Roanoke Island, apologizing for not checking in sooner and blaming her absence on a bit of lingering sadness and a desire for solitude. Helena had been so happy to hear from her, and now that Kate had a new laptop and a secure, well-hidden ISP address, they'd been corresponding on a regular basis.

To: hsadowski@mainstreetfoodpantry.org
From: winealittle@firedrive.com

Dear Helena,

I hope this message finds you well and that the leaves in Minneapolis are just as gorgeous as they are in Indiana. So far

September has been absolutely beautiful, and I hope you're enjoying fall every bit as much as I am.

I got the job at the law firm I told you about in my last message. I'll be in charge of a small caseload of public interest files. It's the type of law I'd hoped to practice after I graduated, and I'm so happy to have finally found a position.

How are Samantha and the kids? Have they been in lately? I hope they're doing well. I bet Georgie is getting so big. When you have a minute, there's another client I was hoping you could check on. His name is Zach Nielsen and he lives with his younger brother and disabled mother. The last time I spoke to him, he mentioned he'd gotten on full-time at his job and might not need any more assistance from the food pantry. Can you pull his file and see if he's been in? I was just thinking about him the other day and thought I'd check. If he has been in, there's no need to let him know I asked.

Please tell Bert I said hello. I sure do miss you.

Hugs,

Kate

Kate's e-mail chimed fifteen minutes later when Helena responded.

To: winealittle@firedrive.com
From: hsadowski@mainstreetfoodpantry.org

Dear Kate,

It's simply beautiful here in St. Anthony Main. The only thing that would make it better is if you were sitting at your desk across from mine. I miss your smiling face. Congratulations on your new job. I just know things are going to work out for you.

Samantha and the kids are doing so well. She told me her situation has improved enough that she's been able to hire a babysitter a few nights a week so she could take a night class at the community college. Eventually she wants to get a degree in restaurant and hotel management. She's so determined, Kate. You should be proud of all you've done for her and the kids.

I pulled Zach Nielsen's paperwork, but it doesn't look like he's been in since the last time you marked his file. See all the good we've done, Kate? Helping people to get back on their feet means we may not see them again, and in this line of work, that's a great thing.

Well, time to get back to work. I'm so happy to hear from you. Please write again when you can.

xoxo,

Helena

Kate breathed a sigh of relief. Phillip and Ian had anticipated that Zach Nielsen would return to the food pantry in an attempt to find out where she'd gone. The trick was to check in with Helena in such a way that it would not arouse her suspicion, because if Zach were to come in and question her, they wanted her response to be natural. If she acted strange, Zach would surely pick up on it. The update on Samantha made her smile. Ian was still giving her money anonymously, and she was obviously putting it to good use.

Kate curled up in one of the new chairs Jade had placed in front of the fireplace. She couldn't wait until it got a little colder and she could light her first fire. In an attempt to stay out of the workmen's way, Kate had been spending most of her time in the kitchen, and it had quickly become one of her favorite rooms in the house. The windows let in an abundance of natural light and gave her a nice view of the pool and patio area. Linda had been right about the changing leaves, and the trees dotting the property and surrounding hills were on fire with the blazing colors of autumn.

As she looked around the room, she admired the shiny stainless steel appliances and the gleaming cherrywood cabinetry, wondering if it was odd to spend so much time in a room she never actually used for its intended purpose. The granite countertops were empty save for a giant silver fruit bowl Jade had brought three days ago that was still empty because she and Ian had fallen into their usual pattern of subsisting on takeout and it had been almost a week since they'd gone to the grocery store.

She found Ian in his office. "I'm going shopping." She came around his desk to give him a kiss. "Back in a couple of hours."

"Buy everything," he said as she walked out the door.

Kate drove down Washington Street and parked near a small home goods store. In the appliance section she selected a panini press, food processor, stand mixer, and Crock-Pot. She bought a set of pots and pans, spatulas and whisks and mixing bowls, and measuring cups. At the specialty market, she bought a crusty loaf of Cuban bread and a pound of roast pork. Before heading for home, she stopped at Safeway and filled a cart to the top with pantry and freezer staples, meat, fresh produce, and dairy items.

She put the groceries away, and after scrubbing the apples, she piled them high in the silver fruit bowl. Then she took the panini maker out of its box and followed the instructions for use. While she waited for it to heat up, she glanced at the recipe on her laptop and laid out the ingredients on the counter: ham, roast pork, butter, mustard, thinly sliced provolone, and dill pickle slices.

I passed the bar exam on the first try, she thought. *I can make a stupid sandwich.*

But it took her three tries to get it right. The first sandwich came out soggy. She burned the second. But the third had the exact firmness she was going for and looked just like the picture. Ian was on the phone when she came in, so she set the sandwich down in front of him and waved. He smiled and blew her a kiss in response.

Five minutes later, the sound of his groaning reached her before he did. He came around the corner, the plate in one hand and the half-eaten sandwich in the other, a look of absolute bliss on his face. He took another bite and groaned again. "Where did this come from?"

"I made it."

"You made me a Cuban?"

"I made you a Cuban."

"Have you always known how to cook?" He set the plate and sandwich down on the counter and tickled her. "Were you hiding this amazing talent for sandwich making, Katie?"

She squirmed out of his grasp, laughing. "No. I've honestly never had much interest in cooking. I know how to make a few things, and I'm good at helping my mom when she cooks, but since we have this gorgeous kitchen, I thought I could teach myself how to cook. You know, the way I honed my skills in other ways by clicking on those handy links."

"That did work out rather well for me." He picked up the sandwich and took another bite. "You don't have to cook if you don't want to. I don't mind takeout."

"I think it might be time I learned. Grown-ups should not eat cereal for dinner like we did the other night." It had been pouring rain, and neither of them had felt like getting in the car and going in search of food.

"This is the best sandwich I've ever eaten."

Kate smiled. "You're just saying that because I'm your wife."

"No, I'm not," he said, taking the last bite.

"It wasn't that hard," Kate said. "I might tackle something a bit more involved. I like the thought of cooking for you."

"Good, because I would not say no if you wanted to make me another sandwich."

"You got it."

CHAPTER FOUR

IAN BURIED HIS FACE IN Kate's hair. He knew by the sound of her breathing and her lack of movement that she was still deeply asleep. Slowly he removed his arms from around her and eased himself from the bed. In the kitchen he made coffee, and on his way back to the bedroom, he retrieved the ring from the desk drawer where he'd stashed it the night before. He set the coffee down on the nightstand and opened the curtains, sending sunlight streaming into the room.

She was still sleeping, but she'd rolled onto her back, which he appreciated because the sheet had pooled at her hips and she was naked from the waist up. He slipped back under the covers and gently rubbed her cheek with his thumb. "Happy birthday, sweetness."

She opened her eyes and smiled at him, her eyes half-lidded in that way that drove him wild. "Is that today?"

"I believe so."

She stretched like a cat and turned toward him, tucking her head under his chin. He held her tight and ran his hands up and down the soft, smooth skin of her back.

"I smell coffee."

He picked up one of the mugs from the nightstand and handed it to her when she sat up. After she took a sip, he said, "Give me your right hand." She let out a small gasp when he slipped the sapphire ring onto her finger.

"Do you like it?" He hadn't gone overboard on the size of the stone, and it suited Kate's slim, delicate finger perfectly.

"I love it. It's beautiful."

"It goes with another gift I have for you. That one should be here later this afternoon."

"I can't imagine what you have up your sleeve."

She laid her head on his shoulder and extended her arm so she could continue admiring the ring.

"I think you're really going to be surprised."

At breakfast, Ian handed her a rectangular box wrapped in silver paper and tied with a blue ribbon.

"Another present?" Inside, she found a gift certificate for a Loudoun County limo wine tour. "You didn't."

He grinned. "I did."

"Someone to drive me around in style after I've done nothing but sample wine all day? It's like I've died and gone to heaven."

"There's more. Your mother is going with you. She arrives tomorrow and is staying through the weekend."

Kate's face lit up. "She's coming?"

"Yes, and she's pretty much beside herself."

"I knew she'd never be able to hold out until November."

Though Jade had worked wonders in a short period of time, there were several rooms that still needed fresh paint and carpeting. Not all the furniture was in yet, and the workers hadn't even started on the walkout lower level. Kate had wanted Diane to wait to visit until it was finished, so they'd invited Kate's parents, and Chad and Kristin, to join them for Thanksgiving.

"Thank you," Kate said, leaning across the table to kiss him. "I don't know why people complain about milestone birthdays. So far turning thirty has been absolutely painless."

Late that afternoon, Ian informed Kate that her gift had arrived. "Keep your eyes closed. No cheating." He led her out the front door, holding tightly on to her hand to make sure she didn't run into anything. When they reached the driveway he said, "Okay. You can look now."

Kate opened her eyes. "Oh my God."

"Do you like it?"

"Oh my God."

"Does that mean, 'Yes, Ian. I totally love it'?"

"It's amazing. What kind of car is that?"

"A Porsche Spyder 918. Gorgeous, isn't it?" The only thing that would enhance its appearance was his beautiful wife sitting in the driver's seat.

"But I already have a car."

He'd bought her a Tahoe to replace the TrailBlazer he'd asked her to sell. "That's your everyday car. This is your fun car."

She walked around the outside of the vehicle. "Nothing says keeping it on the down low like a Porsche."

Loudoun County was no stranger to luxury vehicles, and Kate's Tahoe probably stood out more than a Porsche would. "It's not registered in either of our names."

She grinned. "Of course it isn't."

The bright blue car sparkled in the late-afternoon sun. "I hope you don't mind that I didn't consult you on the color."

"I love the color. It's just like the Shelby."

"The Shelby was Guardsman Blue. This is *sapphire*-blue metallic."

Kate laughed and held up the hand with the sapphire ring. "Ah, I see the connection now. Where did it come from?"

"I bought it online and had it shipped to a local dealer."

"Don't tell me how much it cost. I might not be able to handle it."

He'd paid just under a million for the car. It was six million less than he'd paid for the Shelby, but somehow he didn't think Kate would consider it the bargain he did. "All right. I won't tell you."

He'd always known it would take Kate a while to get used to his money, but he wanted her to think of it as *their* money. A week ago he'd handed her their credit card bill. "Look at this."

She'd scanned the bill and handed it back. "I don't understand. Did we get overcharged for something?"

"You're not using the card."

"Yes I am. I'm using it at the grocery store, and I bought a bunch of cooking stuff online. And I've spent a lot on the house. I don't think Jade is sticking to my budget as well as she could."

"But you've bought nothing for yourself. Would you rather I shopped for you? I do enjoy it."

"Thanks for the offer, but I cannot wear pajamas and lingerie to the grocery store. Silly."

He never took his wealth for granted, and he appreciated the freedom it allowed him and the safety it provided. Now that he had a wife, those things were more important than ever. Kate had handled the price of the house better than he'd expected, but that was more than likely because she knew how important the security and privacy were to him. He'd discovered the hard way what access to unlimited funds could do to a woman, and it wasn't pretty. The fact that Kate had never been interested in his money and didn't want expensive things only made him want to buy them for her.

She rested her hand on the hood of the car. "This is a very extravagant gift."

His expression grew serious. "I've never had a wife to spoil before. Let me spoil you a little. It makes me happy."

"Okay," she said. "But this car is ours to share, and you have to promise me one thing."

"Anything."

"Promise me that it will never end up in the Potomac, no matter what. My heart couldn't take it."

He could see the apprehension on her face, and it bothered him that he'd been the one to put it there. She needed to know that whatever happened, he would never let her go it alone. Never put her through something like that ever again. He looked into her eyes. "I promise, Kate."

She peered in the window. "I've never seen a gearshift like that."

He smiled.

She opened the driver's side door and slid behind the wheel to get a better look. He walked around and sat down in the passenger seat.

"How many speeds?" she asked.

"Seven. And it's a hybrid."

"Really?"

"Yes. This car is *spectacular*. It's no Shelby, but I think you're going to love it."

"You miss the Shelby, don't you?"

"I would like to have driven it one more time." Unfortunately, his beloved car hadn't survived the dip in the Mississippi. She'd run again, but the water hadn't been kind to the electrical systems, and she'd never be the same. He'd donated the car to an auto museum in Nashville.

She started the car, and he could tell by the way she listened intently as he explained the dual-clutch and shift paddles that she was itching to drive it. She leaned over the gearshift and kissed him. "Prepare yourself for an *amazing* ride."

"Okay, but I think the only way we can do this with any finesse whatsoever is if you're the one riding me, because I'm too tall to be on top. You'll have to straddle me, and even then it's gonna be tricky, but if I recline this seat all the way back, I think we can make it work. No one can see us, so I want all your clothes off. From my vantage point, the view will be absolutely incredible."

"You kill me. You really do." She laughed and shook her head. "I hate to break it to you, but that's not the kind of ride I meant."

"No? Damn. How about later?"

"Absolutely. But maybe not in the car. This leather is *pristine*."

For over an hour they traveled the winding roads of the northern Virginia countryside. He turned on the stereo and cranked it to an earsplitting decibel level as they got lost in their own little world. The smile never left her face, and he felt an immeasurable amount of love for the beautiful, carefree woman he'd had the good sense to marry.

When they got home, Kate dug her phone out of her pocket and handed it to him. "Take a picture of me. I want to send it to my brother."

He snapped a picture of her leaning against the car, and when he handed the phone back, she fired off a message to Chad.

She laughed when he responded. "Check it out," she said, handing the phone to Ian.

Chad: *Of course it's a Porsche. If you weren't my sister, I'd hate you a little.*

He'd used his own phone to take several pictures of her while she was driving, and she'd been so engrossed she hadn't even noticed. He scrolled through them until he found his favorite. He'd caught her smile at just the right moment, and the sunlight had been streaming through the window, lighting her up as if she glowed.

He made it his lock-screen photo.

CHAPTER FIVE

WHEN CLASS ENDED, KATE rolled up her mat and tucked it under her arm. She'd found the Pilates studio one day shortly after their move when she'd been exploring the downtown area, and she'd started attending the late-morning class. A few of the regulars stood chatting in the back of the room. The first time Kate said hello to them, they must not have heard her because they didn't say anything. Today, on her way to the locker room, she received a cool hello in response to her cheerful greeting, but that was as far as it had gone. She didn't really mind, but it would have been nice to have someone she could meet for lunch or coffee.

After showering and changing back into her clothes, she stopped at the supermarket and then drove home, the Tahoe loaded down with grocery bags.

Ian smiled, took off his glasses, and pushed his chair back when he spotted her in the office doorway. He always kept the door open, and he never minded when she interrupted his work. "Hey, sweetness. C'mere and give me some sugar."

She walked to his desk and he pulled her onto his lap. She gave him several number four kisses, soft and gentle. He kicked it up a notch by reciprocating with a number six, holding her face tenderly as he gave her a deep, openmouthed kiss with tongue. A logical progression considering she was already sitting on his lap.

When the kiss ended, she looked into his green eyes and covered his face with her hands, pretending she couldn't stand to look at it. "Put your face away. I can't handle this much handsome."

"It's blinding, isn't it?" He grabbed her wrists and removed her hands from his face, smiling wide.

She laughed. "Humility. You should look into it."

"That's probably the only thing I wouldn't be good at. How was Pilates?"

"Still tough. That's what I get for taking the summer off."

"Made any friends?"

"The women don't seem very open to outsiders. It's quite cliquey."

"What do you mean, they're not open?" The pained expression on his face, as if he couldn't handle someone being unkind to her, warmed her heart.

"I mean that sometimes grown women act as if they're still in high school, and I'm the new girl. Don't worry about it. Maybe I don't want to be in their club."

He laughed. "What are you up to for the rest of the day?" He ran his hands up and down Kate's arms as if he couldn't stand not to be touching her in some way.

"I've got groceries to put away, and then I'm going to make us something to eat." Ian loved any sandwich she made with the panini press, so that's what they usually ate for lunch. "After that, I think I'll take my birthday present for a drive."

He broke into a wide grin. She knew it made him happy to see her enjoying the car, and besides, he'd been right about the Spyder: it *was* spectacular.

"But first, lunch," she said, climbing off his lap and letting out a squeal when he gave her a friendly little goose. "I'll call you when it's ready."

After they finished eating, Kate grabbed her keys and backed the Spyder out of the garage. When she was working at the law firm, she'd driven a two-door Accord, but she'd traded it in for the TrailBlazer when she opened the food pantry because she needed a vehicle with enough room to collect and transport donations. She was used to driving an SUV, so when Ian suggested another one, mentioning how much he liked the safety aspects of a larger vehicle, she'd readily agreed. Virginia's winter weather could be fickle, and the Tahoe's four-wheel drive would come in handy if there were higher than average amounts of snowfall. But once she'd taken the Spyder out a few times, she remembered how fun it was to drive a car.

Working with Jade to redecorate the house took up some of Kate's time. Her Pilates classes, household tasks, trips to the grocery store, and experimenting with new recipes took a bit more. But there were still too many hours left in the day, and she'd discovered that taking the Spyder for a nice long drive was a good way to fill them. She mostly avoided driving down Middleburg's main street, not that a Porsche would cause any of the affluent residents to bat an eye. But driving the Spyder had become a solitary endeavor for Kate, and she had no desire to draw attention to herself.

And the Spyder wasn't just a car. It was an *experience*.

She'd begun testing the car to see what it could do. For starters, it could go from zero to sixty in about four seconds according to her rough calculations. It hadn't taken long for her to become comfortable with the shift paddles, and she loved the way she could toggle back and forth between the automatic and manual transmission modes. Each time she took the car out, she went a bit farther and a bit faster. Driving the Spyder felt like driving a racecar, which she supposed wasn't far from the truth. The two-lane roads of northern Virginia were perfect for her excursions because they never seemed to be heavily traveled, at least not in the middle of the day.

She pushed the button for the driving playlist she'd compiled, and the opening notes of Aerosmith's "Dream On" filled the car. The early fall day was sunny and warm, and the trees were still holding on to most of their leaves. She'd recently discovered a rural Virginia byway known as the Snicker's Gap Turnpike that passed through Mountville and Philomont and would take her all the way to Berryville twenty-five miles away. It was one of her favorite routes.

She increased her speed, loving the way the Porsche's tires hugged the pavement. When she glanced down at the speedometer, she was shocked to realize she'd been humming along at a cool 107 miles an hour, which was the highest reading the gauge had ever shown. The superior suspension and modern engineering of the Porsche made for a much smoother ride than the Shelby, and it hadn't seemed like she was going that fast. Instead of slowing her speed, she pressed down on the gas pedal until the needle rose to 115. She'd never thought of herself as an adrenaline junkie, but the feeling of being in control of that much speed invigorated her, and the vibrant colors of the leaves on the trees whizzed by her in a sunlit blur of orange, yellow, and red. Aerosmith gave way to Boston's "More Than a Feeling," and she cranked the volume and got lost in the music.

In Berryville, she pulled into the small coffee shop she'd discovered during her first visit. The pecan chocolate chip cookies they made fresh daily were the best she'd ever tasted, and in addition to her freshly brewed Americano, she bought two of the cookies to take home for Ian.

On the way back, she spotted a sign she'd never noticed before that read Goose Creek Stone Bridge. Feeling a pang of nostalgia for the Stone Arch Bridge and St. Anthony Main, she turned down the narrow gravel road and followed it until she came to a small, deserted parking lot. She locked the car and set off on foot to explore.

To her right, a wooden fence with a sign that said Wildflower Walk bordered an observation area with an informational plaque stating that the bridge had once been the site of a Civil War battle. In the distance she could see the four arches of the abandoned bridge, and the sight of it—moss covered and crumbling—seemed ominous and filled her with dread. The sun had moved behind a cloud and the wind had picked up, making her surroundings feel even less welcoming.

She headed back, bypassing the parking lot and walking down a wide path toward the bridge itself. A wild turkey darted from between the trees in the woods to her left, startling her. On the bridge, she peered over the edge at the fast-moving, muddy water. The last time she'd stood on a bridge like this, she'd been more than a little concerned about her mental health, and when she'd thrown her phone into the Mississippi, she'd been certain the likelihood of ever being happy again had sunk with it.

Now she and Ian were here, together. Married and blissfully content. She felt guilty for her restlessness and the faint tendrils of boredom that had crept into her daily life. Who was she to complain about anything? The husband she thought she'd lost loved her every bit as fiercely as she loved him. They had a beautiful home. A life of luxury. Had she forgotten how fortunate she was? A feeling of foreboding followed the revelation. Maybe they'd cheated fate. What if something happened that would take Ian away from her for real? *Don't buy trouble*, she told herself. *Be grateful for everything you have.*

He was in the kitchen grabbing a bottle of water from the fridge when she returned. "How was your drive?"

She went to him, throwing her arms around his neck and knocking him slightly off-balance.

"Hey," he said, steadying himself and wrapping his arms around her. "What's wrong?"

"I just love you so much."

"I love you too." He squeezed her tight, and when she showed no sign of moving away from his embrace he said, "Are you sure you're okay?"

She lifted her head from his chest. "I found a bridge. A stone one with arches. The last time I stood on one of those, I thought you were dead. It seemed like a bad omen." She felt a little foolish admitting her feelings now that she was home.

"I don't want you to worry about anything, sweetness. Nothing is going to happen to me." He kissed her forehead tenderly, and she believed him.

She nodded. "Okay."

"Other than the bridge, did you have a nice drive?"

"Yes." She felt a twinge of remorse. She'd been driving way too fast, but both she and the car had made it home in one piece, so there was really nothing to worry about. "I brought you some cookies." She pulled the small white bag from her purse and handed it to him.

"All I can say is it's a good thing we have a home gym. Speaking of exercise, I think I'm done for the day. Do you want to go for a walk?" They often explored the property, their fingers interlocked as they followed the fence line, the leaves of the oak trees rustling overhead.

"I'd love to." A lingering restlessness remained, as if she hadn't quite shaken her anxiety. A walk was just what she needed.

"Give me ten minutes to finish up." He kissed her and pulled a cookie from the bag, taking a bite of it as he walked toward his office. "Excellent cookie," he said over his shoulder.

Kate sat down at the island, opened her laptop, and scanned her e-mail. Jade had sent a message with several attachments showing different pieces of furniture for Kate to look at. She made her selections and sent a cheery message back, telling Jade how pleased she and Ian were with the way the house had come together.

Audrey had sent some pictures from a couples' weekend trip to Vegas that she and Clay had gone on with Paige and her husband. They looked like they were having a great time, and Kate would be lying if she said she didn't miss her friends. She would write a nice, long response when she and Ian returned from their walk.

Kate smiled when she scrolled through the remaining messages and spotted a response from Helena to the e-mail she'd sent that morning.

To: winealittle@firedrive.com
From: hsadowski@mainstreetfoodpantry.org

Dear Kate,

It's always so wonderful to hear from you. I've been thinking about you a lot lately. I hope you had a great birthday and are getting out more. I know you said things were better and not to worry about you, but I still do.

The food pantry is doing well. The new director is every bit as dedicated as you were, and we even have a bit of a surplus right now. We're in good shape as we head into the colder months. Do you remember how worried we were last year at this time?

Forgive me if I'm being insensitive, but I can't help but think of Ian and how much he helped us. I hope that someday you'll meet a man just like him. Someone who is kind and generous and will light up your face the way he did.

Take care, Kate.

Love,

Helena

To: hsadowski@mainstreetfoodpantry.org
From: winealittle@firedrive.com

Hi, Helena,

Please don't worry about me. I've found that keeping busy really helps. I love my new job, and I've made some friends who enjoy going to Sunday brunch as much as I do. Mimosas for everyone! I've also been helping Kristin and Chad with the preparations for their New Year's Eve wedding. And last weekend my mom and I celebrated my birthday by visiting a local winery. I've attached a picture so you can see for yourself how much fun I'm having.

I'm so happy to hear the pantry is doing well, and I'll never forget how worried we were in the days before Ian made his first donation. Yes, he did help us, and you're not being insensitive for hoping I'll meet a man like him someday. I really do think I will. It's just a feeling I have.

It's always so wonderful to hear from you.

xoxo,

Kate

She scrolled through the pictures on her computer and selected one of her and her mother on the wine tour that they'd asked the guide to take. They were sitting at an outdoor table, both smiling, glasses held aloft. She cropped the picture so Helena wouldn't see the limo parked in the background, the one with the sign on the side that said Virginia Wine Country Tours. Then she attached it to the e-mail and hit Send.

CHAPTER SIX

ALMOST EVERY NIGHT KATE WOULD pour a glass of wine, turn on some music, and try out another new recipe, and when dinner was ready Ian would join her and they'd sit down together at their new kitchen table. He rarely worked past seven, and after they finished eating, they spent their evenings much the way they had in Minneapolis: watching TV or a movie. Talking and cuddling. Thankful just to be in each other's company.

That night they were having Phillip and Susan over for dinner, and she'd decided on a menu of Caesar salad, creamy risotto, seared sea scallops, and roasted brussels sprouts. Kate had made the meal once already, and since Ian had raved about it, she felt confident serving it to guests.

"This is delicious, Kate. You've become quite an accomplished cook in a very short period of time," Susan said when they were halfway through dinner.

"You have no idea," Ian said. "She makes it look easy too."

"Thank you, but not all my attempts have been a success. The roast I burned set off every smoke detector on the main floor, and it took days to get rid of the smell. I'm still not sure what went wrong."

"How was your visit with your mother?" Susan asked.

"It was wonderful. She was so excited to see the house." Kate and Diane had spent a whirlwind four days together. They'd shopped for additional household items—especially for the kitchen—and in addition to the wine tour, they visited a museum, checked out a few new restaurants, walked into every single establishment on Washington Street, and spent an entire day sightseeing in DC. At the airport, Diane tearfully hugged Kate and told her she couldn't wait to return for Thanksgiving.

"How are things coming along with your company, Ian?" Susan asked.

"I'm starting to think I picked the wrong name for it."

Susan's forehead creased in confusion. "What do you mean?"

"Succedo is one of several Latin translations for succeed. I think it would be a stretch for me to claim any kind of success at this point. Since I'm supposedly dead, I can't use the Privasa name or rely on my reputation, which means I'm just another hacker who's thrown his hat into the security ring." Ian had told Kate how disappointed he was in the slow growth of the company.

"There's definitely more competition now," Phillip agreed.

"And they're all offering something I don't. Unfortunately, most of the companies I've pitched to won't even consider hiring a security firm unless they include social engineering as part of their pentesting."

"What is social engineering, exactly?" Kate asked. She had a vague notion but wasn't clear on the details.

"Social engineering is human hacking," Phillip said. "It can be computer based—sending someone a phishing e-mail with bogus links—or it can be done in person using human interaction and manipulation to gain physical entry or access to information. You've actually done it yourself, Kate. Remember when you went to the auto-storage facility and talked to the employee to find out if anyone had been there asking questions? You were pretending to be someone else in order to get the facts you needed."

"I said I was Ian's attorney. I also let the guy look down my shirt."

"What?" Ian said, turning his head sharply to look at her. "You never mentioned that."

"He was like, nineteen." Kate shrugged as if it were an inconsequential detail. "And I was in dire need of information, *Rhion*." She looked at him pointedly.

"Let me top off your wine, sweetness."

She smiled and handed him her glass.

Phillip continued. "The man who came into the food pantry was more than likely the hacker who doxed Ian, and I think we can all agree that Zach Nielsen was *not* his real name. He was using social engineering tactics to try to catch Kate in a lie."

Ian draped his arm across the back of Kate's chair. "He had no idea how smart you were."

"You could outsource your social engineering, especially the physical entry portion," Phillip said.

Ian shook his head. "I could, but the only three people I trust with any of my business—professional, personal, or otherwise—are sitting at this table."

"Maybe the solution is right in front of you," Phillip said tilting his head toward Kate.

When Kate realized what Phillip meant, she almost flew out of her chair. "Yes! I could help you."

"Why, thank you for opening this can of worms, Phillip," Ian said.

"Phillip," Susan said, gently admonishing him.

"Women make great social engineers," Phillip argued. "I'd go as far as to say they're better at it than men. People are more trusting of women."

"This particular woman is my wife."

"It was just a suggestion."

"I'm sure things will turn around eventually. I'll just keep plugging away."

Ian must have noticed the disappointment on her face because he squeezed her shoulder and said, "I *will* think about it, okay? But right now what I'm really interested in is that pie Susan brought for dessert."

The next morning Kate read everything she could find on social engineering. The art of talking your way past a company's receptionist or entering a building without a badge sounded wildly exciting to her.

She went into Ian's office and sat down on the new leather couch Jade had delivered, which they'd placed adjacent to his desk. It was the perfect addition to the room, and Kate could occasionally be found lying on it, reading a book while Ian worked. "I could do the social engineering for you."

"I know you could, but I don't *want* you to."

"But Phillip said you needed help."

"Listen, Phillip is the closest thing I have to a father figure, but he's very 'goal oriented,' which is fine, but not when it involves my wife. And we both know it doesn't matter if this company is successful or not."

"Of course it matters."

"It's not like we need the money. If I lose out on a few clients, so what?"

"It's not about the money. It's about your happiness."

"I'm not unhappy. A little frustrated maybe, but it's not a big deal."

"The thing is, I think I'd be really good at it."

"I know you'd be good at it."

"Then *why* don't you want me to do it? I read everything I could find. It's not dangerous." The best part about social engineering was that the client *wanted* to see if you could get past their employees, and they gave you explicit permission to try.

"I just don't."

When she didn't say anything, he pushed his chair back and sat down next to her on the couch. He reached for her hand. "The morning you brought me your laptop and asked me to take a look at it because it was running slow was one of the worst moments of my life. It felt like being sucker punched. I'd always assumed that being doxed meant they'd come after me. The way I felt when I realized it was you they'd targeted was like nothing I'd ever felt before, and I will carry that guilt with me for the rest of my life. Social engineering might not be dangerous, but it requires a considerable amount of deception, and people have been known to get angry when they catch you doing it even if you have every right to be there. I don't want to put you in that kind of situation."

She didn't push because she knew there would be no convincing him. "You'll let me know if you change your mind?"

"Of course," he said earnestly. But she knew he wouldn't. "You're not upset with me, are you?" *Please, Kate,* his expression said. *I hate telling you no, but I can't agree to this.*

"No. I understand why you don't want me to do it."

"You mean the world to me, and every single day I remind myself how fortunate I am that you agreed to become a part of this crazy life I lead."

"You provided a pretty convincing argument. I've never regretted my choice."

He brought her hand to his mouth and kissed it.

"I'll let you get back to work," she said.

CHAPTER SEVEN

KATE AND IAN ARRIVED AT the black-tie dinner and silent auction for juvenile diabetes research. Susan had acted as chairwoman for the past six years, and when Kate opened the invitation, addressed to Mr. and Mrs. William Smith, she smiled when she remembered how irresistible her husband looked in a tux. She'd called Susan immediately to RSVP. She was dying to put on a fancy dress and get out of the house and knew Ian would agree to attend any event Susan was involved in. It was also one of the few places they wouldn't have to worry about running into the wrong person, as whoever had doxed Ian was unlikely to be there.

"I'll be right back," Ian said once he'd handed his car keys to the valet and they'd made their way inside the crowded ballroom. "I'm going to fight my way to the bar and get us some drinks."

As she waited for Ian to return, she sensed that someone was watching her. The tuxedo-clad man standing a few feet away was indistinguishable from the others except for the fact that his eyes seemed to be trained on Kate. He was handsome. Tall, late thirties, short hair, clean-shaven. A younger version of Phillip. She fidgeted awkwardly under the relentless weight of his stare, and her discomfort intensified when he walked toward her, head tilted slightly as if he were trying to place exactly how he knew her. Ian reached her side at the same time the mysterious stranger did.

"Out of all the women in this room, you have to zero in on my wife?" Ian said, but he was smiling widely when he said it.

A surprised look appeared on the man's face. "This beautiful creature is your wife?"

"Yes, and she's off-limits," Ian said, handing Kate a glass of wine. "Especially to you."

He clutched his chest in mock despair. "That hurts, man."

Ian's grin grew wider as the men shook hands and clapped each other on the back.

Ian turned to her. "Kate, please meet Charlie Wittkop. Hacker, task force member, and relentless womanizer."

"This is Charlie?" It delighted Kate to finally meet someone Ian shared a history with.

"Pretty enthusiastic greeting from your wife, Merrick. My reputation precedes me."

"I've mentioned you exactly once, and it's Smith now."

"Of course it is."

"It's very nice to meet you," Kate said.

He shook her outstretched hand. "The pleasure is all mine."

Charlie raised his glass in Ian's direction. "Congratulations. Girlfriend and now wife. Must have been quite the whirlwind romance. I'll assume my wedding invitation got lost in the mail."

"It was a small, private ceremony." The look they shared told Kate that despite their verbal sparring, these two men cared about each other. "I didn't expect to run into you here."

"I've attended the past three years. My cousin's little girl has diabetes."

"Then I hope Susan raises lots of money tonight."

Ice rattled as Charlie drained the last of his drink. "I figured you'd go underground for a while and knew you'd pop up eventually. Had no idea it'd be right in my own backyard."

"I thought Phillip might have said something to you."

"He said you were doing the pentesting, but since you flit around the country like a damn gypsy, I had no idea where you might actually be living. Plan on sticking around for a while?"

"Looks that way. It gets much too cold here, but I've got this stunner to keep me warm at night." Ian slid his hand around Kate's waist, and there was something slightly proprietary in his touch.

"She's a beauty." Charlie grinned. "So, are you seriously not coming back to the task force?"

"I'm going to sit this one out." When Ian had surprised her in the airport and promised not to work undercover anymore, she'd felt relieved. But it had to be difficult for him to be in such close proximity to headquarters yet not be able to participate.

"Lots of trouble brewing. We could sure use you."

For a split second, his desire to jump right back into the fray showed on his face. "Yeah, well. You'll have to get along without me."

A gorgeous blonde walked by and gave Charlie the eye.

"Excuse me," he said to them. "If I want to wake up next to that woman tomorrow morning, I should really go introduce myself. Incredibly nice meeting you, Kate. I hope I get to see you again."

"I hope so too."

"Good luck," Ian said, gesturing with his glass toward the woman.

"Thanks. I won't need it."

Kate watched as Charlie caught up to the blonde, who seemed thrilled to make his acquaintance. "Are you all this cocky and self-assured?"

"Well, I'm the cockiest."

Kate took a sip of her wine. "You are a special snowflake indeed. Is Charlie a"—she made air quotes—"special consultant like you?"

"No, he actually works *for* the FBI. Has a badge, wears a tie." Ian shuddered as if he couldn't fathom such a thing.

"You like Charlie," Kate said.

"Sure. I like him as much as I like anyone who isn't you."

"How long have you known him?"

"I don't know. Ten years? He's been on every task force I've ever been a part of."

"Ian, you have a friend." It was clear the two men were competitive, but she'd sensed the genuine affection they felt for each other.

"You sound so surprised."

She laid her hand on his arm. "You may not be aware of this, but you're a bit of a loner."

"No I'm not. I have lots of friends. I just don't need to see them in person all the time. I talk to them online."

"Why didn't you tell Charlie we live here now?"

"I haven't told anyone."

"But he knows about me, right?"

"Everyone on the task force knows about you."

Across the room, Charlie put his arm around the woman and said something in her ear that made her laugh.

"Has he ever been married?"

"His wife cheated on him with another agent, and he got divorced about three years ago and swore off relationships. Looks like he's still in the 'sowing his wild oats' stage."

"When you were at the bar, he was looking at me so intently, almost as if he thought he knew me."

"Yes, I'll be keeping an eye on you both," Ian said.

"You have nothing to worry about. You have much better hair."

"When we get home, I've got something to put in that smart mouth of yours."

"You're a brave man. This smart mouth has teeth."

"You'd never use them. It might jeopardize your reputation as the reigning queen of blow—"

"There you are," Susan said, cutting off Ian's words as she and Phillip suddenly appeared next to them. "You look beautiful, Kate."

"So do you." The two women hugged, and then Ian kissed Susan on the cheek and shook Phillip's hand.

"What a gorgeous dress," Susan said.

"Thank you. Ian picked it out." Kate had promised Ian she would start buying things for herself if there was ever something she wanted, but she'd admitted that she liked it when he shopped for her. Knowing he was looking at the clothes and imagining them on her body aroused her in a way she hadn't expected. And telling him that had the same arousing effect on *him*, which meant she now had a closet full of new clothes. Some were casual, jeans and tops similar to what she normally wore on a day-to-day basis. Some were elegant and classic. A fitted black pencil skirt. A white silk blouse with french cuffs. He was partial to dresses, especially sundresses with a slightly bohemian flair. And all the while, the lingerie and pajamas kept coming.

The strapless black gown he'd bought for tonight had a tightly fitted bodice and a long, full skirt with layers of gauzy black tulle underneath. Her hair had been styled in an elegant updo that showcased the diamond choker Ian had placed around her neck when she was standing in front of the dresser mirror in their bedroom. "It's absolutely beautiful. I'm afraid to ask if it's costume or the real thing," she'd said as she touched the triple row of delicate stones.

"Then you probably shouldn't," he'd murmured in her ear as he fastened the choker.

"You spoil me," she said.

"In all fairness, I did say I was going to."

At the end of the evening, while Kate and Ian waited for the valet to bring Ian's Navigator around, they watched as Charlie—a few spots ahead of them in line—tucked the blonde into the passenger seat of a sleek black Mercedes.

"What is it?" Kate asked, noticing how intently Ian was watching them.

"I never knew what Charlie drove. Pretty nice car for a fed."

She shivered in the late-October air, and Ian wrapped his arms around her from behind. He placed a lingering kiss on the side of her neck, and she let out an almost imperceptible moan because he turned her into a puddle of need whenever he kissed her there.

"I heard that, sweetness. I want to hear it over and over before we finally go to sleep."

As he drove them home, all Kate could think about was how nice it had been to spend a rare evening out with her husband. There was no one she wanted to spend her time with more than Ian, but she wanted to go places with him. Restaurants and movies. Museums and wine tastings. She hoped that someday they could do those things without worrying he might bump into the wrong person.

In the meantime, she would be patient. "I had a really nice time tonight."

He reached over the console and squeezed her thigh. "I'm happy to hear that, sweetness. I did too."

CHAPTER EIGHT

IAN'S DAY HADN'T GOTTEN OFF to a great start. He'd received an e-mail first thing that morning letting him know that a potential client—one he'd been sure would choose his company—had gone with another security firm, citing their need for a full range of social engineering services. He'd then spent the rest of the morning and early afternoon working on the pentesting he was doing for Phillip, and the number of vulnerabilities he'd found in the latest batch of government systems was not only unbelievably high, it was unchallenging for him as well. Nothing made him happier than having to *work* to penetrate a system, to find a way in no one else had thought of. Instead of feeling frustrated, the challenge energized him.

Thinking of Charlie and Phillip and the rest of the task force members only added to his bad mood. He and Charlie had always enjoyed a little friendly-yet-cutthroat competition, but by voluntarily withdrawing from undercover work, he'd catapulted Charlie right into the hot seat.

Where he used to sit.

Where all the action could be found.

And the task force needed him. Charlie had said so himself. But he'd told Kate he wasn't going to work undercover anymore, and he wouldn't go back on his word.

The only way to salvage the remainder of the day was to spend it with his wife. She'd left in the Spyder after lunch for one of her drives, but he really thought she'd be home by now.

Ian: *I feel like taking a nap. The kind where we're both naked and neither of us are sleeping. Are you in?*

He returned to his work, but twenty minutes later, he was still waiting for her to respond. He probably should have called because she wouldn't be able to text back while she was driving. He clicked on the locator app to see where she was and blinked to clear his vision because she appeared to be heading west on a rural byway almost *twenty-five miles away*.

What the hell?

He opened another app—the one that had come with the car—and reached for his glasses. He clicked through the pages for distance driven and fuel efficiency, and read the number for her current speed: 112 miles per hour. He reviewed the stats for the past week and was shocked to discover she'd consistently hit speeds in excess of 120 miles per hour. Three days ago she'd reached an all-time high of 132. What was she thinking?

He blamed himself. Giving her an incredibly fast car and then being upset when she drove it incredibly fast was on him. He was the one who'd encouraged her to increase her speed when he'd put her behind the wheel of the Shelby. But he'd been with her then. He driven with her enough to know she was more than competent behind the wheel, but this was nuts.

Her speed slowed to a much more acceptable level as she neared the town of Berryville. It looked as if she was turning around and heading back the way she'd come. He kept the phone in his hand, monitoring her speed all the way home, relieved to see that it never rose above seventy-five.

He was waiting for her in the driveway. When she got out of the car, he held up the phone, the app still open, and said, "One hundred and thirty-two miles per hour? Are you out of your *mind?*"

She looked surprised. "There's an app for that? Dammit. I should've known."

"Kate."

Her smile faded because he'd never spoken to her in that tone of voice, but she'd scared him. He pictured the Spyder in a mangled, twisted, smoking heap of metal and his stomach clenched.

He reached for her hand and softened his voice. "I just want you to slow down before you get hurt. Or worse. You're married to a man who enjoys driving fast, but come on. Do you have a death wish I don't know about? What were you thinking?"

"I'm bored," she blurted.

He'd promised Kate that life with him would never be boring. Boring was bad. "Bored like you were bored with Stuart, bored?" He sounded alarmed.

She laid her hand on his arm, quick to reassure him. "No, nothing like that. Maybe bored isn't the right word. More like restless."

A restless wife didn't sound good either.

"It's just that I'm not used to having so much time on my hands."

Ah, so that's what this was about. "Come with me." He led her to the porch, and they sat down on the wicker love seat Jade had delivered the day before.

"If you let me help with your social engineering, I'd have something to keep me busy."

He'd known that's what she was going to say before the words came out of her mouth. "I'm on probation with your dad—for life, I might add. I hurt his daughter and dragged his family down a path I know he'd rather none of you were on. How do you think it would go over if he found out I'd turned his daughter into a hacker?"

Kate looked down at the ground. "I used to be an attorney. Then I built a nonprofit organization from the ground up. I had a board of directors. I had employees and volunteers. I worked hard to provide assistance to my community. Now I'm a housewife who goes to Pilates and makes paninis."

"You're much more than that. And your paninis are *so* good."

She looked up and the yearning in her eyes cut through him. He didn't want Kate to be bored, but more than that, he never wanted her to be unhappy. To have second thoughts about the sacrifices she'd made to be with him. He'd already used up his allotment of that emotion with her, and it killed him to see even a trace of sadness on her face.

"You can't hide me away forever, Ian."

One of the things he'd struggled with the most when Kate had been hacked was that whoever had done it had unlimited access to every photo on her computer. Any picture of her and her friends and family had been right there for them to copy and save. They'd probably also taken pictures of her as she walked down the street. He was convinced that the hacker who'd come into the food pantry was the one who'd doxed him and hacked her, and the thought of the guy saving those images, possessing any pictures of his wife, filled him with rage. He started to say that he wasn't trying to hide her away, but he bit back his words because that's exactly what he was doing, and he of all people should have known that his fearless, adventure-seeking wife was never going to be satisfied with that.

He put his arm around her and pulled her close. She laid her head on his shoulder and neither of them spoke for a while. He'd asked Kate not to seek out any employment opportunities, especially those designed specifically to help others. If the person who'd doxed him ever found out where they'd gone, it would not be inconceivable that the first place they'd look for her would be the local food pantries or comparable nonprofits. He liked having Kate nearby. He liked hearing her puttering in the kitchen or looking out the window and seeing her splashing in the pool when he was working. He liked taking breaks in the middle of the day to spend time with her.

"You heard what Phillip said. Women make really good social engineers. At least give me a chance."

There was no way he was going to tell her no, and they both knew it. He'd put her through the worst kind of anguish when he'd faked his death, and then he'd brought her here, to the rolling hills of Virginia, and stuck her in the kitchen. With a woman who craved excitement, it hadn't been his best move.

"There's a lot I'd need to teach you first."

She lifted her head from his shoulder and looked at him, her expression hopeful. "I'm a fast learner."

"And I have a few conditions," he said. "One, I'd rather you didn't say anything to your family about this, at least not for a while. I hate asking you to keep something from them because I know how close you are, but I'm even more uncomfortable thinking about how they might react to this news, which puts me in a difficult position."

"Considering the fact that my dad is still... coming to terms with our relationship, I don't disagree."

"Two. I insist on paying you the way I would any employee. You'll be well compensated, and I want you to do whatever you want with the money."

"I will gladly accept it."

Her response surprised him; he'd been prepared for her to push back. "Three. I'd like you to keep making those paninis because they're good and I really like them."

She bit back a smile. "I would be happy to make you a sandwich anytime you want one."

"One last thing. You cannot ever drive that fast again."

"What? No!" She sounded like he'd taken away her favorite toy. "That car handles like a dream. Frankly, I never expected to love it so much, but I do."

"I'm glad you love the car, but the speeding is nonnegotiable. You mean the world to me, and I can't have you risking your safety like that. There are other ways to get an adrenaline fix, and if you want to start social engineering, you have to agree to slow down."

"All right. I will agree to all those conditions, but I'd like to add one of my own. I want you to rejoin the task force."

He had *not* seen that coming. "Kate—"

"It's me, Ian. I'd like to think that I know you about as well as anyone does, hopefully more. Are you really going to look me in the eye and tell me you're not dying to go back?"

"It doesn't matter how I feel. I told you I wouldn't do it."

"Of course it matters. I understood why you gave up the task force. I thought it was what I wanted too. But you're not satisfied either."

"I'm not unsatisfied."

She leveled a gaze at him, the kind of look that said *please do not try to bullshit your wife.*

"I don't love the thought of you working undercover. But you've got the same look in your eyes I probably do. You left the task force, but only to put me at ease and prove I meant more to you. I know how much you love it, and I never asked you to give it up."

He decided he might as well come clean. "I miss it, more than I ever thought I would. I can't stand being left out. I hate that Charlie's working so closely with Phillip. I keep thinking of all the things they must be working on, and I wish I was working on them too."

"Do you know what else I think? I think the reason you didn't get in touch with Charlie to let him know we'd moved here is because you didn't want to hear anything about the task force if you couldn't be a part of it."

"Can't get anything by you, can I?"

"I certainly hope not."

"Are you sure about this?"

"I'm sure. That doesn't mean I won't worry, but I love you and that means accepting the things that drive you, even if they scare me. Love requires compromise. Maybe—in our case—it also requires bravery."

"I think you're right about that, sweetness." No one had ever understood what made him tick like she did, and marrying her had truly been the smartest thing he'd ever done.

"So I guess things are about to change."

"Maybe just a little. You already know what it's like to be with someone who works on an undercover task force. As for social engineering, I'll mostly be teaching you how to convince people to give you what you want. Something tells me that'll be very easy for you."

She gave him an innocent look, as if she had no idea what he could possibly mean by that, and he wanted to kiss it right off her face.

"There is one thing we might have to change though." He grabbed a lock of her hair and slid it through his fingers, imagining what she'd look like and wondering if she'd agree.

She looked at him strangely and shook her head. "No way."

He smiled and put his arm around her. "We'll see about that." He pulled her close. "Did you get my text about that nap?"

"I did."

"What did you think about it?"

"I think you should know I'm not tired at all."

He kissed her forehead, took her by the hand, and led her inside. "Neither am I, sweetness. Neither am I."

CHAPTER NINE

THE NEXT MORNING, IAN was on his way to meet with the task force by ten o'clock. It was true that in the past, visits to FBI headquarters weren't often at the top of his list of favorite activities. He chafed at the structure.

The hierarchy.

The *rules*.

After the first year or two of working with the FBI, Phillip had stopped asking him to come on board as an official agent because he knew Ian would never say yes, but today he might have considered it if Phillip were to suddenly ask, such was his excitement to be part of the task force again. He couldn't wait to hear what Charlie and the others were working on, and he would forever be thankful for Kate's blessing.

The task force was a subset of the FBI's Cyber Action Team, which was housed under the National Cyber Investigative Joint Task Force. Under Phillip's stellar guidance, they'd worked their way up until they were the premiere task force for domestic cybercrime. If there was a cyber equivalent of the Navy SEALS, they were it. The five-member team—six now that Ian had returned—included some of the nation's top experts in criminal investigation and code analysis, and no other team was more proficient in identifying cybercrimes that were an emerging threat to the American people.

Before he'd started working with Phillip on the pentesting, they'd spoken at length regarding Ian's concerns about being seen at headquarters. The FBI often attended hacker conventions such as Def Con and Black Hat and recruited hackers as special agents—hackers who might have once worn black hats or at the very least had friends who still did. The last thing Ian needed was to bump into whoever had doxed him when they passed each other in the hallway. Phillip had shared Ian's concern, so instead of meeting in his office at headquarters, they'd met off-site in the conference room of a large, nondescript office building half a mile away, kept by the FBI for this very reason. From now on, the task force meetings would also be held there.

Everyone looked up when Ian walked through the door.

"Somebody call it," Charlie said.

Tom, a seven-year veteran of the task force, raised his hand. "Right here."

Charlie withdrew a stack of bills from an envelope and shoved the money across the table.

"Thank you, gentlemen," Tom said as he pocketed the cash.

"You placed bets?" Ian said.

"You didn't think anyone believed you when you said you were quitting, did you?" Charlie asked. "I gave you ninety days. Clearly I underestimated how long you could hold out."

"Do you all not remember the part where someone doxed me and hacked my girlfriend—who is now my wife—and I had to break her heart into a million pieces by pretending I was dead? Not to mention put my beloved car in the Mississippi and throw away a company I'd spent ten years building?"

"And yet here you are," Charlie said with a giant shit-eating grin.

"That's because Kate insisted I rejoin you." He sat down and pointed around the table. "May you single men marry half as well as I did."

Phillip opened the door and hurried into the room. "Welcome back, Ian," he said as he sat down and pulled a sheaf of papers from his briefcase.

"Did you know they placed bets?"

"Oh, who won?" Phillip asked with interest, looking up from his notes.

"Tom," Charlie said.

Ian frowned. "I'm disappointed in you, Phillip."

"All I can say is you'd better hold on to that wife of yours. She's one of a kind. Okay, we've got a lot to discuss, so let's get to it. Charlie, bring Ian up to speed please."

"In the past three months, there's been a string of cyberattacks on several high-profile websites, mostly banks and credit card companies. What appeared last summer to be a series of random hacktivist activity has recently become more organized. In the past month there have been cyberattacks on both the CIA and NATO, which were thankfully unsuccessful. We have reason to believe the same group is responsible for all of them."

"Sounds familiar," Ian said. Phillip had been smart to focus on making sure the FBI's current systems were secure, and the reason he'd asked Ian to do the pentesting was clearer than ever.

"Exactly," Charlie said.

Several years ago a hacktivist group led by a man named Joshua Morrison had done virtually everything Charlie had just said, right down to the CIA and NATO attacks. The group was already a major thorn in Phillip's side when they took things one step further and pulled off a successful cyberattack on one of the FBI's own affiliates, defacing the website and stealing passwords and other sensitive information. Their retaliation had been fierce, and Ian's infiltration of the group had garnered enough evidence to arrest Joshua and send him to a medium-security federal prison in Oklahoma where he was currently serving a ten-year sentence.

The backlash had been severe as the hacktivists felt the FBI used entrapment in order to secure the evidence needed to make the arrest. Ian hadn't been kidding when he'd told Kate the hacktivists made the carders look like Boy Scouts. He'd been on the receiving end of death threats too numerous to count, and the only saving grace was that the court records identified him by a screen alias and not his real name. If they ever did find out who he was, their vengeance would be immediate.

Phillip had shifted the entire task force over to the carding ring to give them a chance to lie low for a while. Ian hadn't minded the lower-profile work, but near the end, after spending so much time trying to bring down the carders, he felt a bit unchallenged. He believed wholeheartedly that they needed to be stopped, but he couldn't help but think of them as low-life crooks that needed babysitting more than anything. Ironically it was more than likely a carder who'd proven to be the biggest threat to Ian's anonymity, if in fact it was a carder who'd doxed him.

"Anyone paid a visit to Joshua?" Ian asked.

"Yes, and he's not talking of course," Charlie said. He passed a thick file to Ian. "Here are the printouts of the evidence we've gathered so far."

"I'll take a look at it and let you know what I find," Ian said.

"Why didn't you tell me this was happening?" Ian asked Phillip after the other members of the task force had filed out of the room to head back to their desks at headquarters.

"Because I knew it would make it hard for you to honor your promise to Kate about leaving the task force, and I didn't want to be responsible for that," he said. "You fought hard for her, and I didn't want to do anything that would jeopardize your relationship. I feel like I've gained a daughter-in-law. I want her to be happy the way I want you to be happy, which is why I suggested you let her help you with your company. You two are more alike than you know. Maybe that's why you get along so well."

Phillip had never seemed more like a father figure than he did at that moment. "Kate's the best thing that ever happened to me," Ian said.

"I think she might say the same."

It was pouring rain when he got back into his car and headed for home. Lightning streaked across the sky, and he crackled with a similar energy. He hadn't felt this way in months, and only in its absence did he understand how much the task force made him feel alive. It had become a major part of who he was and how he identified himself.

He found Kate in their bedroom curled up on the couch that used to be in her old apartment. She was reading a book, and he stood in the open doorway watching her, thinking once again how lucky he was to have her. If she had reservations about the task force—and he was certain she did—she was willing to set them aside to make him happy.

As if sensing his presence, she looked up and smiled. "Hello, lover. I've been expecting you."

Grinning, he leaned against the doorway. "Were you tracking me, Katie?"

"You bet I was. That's quite a storm." She put down her book. "Why are you not over here showering me in kisses?"

"Unbutton that a little for me." She was wearing leggings and one of his button-down shirts.

Holding his gaze for a second, she brought her fingers to the buttons and undid two of them. "Like that?"

He could see the lace of her pink bra. He pulled his phone out of his pocket, zoomed in and clicked. "Maybe a couple more."

He crossed the room to the curtains and closed them. When he turned around, her shirt was open nearly to her waist; a few more buttons and it would hang freely at her sides. "Now the rest."

She sat up and unbuttoned the shirt all the way.

After snapping a few more pictures, he sat down beside her and twisted his fingers in her hair, pulling her closer and kissing her hard. Then he slipped the shirt from her shoulders, pulled her arms free, and tossed it on the floor. "Lie back."

She did as he asked. He loved the way she looked in the pink bra he'd bought her. God, she was so beautiful. Her eyes tracked his movements as he ran his hands through her hair to fan it out. He loved her like this: trusting and secure in the knowledge that he'd never do anything she didn't want him to do. Would never do anything she didn't like. Again, he pointed and clicked.

Reaching for her feet, he set down the phone and took off one sock at a time. He tickled the arch of her foot, and he smiled when she laughed and tried to pull her foot away. He gripped it harder but didn't tickle her again.

He leaned over her body, and she wrapped her arms around his neck, pulling him closer and squeezing him tight. She was always so eager, so receptive to his attention and affection, and her desire for him made him feel ten feet tall. He kissed her again, even harder than before. She slid one hand into his hair, closing her fist, and then twisted the other in his shirt to hold him there.

He dragged his mouth away reluctantly because he had other things on his agenda and there would be plenty of time for kissing later. It took him no time at all to strip off the leggings, and he knew he would find pink boy shorts under them because the bra he'd bought her had been part of a matching set. He turned her slightly onto her side, with one arm under her head and the other lying on her hip, and took several more pictures.

"Kiss me again," she said, turning onto her back.

How could he not oblige? He covered her with his body, and the sound she made when his mouth met hers was somewhere between a whimper and a groan. After a few minutes, he made his way to her neck, and the way her skin felt under his lips, delicate and smooth, her pulse beating rapidly beneath it, made him want to be rough with her. He sucked the tender skin hungrily into his mouth, stopping just short of leaving a mark.

He placed his knees on either side of her and sat up, pulling the phone from the front pocket of his jeans. "Take off your bra." It didn't matter that he saw Kate's breasts every single day, often more than once. He would never tire of seeing them, and certainly not like this. She reached around to unhook it, and his breathing grew ragged when she tossed the bra on the floor. He wanted to touch her, but he wanted her to touch herself more. She complied as if she'd read his mind, and he fired off multiple shots with his phone, his jeans growing uncomfortably tighter.

When he couldn't stand it any longer, he placed his palms on her chest, his hands gliding over her skin. Her body was firm and strong, but the softness that covered its surface captivated him, and he could spend hours happily tracing the curves and hollows with his fingertips. Kate reached for the hem of his T-shirt and pulled it off. He leaned forward until they were pressed skin-to-skin, and he raised her hands above her head as he kissed her, their fingers intertwined as she arched her back underneath him. He listened to her ragged breathing, gauging how much time he had left. Kate was not only open to him taking pictures of her, he'd discovered it turned her on like nobody's business, and he liked to drag it out as long as he could stand, which was only marginally longer than Kate could handle. By the end, she'd be pulling at his clothes, urging him to take her. Her skin was hot, but she shivered as he dragged his mouth from her lips to her neck and finally to her breasts. Cupping them, he knew exactly where to draw the line between pleasure and pain when he took her nipple into his mouth.

She wrapped her legs around his waist and held his head in place, her breath coming in short little gasps. When he pulled away and sat up, he took another picture, not of her body but of her face. Her flushed cheeks, swollen lips, and bright eyes took her beauty to a whole different level.

Gently he turned her onto her stomach. After brushing her hair to the side, he ran his finger down her spine and didn't stop until he'd slipped it down the back of her boy shorts. She trembled when he pulled them off and ran his hands over her backside.

Now he stood next to the couch, looking down at her as she looked over her shoulder at him. He held the shutter down, and the camera took several pictures in rapid succession. He was so hard he couldn't keep his clothes on for one more minute, and she watched as he set down the phone and stripped.

"Sit up," he said.

Now she was facing him, leaning against the back of the couch.

He gently eased her legs apart. "Yes," he said. "Jesus, yes." He took one more picture and then set the phone aside. Softly he stroked her, teasing, working his way toward her center, replacing his fingers with his mouth. Her legs were over his shoulders, and he couldn't get enough of the way she tasted. She twisted her fingers in his hair and told him in gasping, sputtering bursts how good it felt.

"Please, now, Ian."

He picked her up and carried her to the bed, laying her down on it and entering her in one fluid movement. She came immediately, screaming out his name. He held back his own orgasm, prolonging his release because she felt so good and he didn't want it to be over. But to hold off much longer would require a Herculean effort, and if past experience had shown him anything, there would be another round after this one. He let himself go, shuddering and shaking, collapsing onto her because she'd told him she loved it when he did that, assuring him she wouldn't break. She wrapped her arms around him as he buried his face in her neck, breathing in the smell of her damp skin. In time he shifted and pulled her over so that her head was lying on his chest.

He couldn't hear the rain anymore. He felt drowsy, as if all the excitement of the day had sapped him of his energy. He wanted to lie in their bed, wrapped around Kate, until one of them came up with a good enough reason to leave it.

"How did it go with the task force?" she asked, and she sounded as drowsy as he felt.

"They placed bets on how long I could stay away. Can you believe it?"

"Absolutely. Your face lights up when you talk about anything related to the FBI."

"Really?"

"Yes."

"Before we started working to break up the carding ring, the task force brought down a group of hacktivists. We sent one of them to prison where he's currently serving a ten-year sentence. There's reason to believe the same group is responsible for a string of recent cyberattacks on banks and credit card companies.

"You said hacktivists aren't interested in stealing. Why would they hack banks and credit card companies?"

"Because they like to show how easy it is to obtain information. They steal the data and share it with whistle-blower organizations. And some of the attacks have been on government agencies, which is why Phillip wanted me to do the pentesting."

"That sounds troubling. No wonder he's so worried."

"It's a serious threat to national security."

She let out a surprised chuckle. "Do you have any idea how excited you sound?"

"I can't help it. I find it exhilarating."

"I know you do. This is exactly the kind of challenge that makes you happy."

Opening himself up to Kate, sharing his feelings and letting her see who he really was, had been one of the wisest things he'd ever done. "You make me happy."

"I'm just the cherry on top."

"Yes you are." He ran his fingers through her hair, idly wrapping the strands around his fingers. "Do you know why I call you sweetness?"

She propped herself up on her arm and smiled down at him. "I thought it was just your preferred term of endearment."

"It is, but I call you sweetness because everything in my life got sweeter the minute you became a part of it. You're exactly the woman I always hoped I'd find."

"I love you," she said, giving him one hell of a hot kiss.

"I love you too."

She laid her head on his chest and snuggled closer.

He put one arm around her and reached for his phone with the other.

"Are you looking at the pictures?"

"Hell yes, I'm looking at them."

"Let me see."

She shifted a bit and he brought the phone down so the screen would be visible to both of them, and five minutes later it seemed he'd been absolutely right about that second round.

CHAPTER TEN

IAN DID A DOUBLE TAKE when Kate walked into his office two days later and stood before his desk. Her long dark hair had been dyed a golden blond, a shade or two lighter than his. Before, it had reached almost the middle of her back, but she'd cut some of it and now it fell in long layers several inches below her shoulders. He'd contemplated asking her to dye her hair when they returned from Roanoke Island, but after discussing it with Phillip, they'd decided it probably wasn't necessary, especially if he wasn't also going to dye his. But now that she was going to be seen in public more often, he'd decided he'd feel more comfortable if she altered her appearance a bit.

"All right," she said. "Let's just get the carpet not matching the drapes jokes out of the way right now."

"I'm not sure that tiny landing strip of yours actually qualifies as carpet, but okay. It's not going to match." He pushed his chair back and studied her. For as long as he could remember, certainly as long as he'd been aware of the opposite sex, he'd preferred a certain type: long-legged brunettes with dark eyes. But his wife had just shattered that all to hell, and no one was more surprised than him.

"I know that look," she said.

"I should hope so." The truth was there was never a time, day or night, when he didn't want her at least a little bit. And right then he wanted her more than ever. "I never pictured you as a blonde, but this is a superhot look on you, and I pretty much want to lay you across my desk."

She grinned. "So I guess you like it."

"You look beautiful. Thanks for agreeing to do it."

"Well, blondes do have more fun."

He came around from behind his desk and sat on the edge of it so that he was facing her. "I know you're all about using your sex appeal for personal gain, but I do not want those"—he pointed to her breasts—"or those"—he pointed to her legs—"or this"—he reached behind her and palmed her ass—"being used as an incentive in any way. The only person who should be looking down your shirt is me. You are not bait."

She shook her head. "I promise I'll never do that again."

"Are you ready to go over scenarios?" He'd given her a stack of three-ring binders overflowing with information on social engineering attack vectors and asked her to study them. Maybe when she saw what it really entailed, she'd change her mind.

"I want to look over some of the materials one more time. Give me half an hour and then come to my office. I'll be ready for you."

"You got it."

Kate had quickly turned the small sitting room off the formal living room into her office once Ian agreed to let her help him. The walls had been freshly painted when the main level had undergone its remodeling, and at Kate's request, Jade had delivered a desk and a small chair and ottoman. Together they had selected brightly colored art for the walls, and Kate placed the rug from her apartment in Minneapolis on the floor in front of the desk. She loved it.

In law school, she'd had to commit copious amounts of information to memory, and Ian probably had no idea how eagerly—and thoroughly—she'd immersed herself in the study materials he'd given her. Phillip had said that social engineering was human hacking, but Kate soon realized it was much more complex than that. Ian preferred using his technical skills to penetrate and scan a company's computer systems for vulnerabilities from the *outside,* but Kate would focus primarily on human-based techniques directly involving a company's personnel. That might entail sending a phishing e-mail with a malicious link to someone within the company or convincing them to accept malware via a USB drive. In addition, she would become an expert in the art of pretexting, or conducting prior research that would lend legitimacy to an invented scenario in order to convince the victim to release the desired information or agree to a specific action. Kate had studied every possible situation and its consequences and couldn't wait for her first assignment to try out everything she'd learned.

She was sitting in the chair with her feet on the ottoman, flipping through one of the binders when Ian appeared in the doorway.

He sat down on the ottoman and put her feet in his lap. "Ready?"

She handed him the binder. "Hit me."

"Office building, badge access only, receptionist."

"I'll say I'm there for an interview."

"What's your attack vector?"

"USB-delivered payload."

"How are you going to do it?"

"I'll spill my coffee on my résumé or claim I've forgotten it. Then I'll ask them to print me a copy."

"How will you build rapport?"

"I'll look for common ground, a vacation photo or a picture of a child on the desk. I'll say how much I enjoyed that particular location when I visited last year, or I'll mention how cute the child is."

"What if the child isn't cute?"

"Ordinarily I'd argue that all children are cute, but Chad looked pretty goofy until he was about five, so I know that's not one hundred percent true and people will question my motives if they think I'm not being authentic. So if the child isn't cute, I'll find an individual characteristic that is. Chad, for example, had adorable dimples."

"What if it's a picture of a dog and not a baby?"

"I'll tell them about Scooter and how I rescued him from the pound after he was dumped along the side of the road along with three of his siblings. He was in such bad shape, but he's four now and thriving."

Ian sat up a little straighter and looked at her curiously. "Cat."

"My Fluffy recently had a litter of kittens right underneath my bed. It was truly amazing, and I'm so glad I got to experience it."

"What if it's one of those hairless cats?"

She didn't miss a beat. "Technically they're called sphynxes, and they're not totally hairless. They're also very friendly. Mine greets me at the door every day when I get home from work. It's so rare that I connect with other sphynx owners."

"I'm amazed at how quickly you think on your feet, which is a very important and valuable skill for a social engineer to have. Did you actually research hairless cats?"

"I researched every kind of pet anyone might possibly have a picture of on their desk. You could have asked me about fish, hamsters, guinea pigs, or snakes. I'd have nailed it."

"But what if there are no pictures of children or pets?"

"Then I'll look for a knickknack, postcard, logo on a coffee cup. Anything that will give me a jumping-off point."

"What if you fail in your attempts to deliver a payload to the gatekeeper?"

"Then I'll have to tailgate my way into the building. Once I'm inside, I'll have several options for collecting information, like shoulder-surfing or impersonating an employee." The clients who hired Ian would expect his firm to make repeated attempts to penetrate their networks from several different angles. The practice, known as red-teaming, would allow Ian to analyze the vulnerabilities they discovered, which he would then share with the client in order to assist them in tightening their security.

"What if you get caught?"

Not getting caught was the primary goal of any social engineer, and the more outrageous the intrusion, the bigger the bragging rights. No one wanted to get caught, but playing it safe wouldn't show a company the holes in their security.

"I'm not going to get caught."

"I admire your unwavering confidence, really I do. But let's just say—hypothetically—that an overzealous employee is bored and decides to play 'spot the social engineer.' What do you do?"

"I give them my letter. Because I've *failed*."

Before beginning any social engineering assignment, Kate and Ian would have in their possession a letter from the client stating that Diane and Will Smith had the legal right to be on the premises. It was standard operating procedure, and every white hat security firm insisted on it because it offered them protection from any employee who might become suspicious and attempt to stop them in their tracks or haul them off to security.

"Try to think of it as your get-out-of-jail-free card."

"Have you ever had to use it?"

He gave her a look like *surely you must be kidding.* "No."

"Of course you haven't."

"Aw, sweetness. I never knew you had such a competitive side."

"Neither did I."

He smiled and gave her back the binder. "I'm extremely impressed. You've got this down cold."

"Thank you. There's nothing in that binder I don't know. You could quiz me for another half hour and I'd never miss a beat."

"Ferret."

She struggled to suppress a grin and he thought he'd finally succeeded in tripping her up, but she quickly composed herself. "These cuddly animals are so unfairly maligned. Only a fellow ferret owner understands how truly special they really are."

"Who *are* you?" he asked, his own laughter finally overtaking him.

"Isn't it obvious? I'm your new social engineer."

CHAPTER ELEVEN

"WE SHOULD MOVE THESE meetings to Applebee's," Tom said when Ian and the rest of the task force filed into the conference room where Phillip was waiting. "If we can't hold them at headquarters, we might as well take advantage of the two-for-one happy hour that starts"—he glanced at his watch—"in about forty-five minutes."

"Not to mention the hot wings and free Wi-Fi," said Brian, the newest member of the group.

"That's hilarious," Ian said. "I'll remember that next time one of you needs to be on the down low." He pulled out the printouts Charlie had given him at their last meeting. They were covered in notations identifying the markers that proved the attacks were the unique work of the same hacktivist collective they'd already brought down once. "I've read through all the evidence and analyzed the code. I know for a fact the attacks were carried out by Joshua Morrison's group."

"Same signature?" Charlie asked, his forehead creasing in concern. Hackers often left TTPs—tools, tricks, and procedures—behind that pointed to the work of a certain person or group.

"Yes," Ian said. "They appear to be pulling together, organizing, but their goal isn't clear."

"How are we going to proceed?" Tom asked.

"Now that we know for sure it's the same group, a task force member will infiltrate," Phillip said. "It's our most efficient way of uncovering their agenda."

"Don't worry Merrick," Charlie said. "You've more than paid your dues, and I already volunteered."

Ian took the teasing in stride. He had no problem with Charlie going undercover and knew Kate would be very happy to hear it wouldn't be him. "I appreciate that, and it's *Smith*, remember?"

"E-mail me a spreadsheet with your names. I can't possibly be expected to keep them all straight."

"I wonder what they want," Tom said, looking contemplative.

"Could be anything. I want everyone to be thinking about possible attack vectors," Phillip said. "Charlie, start monitoring the channels and planning your entry. We'll reconvene in a week."

"Will do." Charlie closed his laptop and turned to Ian. "Let's go get a drink."

Ian followed Charlie to the bar he'd chosen, hoping the Navigator would still be there when he came out because the location was neither trendy nor particularly desirable. One might even say it was downright sketchy. His misgivings were compounded by the surly bartender who barked out, "What do you want?" upon their entrance and the fact that their shoes stuck to the sticky floor as they carried their drinks to a table in the back.

"Jesus, Charlie. Don't tell me this is your regular hangout, because I fail to see the draw."

Charlie knocked back half his drink in one swallow. "Are you kidding me? This place is perfect. The drinks are strong and there's never anyone around to eavesdrop on my conversations."

"You better pace yourself. We just got here."

"My tolerance for alcohol has already increased significantly thanks to the hacktivists. Damn carders never made me want to drink like this. I'm going to require a liver transplant by the time this task force wraps up."

Ian raised his glass and then took a drink. "I hear that." He'd been in Charlie's shoes before and knew how intense it could be. The sheer number of hours he'd put in and the constant threat of blowing his own cover by saying the wrong thing or not covering his tracks well enough had worn on him. He'd cut Charlie some slack on the drinking.

"It's great to have you back, man."

"Thanks. I didn't realize how much I'd missed it until I ran into you."

"Kate seems like a great girl."

"She is."

"How'd you convince her to marry you?"

"Women are powerless when it comes to my charms."

Charlie snorted and took another big drink. "Still wearing 'em down, I see."

"It took a little persuading, but she came around."

"I'm happy for you. I'll admit I wasn't sure about any part of that crazy plan working out. But here you are, Kate by your side."

"Yeah," he said. "Here we are."

"You buy a house?"

Ian nodded. "We planned to buy something closer to headquarters, but we ended up on a horse farm in Middleburg."

"How did that happen?"

"Seventy-five fenced and secluded acres and a top-of-the-line security system, which I modified to make even better."

Charlie's glass had been empty for five minutes when Ian finished his drink.

"Want another? I'm buying."

"Thanks, but I'd better head home. Kate taught herself how to cook and undoubtedly has some sort of gourmet dinner on the stove. It's going to take me a while to fight my way through the traffic."

"Beautiful and she can also cook? Boy, you really did hit the jackpot, didn't you?"

"I remind myself of that every single day." He stood and put on his coat. "Thanks for the drink. I'll see you around."

CHAPTER TWELVE

AFTER KATE'S FIRST SOCIAL ENGINEERING assignment went off without a hitch, they celebrated by spending the afternoon in bed and the evening enjoying a bottle of champagne in front of the fireplace. It was true that the kind receptionist and the world's cutest baby had made for one of the most ideal scenarios for a successful hack, but she'd used the USB attack vector successfully two more times since then—one receptionist had a picture of a Hawaiian beach and the other a golden retriever. Ian had been able to bring on two new clients now that he could offer social engineering as part of his audit package, and that made Kate very happy. She might not be using her law degree anymore, and the food pantry was no longer hers to run, but she added value to Ian's company and she enjoyed the work. And she hadn't balked when Ian insisted on paying her because her first paycheck, and every paycheck after that, had been donated anonymously to the Main Street Food Pantry.

It wasn't quite the same as being there, but it was still a contribution, and surely that counted for something.

She'd hired a housekeeper, a nice woman named Renee who would come a few days a week to clean, do the laundry, and buy the groceries on the list Kate left for her. Cooking was the one thing she had no desire to give up, and at the end of each day she looked forward to pouring a glass of wine, rolling up her sleeves, and making dinner. She was currently working her way through a series of Thai recipes, which pleased Ian immensely.

He had insisted on accompanying her on all of her previous social engineering assignments, but lately he'd needed to spend more time with the task force, so she'd convinced him she could start going on assignments alone. He'd reluctantly agreed. She thought it might actually be *easier* without him watching her because she wouldn't have to pretend they didn't know each other. Besides, having an audience to her potential failure, even if that audience was her husband, made her slightly nervous.

Her phone pinged with an incoming text as she was pulling into the parking lot fifteen minutes before her appointment.

Ian: *I might have forgotten the new housekeeper was starting today.*

Kate: *Oh God. How naked were you?*

Ian: *Everything was just swinging in the breeze when I walked into the kitchen.*

Kate: *Now she'll be with us forever.*

Ian: *My naked body does have that effect on women.*

Kate: *It's why I'm with you.*

Ian: *I thought you were with me because of my hair?*

Kate: *Your hair is just a bonus.*

Ian: *Are you in the parking lot?*

Kate: *Just arrived. I'm sitting in the car until it's time to go in.*

Ian: *Don't be nervous. You can always retreat and try again if it doesn't feel right.*

Kate: *Okay. Wish me luck!*

Ian: *You'll do great. Go get 'em, sweetness.*

It had taken Kate over a week to complete the pretexting for this particular assignment. She'd started by identifying her target—Garrett Linder, the VP of marketing. Then Ian hacked the DMV to determine the make, model, and license plate number of his car. For several days in a row, when Garrett pulled out of his work parking lot, Kate followed him. She knew an amazing number of things about him by then: phone number, personal e-mail address, college major and GPA, social media accounts and passwords, hobbies, and his favorite genre of music. He was divorced but in a new relationship, and he liked to stop at a small upscale bar every night on the way home where he appeared to know the bartender personally. He never stayed for more than two drinks.

One night soon after, she was sitting at the bar when Garrett came in. Pretending to be engrossed in her phone, she let her hair fall across her face and never looked directly at him as she sipped the glass of wine she'd been nursing for the past forty-five minutes. She was close enough to his stool that she heard him order a gin and tonic and watched as the bartender reached for the Hendrick's.

The next night, Kate and Ian waited in the parking lot until she saw Garrett walk through the front door of the bar. Ten minutes later, she went inside and sat down at the bar, leaving an empty stool between them. She was wearing her wedding ring because Ian wanted there to be no doubt about her marital status or for her to inadvertently send the wrong signal. "Gin and tonic," she said when the bartender asked for her order. "Hendrick's, please."

Garrett glanced over at her and raised his glass. "A fellow gin connoisseur."

She smiled at him. "If you're not going to drink Hendrick's, why bother?" The bartender set the drink down in front of her and she took a sip. "After the day I've had, I deserve it."

"Tough one?"

She took a long drink and sighed. "Mostly frustrating."

"What do you do?"

"I was an account executive, but my employer implemented some budget cuts and laid off almost the entire department. Now I'm temping as a receptionist until I can find another position."

"I'm in marketing too." He dug out a business card and slid it across the bar to her.

She pretended to read the words because she already knew what they said. Then she turned to him and smiled. "I really wanted to apply for a job there, but I didn't see any openings on the website."

"We do a lot of promoting from within, but we still hire from the outside."

"Do you think—" She stopped speaking suddenly as if she were embarrassed by the request she'd been about to make.

"What is it?"

"I was just wondering if I could drop off a résumé. I know I'd have to go through the proper channels and fill out an application, but it would be great to have a professional contact."

"Sure. No problem. Just check in at the front desk and tell the receptionist you're there to see me. I play squash from one to two on Tuesdays and Thursdays, but otherwise I should be there. If not, my assistant Sheila will be."

"Thank you. That would be great. I really appreciate it."

"Sure. No problem."

She nursed her gin and tonic while he conversed with the bartender and waited patiently until he finished his drink and left.

"All set?" Ian asked when she got back in the car and they drove away.

"Yep."

"Any roadblocks?"

"None. I'll be paying a visit to the company on Tuesday between one and two."

"When he's not there."

"Exactly. But his assistant Sheila will be."

"Nicely done."

"It was actually very pleasant. He's a nice guy, easy to talk to. Do you know what the worst part was?"

"What?"

"I discovered I really hate gin."

Kate watched the minutes tick by on the dashboard clock. At exactly 1:50, she walked into the building and approached the reception desk. There were public restrooms in the lobby— a separate one for men and women—but to Kate's relief they looked as if they could only accommodate one person at a time, and both doors were closed. Just beyond the reception desk to the right was a long hallway. She spotted the conference rooms Ian had noticed when he'd visited the company to obtain the CIO's signature on the audit agreement. Next to them, a drinking fountain separated a set of larger employee restrooms.

"Good morning," she said, careful not to sound too chipper. "Garrett Linder asked me to drop off my résumé."

The receptionist dialed a number, and when no one answered, she hung up the phone. "I'm sorry. Mr. Linder is not answering his phone."

"Oh, right. He mentioned he plays squash on Tuesdays and Thursdays and if he wasn't here I could walk it back to Sheila."

"I'm sorry, but that area is restricted and I'd need his approval to issue a visitor badge." The receptionist smiled and extended her hand as if she was happy to accept the résumé. "I can hold on to it and make sure he gets it."

"That's very kind of you, but I really wanted to give him the résumé personally. He was so nice to agree to take a look at it." Kate glanced at her watch. "I'm sure he won't be long."

She swallowed hard and covered her mouth with her hand. She'd applied foundation that was two shades lighter than she normally wore, and she'd skipped the blush entirely. The result had been a paler-than-normal complexion. She'd come up with the idea on her own, and if it worked, she'd be sure to use it again.

"Are you okay?" the receptionist asked.

Kate leaned in, lowering her voice a little. "Morning sickness. The name's a bit of a misnomer because I seem to have it all day long. It's especially bad today, but I was in the area and really wanted to cross this off my list."

"I know exactly how you feel. I had it something awful with my daughter." She looked at Kate sympathetically and motioned to a row of chairs. "You can wait over there if you'd like. Hopefully he'll be back soon."

Kate waited five minutes and approached the desk again. "I think I'm going to be sick, and someone is already using the lobby restroom," she whispered urgently. "Do you have a garbage can?" There were tears in her eyes, and she hoped her expression conveyed her mortification at something so embarrassing happening in such a public place.

The receptionist looked at Kate in horror and pointed toward the conference rooms over her shoulder. "There's another set of restrooms back there. I'll buzz you in."

Kate took off and right when her hips hit the low metal turnstile, she heard a buzzing sound and it swung open. Running, she ducked into the bathroom, and as soon as the door closed, she smiled and nonchalantly walked over to a stall and locked herself inside. From her bag, she pulled a USB drive, pen, and notebook and placed everything on the floor. On the first page of the notebook she'd jotted a to-do list. The first two items were mundane, scheduling meetings and replying to e-mails. The last item was starred and said in all caps: RUN REPORT FOR TED BROWN, which was the name of the CEO. She left another USB drive and notebook with a similar to-do list but a different name on the counter next to the last sink. When she left the bathroom, she ducked into one of the conference rooms and left a third set of materials on the table.

On her way out, she kept her head down as if she were too embarrassed to make eye contact with the receptionist and walked out the door.

It was over an hour's drive home, and her phone rang when she was almost there. "Yes, lover," she said.

"Hello, sweetness. I'm calling to congratulate you on a job well done. You know how happy it makes me to have control of a client's network."

"All of them?"

"Two out of three. I expect the third will soon follow. The bathroom drives were used first. They always are."

"I can't believe people will stick an unmarked USB drive they found in a bathroom, one of them on the floor next to a toilet, into their work computers."

"Unbelievable, isn't it?"

"And gross."

When she got home, she walked into Ian's office and leaned down to give him a kiss.

"Do you feel okay?" he asked.

She threw herself down on the couch and sighed as if she felt terrible. "I'm in the throes of a wicked bout of morning sickness."

An affectionate smile appeared on his face. "Are you trying to tell me something?"

She could not love him more.

"Your reaction is the sweetest thing I have ever seen and my heart just melted, but unless we've recently had a birth control failure I'm not yet aware of, this baby is only the pretend kind. I used foundation to make myself look pale so the receptionist would think I wasn't feeling well. I dropped the VP's and his assistant's name so she'd buy that I had a legitimate reason to be there. But then I worried she might not let me walk it back to Sheila, which is exactly what happened. Plan B involved forcing her to buzz me back by telling her I had morning sickness and making it seem like I was about to throw up all over the lobby."

"Man, you're good."

"That ruse is definitely going in my arsenal. I have a feeling there will be a high rate of success with it."

"Are you up for a team assignment?"

She'd never considered the possibility of the two of them partnering on a social engineering job and could not think of anything more entertaining than working with her husband.

"I just brought on a new client, and I have to tell you, Katie, his smug arrogance is bugging me a little bit."

She laughed. "He must *really* be arrogant if it bothers you."

"The last two firms he hired were unsuccessful in their penetration attempts. I got the feeling he gave me the business solely for the satisfaction of making us number three."

"Oh, it is *on*, Ian."

"That's what I thought, sweetness. I'll have the pretexting done by the end of the weekend. We'll start on Monday."

CHAPTER THIRTEEN

"THOSE ARE SOME SWEET khakis," Kate said.

"Aren't they?" Ian turned in a circle to give her the full view. "Help Desk Todd wears them every day."

"I bet he's a real lady-killer." Ian was also wearing a light blue short-sleeve polo, which he'd told her mirrored the uniform worn by the majority of the male employees who were not part of upper management. His hair had been tamed into some semblance of order, which wasn't easy considering it hadn't been cut in a while.

He took a step back and assessed her appearance. At his directive, Kate had dressed in neutral colors and had chosen a cream-colored cardigan sweater and a pair of pants in a muted tan. Their wedding rings would remain at home because Ian had found they encouraged people to ask questions that they might not want to answer. He'd told Kate that the fewer things people could ask her about, the better her chances were of avoiding a lie that might quickly spiral out of control.

"The clothes are perfect. I just wish we could do something about your face."

She'd applied minimal makeup, and the only thing she'd done to her hair was blow it dry. "What's wrong with my face?" she asked, looking genuinely concerned.

"A good social engineer blends into the scenery, but you—Jeannine from Legal—are way too beautiful. You'll stand out, and they'll remember you." He studied her. "Can you pull your hair back?"

Kate slipped an elastic from around her wrist and scraped her hair into a ponytail with her fingers. Ian slid a pair of black-rimmed Wayfarer-style glasses with nonprescription lenses onto her face and sighed. "I was trying to make you less attractive. It has backfired spectacularly because now you look even hotter."

"Does someone have a naughty librarian fantasy?"

"Come to bed tonight looking like this and you'll find out."

"I'll even bring a book."

He removed the glasses and took Kate's hair down, tucking it behind her ears. "Better," he said. "But still stunning."

"Flatterer."

"Here's your lanyard." Kate slipped the cord over her head and scrutinized the badge attached to it. It looked official, but it was a dummy and incapable of buzzing her through any of the company's doors. What they were about to attempt was the riskiest type of social engineering because it required them to infiltrate a company and impersonate its employees. Ian had told her that wearing the lanyards around their necks in plain sight instead of clipped to their shirts would go a long way toward deflecting suspicion. They might not be able to use their badges, but it would *look* like they could.

"I did some digging, and the reason no security firm has been successful in penetrating this company has less to do with its current security practices and more to do with the fact that the IT manager knows about the audits and likes to leak the news about them so his direct reports will be more vigilant."

"Isn't that counterproductive to discovering their security weaknesses?" Kate asked.

"Yes, but it makes him look like he's running a tighter ship than he is."

Kate looked nervous. "So we're going into this with giant targets on our backs?"

"We would if we were starting the pentesting three weeks from now, which is what the CIO and I agreed on. But I found out last week that he and the CEO will be away at off-site meetings for the next three days, which is why we have to start today."

"The rules just don't apply to you, do they?"

He looked at her as if the answer to that question was obvious and shrugged. "We both know how bad I am at following them."

"Won't the CIO be furious when he finds out what we did?"

"Not after I show him all the ways we were able to penetrate the company. I'm going to drive home the point that black hat hackers aren't going to agree ahead of time to only attack on a particular date. They can strike at any time."

"So the IT manager would rather cheat than let a security firm discover legitimate ways to help his company become more secure. Isn't that a giant waste of money?"

"Yes. And after the CIO tried unsuccessfully to get rid of me by saying they were already secure and didn't need an audit, he admitted their budget wouldn't allow for another one, which is why I told him we'd do it for free."

"Why would we do that?"

"Because we don't need his money, but we do need his referral. Several of his contemporaries at other companies have already turned me down. I don't like that."

Kate shook her head sympathetically. "Of course you don't."

"I was able to overcome his objections by pointing out how much sense it made to take advantage of a service that would cost him nothing, and if we're successful—which we will be—then he'll really be motivated to sing our praises. I used to do this occasionally when I was building my company the first time around. Works like a charm."

"We need to penetrate the hell out of this company, don't we?"

"We've got three days to get way up in there, sweetness. As deep as we can go."

Kate picked up her purse. "Then let's do it."

They drove separately. Though it was unlikely, Ian didn't want to risk someone seeing them getting out of the same car and putting two and two together later.

Kate called him when she arrived. "I'm here."

"I saw you pull in. I'm parked a few rows over. I'll text you when it's your turn. Do it just like we planned."

"I'm ready."

She stayed in her car and watched as Ian walked across the parking lot palming two cups of coffee in one hand and a large white box in the other, the strap of his laptop bag over his shoulder. When he didn't return, she assumed he'd successfully entered the building, and he confirmed it a moment later.

Ian: *Hurry inside before this coffee gets cold. We can drink it with our donuts.*

Kate: *There are donuts?*

Ian: *I bought them when I stopped for the coffee. If I'm going to use the box trick, it might as well have something good inside it. I got you a chocolate one.*

Kate: *You're the best. Where are you now?*

Ian: *I'm in my office.*

Kate: *You don't have an office. Because you don't actually work here.*

Ian: *I've commandeered an empty conference room on the third floor.*

Kate: *Of course you did. Okay, here I come.*

Her heart rate increased as she got out of the car and walked toward the side door, carrying her own large box. She slowed down so her arrival would coincide with a cluster of people who were about to go in. The first person, a man with white hair and a kind smile, swiped his badge and held the door for the others. When he spotted Kate, he waited for her to pass through.

"Thanks," she said.

He gestured toward the box. "Looks heavy."

"Contracts. Took me four hours to get through them last night." She adjusted the empty box, boosting it a bit higher as the lie rolled off her tongue. She remained silent, fighting the urge to add details to her story. *The truth needs no explanation.*

"Where are you headed? I could carry that for you."

She smiled. "Upstairs. Thanks. I've got it."

After watching to make sure he headed in the opposite direction, she got on the elevator. She felt the same thrill she'd experienced during her first social engineering assignment, and every assignment since then, although this time it was heightened. Tailgating her way into a building was definitely the trickiest thing she'd done, and she could see how the thrill of deception could become addicting. On the third floor she got out and walked down the hall, peering into conference rooms until she found Ian. A bite of donut disappeared into his mouth as Kate entered the room and shut the door behind her.

"Excellent job, sweetness. I expected nothing less from you."

"Why don't you like social engineering? Oh my God, it's *exhilarating.*" She set her box on the table and leaned down to kiss him. "Mmmm... You taste like frosting."

He brushed the crumbs from his hands and started typing as Kate reached into the box and grabbed a chocolate donut with pink sprinkles. "I do like social engineering, but I'm not a fan of physical entry and would much rather access the network with my technical skills from the comfort of my home office. But hackers are getting bolder, and when they start walking through the front door, you've got to figure out ways to keep them out so they don't do what I'm about to do."

He removed an Ethernet cable from his laptop bag and plugged it into a jack on the wall. Then he connected it to his laptop. "This is a live network jack. Employees can access the corporate network when they're in here for company meetings. Once a hacker's behind the firewall, it's like giving him the keys to the candy store. I can go anywhere I want." He reached into his laptop bag again and withdrew a small square item. "This is a wireless access device." He bent down and plugged it into the jack. "If someone suspects us and we have to leave the premises temporarily, I can still access the network from my car in the parking lot. Before we leave here, I'll have enough information to access the network from wherever I happen to be."

"What are you going to do if someone's reserved this conference room for a meeting?"

"My first order of business was to move everyone into new rooms. Unfortunately, they'll all think they're losing their minds, but it had to be done."

"What's next?"

"I'm going to run a scan to check the network for computers that aren't protected by a password, and then I'll launch a packet sniffer to capture the traffic moving over the network."

Kate looked shocked. "It's really called a panty sniffer?"

He grinned. "*Packet.*"

"Oh. That makes much more sense."

"Once I've cracked all the machines that *are* protected, I'll give myself administrator rights to the entire network. Should only take about half an hour."

"Wow," Kate said. "All of that before nine a.m."

After Kate finished her donut, Ian sent her out on a recon mission. "Familiarize yourself with the layout of the building. Do a sweep of the break rooms. Be friendly, but not too friendly. If anyone asks you who you are, stick to your story."

"I'm a temp working with Legal on a short-term project to make sure all job descriptions are in compliance. Got it."

Ian had explained to Kate that the trick was not to identify too closely with any particular department because it would raise too many questions and it wouldn't take long for the manager or leader of the department to become suspicious. She would actually be spending most of her time floating around, looking for obvious security infractions like passwords written on sticky notes and left in plain view, and sensitive information that was being disposed of incorrectly. But if anyone doubted her story and started asking legal-type questions, she would be more than qualified to answer them. Meanwhile, Ian would concentrate on the internal network pentesting.

She kissed him good-bye and headed for the door.

Before she left, he said, "Sweetness, find out where the computer server room is located, will you?"

"Anything for you, lover. I'll be back in a little while."

Kate roamed around the building, moving freely from floor to floor. There were no other entry points that required badge access, so after exploring the areas with cubicles, she checked out the break rooms. All had a similar setup: table for six, coffeepot, sink, microwave, vending machine, and fridge. A middle-aged man was sitting at the table reading the newspaper when Kate walked in.

"Good morning," she said.

He looked up and smiled. "Good morning."

Kate was pouring herself a cup of coffee when two women walked in.

They gave her a few sidelong glances, and then one of them said, "Are you new?"

"I'm a temp. Special project for the legal department. I'll be here for a few days. Do you know where I can find the server room that houses the computer systems?"

People were always so eager to share what they knew, and one of the women answered automatically. "It's on the second floor. My boyfriend works in IT."

"Thanks." Kate smiled and swept from the room with a breezy "Good-bye!" before the women could think too much about why a temporary employee working with Legal wanted to know where the computer systems were located.

The server room sat near the back of a large, open-floor-plan space filled with rows of cubicles. Kate walked past the enclosed, freestanding structure slowly, observing the same kind of sensor on the exterior door that she and Ian had successfully bypassed on their way into the building. Unfortunately, she didn't see a single person going in or out of the server room, and the lack of traffic would make it extremely difficult to tailgate in without raising all kinds of red flags. She lingered awhile, pretending she was reading something on her phone. An L-shaped desk with a low partition sat approximately twenty feet from the server-room door, and a young man in his early twenties stared blankly at his computer monitor.

"Can I help you?" he called over after noticing her standing there.

She approached his desk. "Hi. I'm a temp. I'm supposed to join in on a marketing meeting. Do you know if that's going on somewhere down here?"

"No, the marketing department is on the fourth floor. This is IT."

"Thanks.

She returned to the conference room where Ian was still hard at work.

"How'd it go?" he asked. "See anything interesting?"

She pulled out a chair and sat down. "Nothing out of the ordinary. I found the server room. It's on the second floor."

"Freestanding?"

"Yes. How'd you know that?"

"Because no one wants their server room up against an exterior wall that might house water pipes. If they were to burst, it would ruin all their equipment. That's why you won't find many server rooms on the top floor or in the basement. Roofs can leak and basements can flood. Exterior windows can also be a potential security risk. Same with doors. If they can, most companies will try to utilize a room on a middle floor and then retrofit it for their needs by adding cooling and extra security features."

"I noticed it's the only place besides the building's entrances that requires a badge."

"I'm not surprised. Even a company with lax security knows to protect the hub of their operations."

"There weren't a lot of people going in or out. They've also got someone stationed nearby. I'm not sure if he's responsible for keeping an eye on things or if that's just where his desk is located."

"Probably a little of both."

She gestured toward his laptop. "What are you doing now?"

"I'm combing through every file on the network, looking for anything marked confidential or for internal use only. One thing you do not want a hacker to have is access to your private files. It could be a very embarrassing PR nightmare. Not only that, if they're doing any kind of R&D, their secrets could be sold to a competitor."

Ian wanted to take a look at the server room, so he and Kate went down over the lunch hour when there wouldn't be as many people milling about. They walked past slowly, and Ian gave a small nod to let Kate know he'd seen enough. When they returned to the conference room, he told her he wanted her to make the rounds again as soon as everyone returned from lunch, and then they would be done for the day.

"That's it? I feel like I'm just getting warmed up."

"I'm sucking up an enormous amount of their bandwidth with my scans, yet no one seems to have noticed. It's better to quit while I'm ahead. We've got three days, so we'll start small and slowly become more visible. You're going to be mingling among the employees more than I will, and I want them to get used to seeing you. But not *too* used to it. You're very approachable and people will want to make friends with you, but you'll need to keep them at a slight distance so they don't become suspicious. By the third day, we can really push it because by then I *want* them to notice us."

"So what will we be doing tomorrow?"

"Tomorrow you can start shoulder-surfing to see how discreet people are when it comes to typing in their passwords. You can also nose around their desks and eavesdrop on their conversations."

"What about you?"

"I'll finish looking through the files, and then we're going to up our physical-entry game, and by that I mean figure out the best way to break into the server room."

"We're going to break into the server room?"

"You're not. I am. That's another place you don't ever want a hacker poking around, and in order to show the CIO we're truly the best at exposing a company's security weaknesses, I need to get inside. It will prove there's no place in this company we couldn't go."

"There aren't a lot of people going in and out. Won't that make it extremely difficult to tailgate your way in?"

"I'm not going to tailgate. But unfortunately, I can't pick that kind of lock either."

"You know how to pick locks?"

"I can get past a standard lock in about ten seconds if I have my lockpicking kit."

She looked at him like he was crazy. "Your lockpicking kit. This is a thing you own?"

He smiled brightly and nodded. "We used to have contests at MIT. I can break into almost anything."

"Sometimes you straight-up scare me. If you know so much about locks, why didn't you use that knowledge to lock my apartment and go home when I was sick instead of sleeping on my couch and barging in on me in the bathtub?"

"Well, for starters, I wasn't trying to *unlock* your apartment door. And secondly, I didn't have my tools. And thirdly—and most importantly—I didn't want to leave."

"So how are you going to break into the server room?"

"I'm not sure. I'll have to think on it for a while. But never fear. There's a way in. There always is."

CHAPTER FOURTEEN

KATE AND IAN TAILGATED THEIR way into the building on day two. Ian sailed through with his coffee and donuts, but things didn't go quite as smoothly for Kate. As she prepared to fall in with a small group of people bottlenecked near the door, a woman in her early twenties juggling a Starbucks carrier with four cups of coffee, an iPad, and her purse seemed to be waiting for Kate to buzz them in. Trying to remain calm, she smiled and gestured helplessly with her box toward the only other person whose eye she could catch. The young man looked more than happy to help them as he swiped his badge and held the door open until they both passed through.

The girl who had her hands full looked at him with stars in her eyes and said, "Thanks."

He gave her an *aw shucks, it was nothing* grin. "You're welcome."

And they said chivalry was dead.

Ian was already hard at work in the conference room. After they finished their donuts, he resumed scanning the network and sent Kate out to make another sweep of the building. "Today is phase two. You can be a little more visible. Feel free to chat with anyone who strikes up a conversation. Be sure to swing by the IT department to see what they're up to, and make note of how many people you see going in and out of the server room."

"Anything else?"

"Try a little shoulder-surfing. I guarantee you'll enjoy it."

Kate followed the same circuit she'd walked the day before and visited all five floors of the building as well as the break rooms. When she was finished, she made her way slowly up and down the aisles between the rows of cubicles and watched over the employees' shoulders as they typed in their passwords after returning to their desks. Then she went into the break room to get a cup of coffee and check in with Ian.

Kate: *I just watched three employees type in the world's least secure password of #1234. I watched another type in catfetish1@. What is wrong with these people?*

Ian: *catfetish1@ is actually preferable in this scenario. Harder to crack.*

Kate: *I'm going down to the first floor. I'm curious to see how freaky they are in accounting.*

She strolled nonchalantly down the rows of the accounts payable department. A young man returned to his cubicle with a cup of coffee in his hand. Kate was standing a safe distance behind him, watching as he set down his coffee and typed in his password—gamerboystud7—when she sensed a presence next to her. It was the girl from that morning who hadn't been able to buzz them in because her hands were as full as Kate's.

"Hi," she said.

"Hi."

Gamerboystud7 turned around and shot Kate a curious look, so she quickly moved back toward the center of the aisle.

The girl fell in beside her as she walked away. "I'm Ashley."

Kate panicked momentarily because she blanked on the name she was using, but right before the delay in her response would have become awkward, she said, "Jeannine."

"Do you work on this floor?"

"I'm here on a temp assignment. I'm working with Legal on a special project."

"Legal's on the fourth floor. This is Accounting."

"I had to come down for some more files."

Ashley tilted her head. "What kind of files?"

"Job descriptions. I'll be floating around to all the departments, making sure they're in compliance."

"Oh. Sure. That makes sense."

Thank God. Kate decided to change the subject. "It was really nice of that guy to hold the door for us this morning."

"Yeah, he gets here around the same time every day."

Ah, so the girl hadn't been waiting for Kate to buzz them in after all. She'd been waiting for *him.* "And do you always have your hands full?"

She blushed. "Always. My coworkers think I like them so much I'm willing to bring them coffee every day." She lowered her voice. "I don't, really."

Kate smiled. The girl reminded her of her future sister-in-law, Kristin. They had the same spunk. "Do you have plans for lunch?"

"As a matter of fact, I don't."

"I don't know anyone here, and it's boring eating alone. Would you like to go with me?"

"Sure. Meet me in the cafeteria at noon."

Back in the conference room, Kate informed Ian she was meeting someone for lunch. "At first I was worried. She was kind of staring at me with this eerie laser focus, like she was trying to see into my brain. I thought I was going to have to befriend her just to deflect suspicion. But then I learned she has a massive crush on a guy who works here, and frankly she needs help moving things forward."

"See, I knew you'd make friends." He took off his glasses and pushed his chair back from the table. "Are you up for something a bit more challenging? I can do it myself if you don't feel comfortable, but you'll be more inconspicuous because they won't be expecting a woman to do it."

"Are you kidding me? Of course I want to do it." Kate leaned toward him, eager. "What is it?"

"I need you to install this on the systems administrator's computer." He held up a small, cylinder-shaped module with a round opening on each end. "It's a keylogger."

He handed it to her and she studied it.

"What does it do?"

"It records all his keystrokes so I'll know whether he has any suspicion that someone is accessing the network. You'll have to pull the cable that runs from the keyboard to the computer, plug this in, and reconnect the cable."

"I can do that."

"I found an online database that lists the physical location for every employee. He's in the northwest corner, second row over. His name is Nathan Robertson and his cube is slightly bigger than the others. There should be a nameplate on the exterior wall."

Kate took a deep breath. "You always know just how to get my adrenaline pumping, don't you? I may need an extra glass of wine tonight."

"I thought you might. I restocked the wine fridge yesterday."

After locating Nathan's cubicle, Kate walked by slowly, re-lieved to discover it was empty. If she hurried, maybe she could install the keylogger before he returned. She crouched down and darted underneath his desk before she lost her nerve.

It was dark and she worried she might drop the keylogger, so she pulled out her phone and turned on the flashlight, wedging it underneath her chin. Working quickly, she found the correct cable and pulled it from the tower. Then she connected the keylogger and plugged it back in again.

She was on her hands and knees, backing up slowly to avoid hitting her head on the underside of his desk, when a man's voice said, "Excuse me. Why are you under my desk?"

"Oh my God, is this your desk? I'm so sorry!" *Calm down, Kate. No need to shout.* "I lost the back to my earring," she said in a much softer tone. "I saw it hit the ground and roll under here. I chased after it without thinking."

He crouched down. "Do you need help?"

"Thanks, but I found it," she said, scrambling to her feet as she pretended to put the back of the earring on. Her heart thundered in her chest.

"I'm Nathan."

She extended her hand and he shook it. "Jeannine." He was nice-looking, maybe a few years older than her.

"You don't work in IT, do you? I'm sure I'd remember you."

"I'm a temp working on a compliance audit for Legal. I just had a brief meeting on this floor and was on my way to the break room."

"I'm headed there myself. Mind if I walk with you?"

"Not at all." That was the last thing she wanted, but she wasn't willing to jeopardize his acceptance of her explanation for being under his desk.

In the break room, she poured a cup of coffee. She'd had trouble sleeping the night before because her frequent stops in the break room yesterday had caused her caffeine consumption to skyrocket. As soon as she was out of Nathan's view, she'd dump the cup in the garbage.

"How long will you be working on this assignment?" he asked.

"I'm not sure. Probably another day or two."

He leaned against the counter. "Maybe we could grab a cup of coffee before work someday this week."

"Sure."

He pulled his phone from his pocket. "What's your number?"

"I'll give you my e-mail address."

He grinned. "Fair enough."

Ian had set up a bogus e-mail account for Kate to use any-time someone asked for her contact information. She rattled it off and he typed it in.

They left the break room, and when they reached the aisle where his cubicle was located, he said, "Have a nice afternoon."

"Thanks, you too."

On her way back to let Ian know everything had—mostly—gone off without a hitch, she realized Nathan hadn't actually needed anything in the break room.

Ian was leaning back in his chair grinning, arms crossed in front of him when she let herself back into the conference room. "I send you to install a keylogger and you come back with a date?"

"How do you know that?" Her eyes widened. "Hold up. He's already sent an e-mail? I literally just left him five minutes ago."

"Oh, yes. Nathan thinks he's taking my wife to Starbucks for coffee and scones. *Please.*"

Kate clasped her hands together and gasped. "Do you think he'll let me order one of those seasonal lattes from the secret menu?"

"I think he just might. A venti, even." He pulled her down onto his lap and tickled her, making her laugh and squirm.

"Stop that. I had no choice. He caught me underneath his desk, and I'm not wearing a ring. I have to admire his fearlessness."

"I think it's great that you have a date. Really. Couldn't be cooler with the idea."

"You're a horrible liar."

"I'm an *excellent* liar. How do you think Nathan will feel about you bringing your husband along?"

"I think he'll be bummed because that's probably not the kind of three-way he was hoping for."

"It's not the kind any man hopes for."

"Have you ever actually had a three-way? You said most men wouldn't turn one down."

"No, I've never had one. And what I said was that most men probably wouldn't turn one down if the opportunity presented itself, which it never has for me. It's also not the kind of thing I ever went looking for. I can't speak for all mankind, but if I had to guess, I'd say the idea of a three-way is more enticing than the act itself. That doesn't mean there aren't men out there desperately trying to have them, but I'm not one of them. There's only one woman I want in my bed, and there's no room for anyone else. Besides, we're plenty spicy on our own, and you have yet to say no to anything I've suggested. Together we're pretty hot." He slid his hand behind her head and kissed her gently.

"I was just wondering."

"Have you ever had a three-way?"

She shook her head. "Not my jam."

The sound of approaching footsteps halted further conversation, and Kate leapt from Ian's lap. She landed in her own chair mere seconds before the door opened.

"Hey," Ian said, looking up like he was bored. Kate scribbled away on her notepad as if she were too busy to even look up.

"I'm pretty sure I have this room reserved."

Ian tapped on his keyboard. "Is your name Colin?"

"Yeah."

"You're actually in 3A next door. You've got the room from noon until one."

"Okay. Thanks. I could have sworn I booked this one. Sorry to interrupt."

"No problem."

"You have the reflexes of a cat," Ian said after Colin left.

Kate laughed. "I'm also quite bendy."

"Trust me. I thank your Pilates instructor every day for that."

"I have to meet Ashley in the cafeteria. Do you want me to bring you back something to eat?"

"Thanks, but it's time for me to start raising my profile. I think I'll go for a nice long stroll. I'll hit the vending machine in one of the break rooms."

She kissed him again. "Okay. See you in an hour."

She spotted Ashley standing in the cafeteria line and joined her.

"So, what's his name?" Kate asked once they'd carried their trays to a table and sat down.

"Tristan."

"What department does he work in?"

"Marketing."

"What else do you know about him?"

"That's it."

"That's it?" Maybe Ian had rubbed off on her because Kate found Ashley's lack of due diligence somewhat confusing. "How long have you been timing your arrival to coincide with his?"

"I don't know. A month or so?"

"Do you know if he has a girlfriend?"

"I've never seen him with anyone. Sometimes I walk by his table at lunch, but he's always with his coworkers. Just guys."

Kate looked around the cafeteria. "Is he here now?"

Ever so nonchalantly, Ashley looked over her shoulder and did a quick visual sweep of the cafeteria. "I don't see him."

"Maybe we should think about maximizing your potential for a little more interaction."

"That sounds good. I'm really tired of stopping at Starbucks every morning." Ashley unscrewed the cap of her lemonade. "Do you have a boyfriend?"

Kate was supposed to say she was single, but how could she help Ashley if she couldn't even claim a boyfriend of her own? "Yes."

"What's his name?"

"Steve." *Wait, no. Steve is my dad. Oh, God.*

"Where does he work?"

"NASA. He's an astronaut." *Where is this coming from?* No wonder Ian had cautioned her about providing too much backstory. "He's away at training right now. At Cape Canaveral."

Seriously, Kate. Stop.

"Wow. That's really exciting. How did you meet him?"

Kate laughed. "I was on vacation in Florida and I *literally* crashed into him on the street. We've been together ever since."

Ashley's forehead creased in confusion. "So it's a long-distance relationship?"

"For now. I'll be moving there soon. That's why I'm temping. I don't want anything too permanent."

Ashley sighed. "I wish you were staying. I need all the help I can get with Tristan."

After lunch, Kate told Ashley she wanted to grab a bottle of water before she went back to work. They walked into the break room, and Ashley nearly crashed into the back of Kate who'd stopped suddenly because Ian was sitting at the table eating potato chips, surrounded by women. He paged through the newspaper while five adoring sets of eyes tried to cover up the fact they were staring at him.

Kate hummed as she fed quarters into the machine and pushed the button for water.

"Is that "Close to You" by the Carpenters?" Ashley asked.

"It is. Good ear."

"Oh, I love that song."

"Me too."

A few more people filed into the break room, patiently waiting their turns for the microwave or for space to open up at the table. Reluctantly it seemed, the women gathered their trash and headed back to their desks, casting wistful glances at Ian. Kate kept one eye on him as she and Ashley stood there chatting.

She listened as he leaned toward the man sitting across from him. "Who's the tall blonde by the coffeepot?"

The man glanced over his shoulder at Kate. "I don't know."

"Man, I wish she was wearing a skirt. I bet her legs go on for miles."

"Dude. Keep your voice down. You can't say things like that."

"Why, is the sexual harassment policy here pretty strict?"

It was all Kate could do not to burst out laughing because Ian had not lowered his voice *at all.*

"What? Yeah. I mean, I'm sure it is."

"That's good."

The last thing Kate heard as she and Ashley left the break room was Ian wondering aloud about her bra size. "I bet she's a 34C. I have a really good eye for these things."

"Do the potato chips taste better when you're surrounded by your harem?" Kate asked when Ian returned to the conference room.

"Not really, but if one of them asks me out, maybe we can double with you and Nathan?"

"Just keep it in your khakis, Todd, and no one will get hurt."

"How was lunch?"

"Well, other than telling Ashley my boyfriend's name was Steve and he's away at astronaut training, it was uneventful."

He burst out laughing. "What the hell, Kate?"

"I know. It was the first name I thought of and it just tumbled out of my mouth. By the way, can you find out a few things about a guy she likes so I can help her?"

"Really? You're asking me if I can find things out about someone?"

"How silly of me." She tore a piece of paper from her notebook and wrote Tristan's name on it. "He works in the marketing department. I need to know if he already has a girlfriend or if he's just socially inept. Guys sometimes need a little nudge when it comes to making the first move."

Ian seemed confused. "They do?"

"Well, not you. But others sometimes do."

"You're adorable when you play matchmaker."

"These kids need some help. I'm convinced they're star-crossed lovers who need to be together, but Ashley's paralyzed by shyness and Tristan is completely oblivious."

"I'm on it." He folded the piece of paper and tucked it into his pocket. "C'mon. Let's take a stroll."

She had no idea where he was leading her until they reached the second floor. "I assumed you'd want to avoid the IT department?"

"I did at first, but now it's time to start raising my visibility a bit." They walked brazenly through the department as if they had no particular place to go, but no one gave them a second look. They walked by the server room, pausing when someone came out. Ian stared at the room through the open door and didn't start walking again until it closed. Then he led her to the stairwell where they went up three flights to the fifth floor. He stopped in front of a door.

"Whose office is this?"

"The CEO's. I just need a few pictures and we'll be on our way." He fished a small metal tool from his pocket, picked the lock, opened the door, and pulled her inside.

"Is that from your lockpicking kit? Let me see it."

He handed it to her and then locked the door from the inside and started taking pictures with his phone.

"Kate, sit down in his chair." She complied, back straight, hands folded and resting on the desktop.

"What are you going to do with the pictures?"

"Maybe I'll make a slideshow montage. I'll call it 'look at all the places we broke into while you were gone.'"

"I'm sure he'll love that. Let me take one of you."

They swapped places and Ian turned on the CEO's computer. "I'm going to hack into his computer first. Putting some sensitive information on the screen adds a certain flair to the picture."

"Indeed it does."

He finished typing thirty seconds later. "There. The salary breakdown of the entire IT department ought to do the trick."

"Impressive."

Ian shut down the computer and they were about to leave when someone knocked on the door. They froze. The doorknob rattled and Kate shot him a panicked look. He winked and held a finger to his lips.

After not speaking or moving for five minutes, Ian gave the all clear. "Let's go," he whispered.

CHAPTER FIFTEEN

KATE ARRIVED HOME BEFORE IAN. By the time he walked into the kitchen, she'd already poured a glass of wine and started dinner. He dropped a kiss onto her lips.

"What took you so long? I thought you were right behind me."

"I stopped at a hardware store to buy supplies. During our server-room recon this afternoon, I noticed the door had a small gap underneath it. When the door opened, I also made note of the sensor on the wall inside the room, so I did a little snooping around before we left for the day."

"As you do," Kate said.

"Five years ago, a different company occupied the building and they used what's now the server room for some kind of lab. It's perfect, really. Secure. Contained. Except for the small gap between the floor and the bottom of the door they never bothered to close. As for the sensor on the wall, it's heat activated. Say your hands were full of test tubes or some other lab-specific item and you didn't want to put them down to swipe your badge. The heat from your body triggers the sensor and the door opens for you."

"Have I ever told you how much your brain turns me on?"

"I thought it was my hair that did that?"

"Your hair is just the nice packaging. It's what's underneath that really gets me going. Nothing is hotter than smart, my friend." She poured him a bourbon and they clinked their glasses.

"I don't know if it still works. They could have easily disconnected the sensor. They *should* have disconnected it. Either that or sealed the gap under the door. At the very least they're losing some of their cold air."

Kate mulled it over for a minute. "So you're going to trigger the heat sensor from the outside."

"I could not be more proud of you right now."

"Don't be too quick with your praise. I didn't say I knew *how* you were going to do it."

He handed her a paper bag, and she reached in and withdrew a hand warmer. It was palm-sized so it could be slipped inside a glove or pocket. "I think I know where you're going with this."

"I'm going to attach it to a stiff wire and slide it under the door and up toward the sensor. The room is kept so cool that it shouldn't take much to activate it."

"Have you ever done this before?"

"No."

She clapped her hands together. "Can I do it?"

"No."

"Oh, come on. Why not?"

He looked sheepish. "Because I kinda want to do it."

"I'm not surprised. This is some *Mission: Impossible* stuff right here."

"I'll let you do it next time, I promise."

"I'm going to hold you to that," she said as she pulled items from the refrigerator and preheated the oven.

"Are you sure you feel like cooking? We could pick up dinner."

"Cooking relaxes me. Or maybe the wine does. Either way, I've been looking forward to this all day."

"What does my gourmet chef have planned?"

"Beef medallions with blue cheese, roasted asparagus, and baked potatoes. I've never made the beef before, so you might want to lower your expectations," she said, laughing. "I'm making no promises."

"I have faith in you. I'm sure it'll be wonderful."

Ian went into his office after they finished dinner, which he proclaimed was every bit as wonderful as he'd predicted. Kate went in to check on him an hour later, and he handed her a piece of paper with every detail about Tristan that Ashley could ever want to know, including the fact that his girlfriend had cheated on him a year ago with a coworker. When the guy dumped her, she'd come crawling back and Tristan wisely told her to take a hike. Kate smiled as she scanned the information and then looked at him tenderly. "I never thought I'd say this, but I'm actually feeling a bit nostalgic for the first time you hacked *me*."

He grinned. "Maybe Ashley and Tristan will get married someday. You should keep in touch with her."

The next morning, Ian drove them to work and they walked toward the entrance together. They no longer minded if people thought they knew each other, but Kate stopped short of the door. "You can go in without me. I need to wait for Ashley. This shouldn't take too long."

"Check me out. No coffee. No box. I'm not even wearing my lanyard. Watch and learn, Katie."

He sauntered up to the entrance and leaned against the building. When the next cluster of employees reached the door,

Ian fixed them with a bored stare until one of them pulled out their badge and swiped it. Just before entering the building, he turned around and gave her the thumbs-up.

Ashley arrived holding her Starbucks carrier full of coffee, iPad, and purse, and Kate pulled her aside, knowing she had to speak quickly. "Tristan likes visiting microbreweries and watching horror films. He likes dogs more than cats, and loyalty is very important to him, especially when it comes to women."

Ashley looked confused and more than a little wary. "How can you *possibly* know that? Oh my God, did you cyberstalk him?"

Kate felt a momentary twinge of guilt for her actions, but her heart was in the right place and she told herself it was for the greater good. "No, nothing like that. It's all, you know, public knowledge if you're good at reading between the lines. So here's what we're going to do. After Tristan swipes his badge and follows us in, I'm going to ask you if you've decided whether to go on the brewery tour of DC this weekend. You're going to say you'd love to, but you don't know anything about microbrews."

"And then what?"

"Then we cross our fingers that Tristan takes the bait."

They didn't have to wait long.

"Here he comes," Kate said. Watching from the corner of her eye as Tristan walked across the parking lot, Kate pretended to be engrossed in conversation with Ashley. Unlike Ian, she still had her box. Tristan eyed them, and Kate stifled a smile because she could tell by his expression that he was absolutely a willing and eager participant in this daily dance. He swiped his badge and held the door, and after they thanked him, he followed them inside. Kate deliberately slowed their pace.

"So are you going?" she asked in a slightly louder than normal voice.

"I don't know anything about beer, especially microbrews."

"That's the point. The tour is supposed to be very informative."

"I don't mean to eavesdrop, but are you by chance talking about the DC Brew Tour?" Tristan asked.

Well done, Tristan.

"Oh," Ashley said, looking over her shoulder as if she had no idea Tristan was there. "Yes. Are you familiar with it?"

"I've been on it three times. It's awesome. You should totally go."

"Really? How does it work?"

Kate very subtly nudged them out of the stream of traffic entering the building, looked at her watch, and tossed a breezy, "See you later" over her shoulder as she left Ashley and Tristan to their conversation and headed toward the elevator. *My work here is done.*

Ian was waiting in the conference room. "How did things go?"

"I don't want to sound like I'm bragging, but I'm pretty good at this matchmaker stuff."

"Just one of your many talents, sweetness." He sighed. "We should have stopped for donuts. Okay, today is phase three, which means we're going to be the opposite of running silent. We're everywhere."

"Are we trying to get caught?"

"Not exactly, because I still have to break into the server room at the end of the day. And if I'm unsuccessful, we'll have to come back tomorrow so I can try again. But we're going to push the envelope as far as we can. Common sense dictates that our behavior should spark suspicion among the employees of this company. Let's see how much they're paying attention."

"What do you want me to do?"

"See if you can obtain the log-in credentials of five to ten employees on each floor. If they're away from their desks, sit down at their computer and try to log in. If they're at their desks, ask them for their user name and password. Keep track of how many people refuse or ask you why you want to know."

"What will you be doing?"

"I'm going to start by crashing the IT department's weekly meeting."

"You're kidding."

"Nope. Just think how the CIO will feel when he hears about it. After that, I'm going to do the same thing you're doing, although I'll probably be a bit less subtle about it."

"Nooooooooo," she deadpanned.

"Hard to believe, huh?"

She grinned. "Not at all."

He pulled out the neckline of her shirt, looked down it, and let out a low wolf whistle. "That should hold me for a while."

"Plenty more where that came from later," she said as he laughed and headed for the door.

Ian entered the conference room for the IT meeting and took a seat near the back. A few members of the department shot him curious looks; he met them with a cheery smile.

A man dressed in an identical uniform of polo shirt and khakis sat down next to him. "Hey."

"How's it going?" Ian said.

"Not bad. Do you know what we're discussing today? I forgot my agenda."

"I literally do not have a clue." He could have found out if he'd wanted, but that seemed like unnecessary work, especially since he didn't really care.

The IT manager, a man Ian recognized from the picture he'd downloaded from the Internet, hurried into the room. He scanned the attendees as if checking to see if everyone was there and hesitated for a moment when he spotted Ian. He should have asked what someone he didn't recognize was doing there, but Ian had found that most people didn't like asking questions in front of others for fear of looking like they didn't know what was going on. The IT manager was no different, and he moved on and got started with the meeting.

Kate was sitting at an unattended cubicle playing online solitaire when she received a text from her brother. She'd cracked the employee's computer password on her third attempt by using his last name—clearly visible on the name-plate—followed by his first name and the number 1. When would people learn?

Chad: *I want to buy Kristin something really special for Christmas. Can you do some nosing around and get back to me?*

Kate: *I'm on it.*

She placed her queen and sent a message to Kristin.

Kate: *What gift item do you wish you had right now?*

Kristin: *Did Chad ask you for ideas?*

Kate: *You know how shopping paralyzes him. Tell me what you want and I'll make sure you get it.*

Kristin: *Let me think about it and get back to you.*

Kate became engrossed in her game and wondered how far she could get before the employee returned.

Ian: *This meeting is incredibly boring. Sext me.*

Kate: *Remember when you walked in on me in the bathtub at my apartment in Minneapolis?*

Ian: *How could I forget? The image of your left nipple was burned into my brain that day. I'm picturing it right now.*

Kate: *I was absolutely about to touch my breasts.*

Ian: *I knew it! Tell me how it was going to go down.*

Kate: *I was going to pretend my hands were your hands. Then I was going to touch myself the way I imagined you would touch me.*

Ian: *Keep going. DO NOT STOP.*

Kate: *That's as far as I got because then you walked in on me FOR REAL.*

Ian: *How very PG-13. I KNOW YOU CAN DO BETTER.*

Kate: *We're in the conference room. It's dark and empty and I'm stroking you through your khakis.*

Ian: *Zzzzzzzzzzzzzzzzzzzzzzzz.*

Kate: *We're in the conference room, and I've been such a bad girl. You're going to teach me a lesson.*

Ian: *I'm awake now.*

Kate: *We're in the conference room, and you take off all my clothes and lay me down on the table. As you stroke me, you tell me I have to keep quiet or you'll stop. I can't stop making those little noises you like because it feels incredible, so you have to cover my mouth with your hand, which turns me on like you wouldn't believe.*

Kate felt warm and fidgeted in her chair as she hit Send. Two minutes later, her phone buzzed.

Ian: *I'm waiting.*

That was strange. He should have received it by now. She scanned her text log. Why was Chad's name showing up? Her heart began to pound as she checked her last message and saw Chad's name.

Kate: *OMG!!! I accidentally sent that last text to my brother.*

Ian: *What did it say?*

Kate: *I'll resend it. Hopefully to you and not any other member of my family this time.*

Ian: *Like Steve, your astronaut boyfriend/dad?*

Kate: *SHUT UP I WOULD DIE. And I'm trying to erase the dad/boyfriend thing from my memory, so please don't mention it ever again.*

She resent the text and he responded ten seconds later.

Ian: *I predict it's going to be very difficult for Chad to accept that his little sister has a freaky side. And it's all I can do to keep myself from marching you right into that conference room and making this a reality. But I'm a professional who rarely mixes business with pleasure, so I will restrain myself.*

Kate: *That's a first.*

Ian: *I know. It's killing me.*

Chad: *Jesus! Pretty sure that wasn't for me. Really wish I could unsee it.*

Kristin: *HAHAHAHAHAHAHAHAHAHA. Chad just forwarded the best text message EVER. *dying**

"Uh, this is my desk." The employee sounded utterly dumbfounded to find Kate sitting in his chair.

Kate looked up from her phone. "Oh, hey. Sorry. I felt like playing solitaire and my desk is, you know, *clear on another floor.* You need to change your password because it only took me three tries to figure it out. Feel free to finish my game."

She dashed off before he could ask any questions and took the stairs to the fourth floor. She'd brought a small notebook with her, and she made her way up and down the rows asking employees for their passwords. Each time, she gave them the same spiel: *I'm working on a project with Legal. I need your user name and password.* Most of them gave it to her without a single protest, but a few of them refused.

"Excellent," she told them. "You shouldn't give that information to anyone."

She received another text from Ian.

Ian: *The IT department is having something called food day tomorrow. They passed around a sign-up sheet. I said I'd bring cheese dip.*

Kate: *Of course you did.*

Ian: *If we have to come back tomorrow for another crack at the server room, can you please make some? I told everyone I was world famous for it. I can't believe how excited they got.*

Kate: *You're killing me.*

Ian: *Does that mean yes?*

Kate: *Yes, I will make you some cheese dip.*

Ian: *Best wife ever.*

After the meeting, as his employees filed out the door, the IT manager walked up to Ian and said, "Excuse me. Who are you?"

Ian stuck out his hand and they shook. "Todd Smith. Help desk administrator."

"Who hired you?"

"I had a phone interview and then HR asked me to come in for a face-to-face with one of the supervisors. I forget his name, but he was just in this meeting. I got the job offer two days later." Watching the manager rack his brain as he tried to recollect any of this amused Ian immensely.

"Yeah, okay. Sorry. Didn't know they'd already set a start date for you. Welcome aboard."

"No problem. It's great to be here. I can't believe how much I've already learned."

Kate and Ian ate lunch together in the cafeteria, and she smiled when she noticed Ashley and Tristan talking animatedly at a table for two.

Ian unwrapped his sandwich. "This afternoon we'll be collecting more user names and passwords. I'd like to take a look at the copy rooms on each floor. The recycling and shredding bins should be located there and clearly marked, and I want to see if the employees are disposing of documents the way they should."

"What if someone suspects what we're doing?"

"If it looks like one of us has gotten cornered by someone who's figured out what we're really up to, the other can confirm it by casually asking, 'How's it going?' If the answer is 'Great,' then there's nothing to worry about. If the answer is, 'Couldn't be better,' shit's about to hit the fan and you should calmly—but very quickly—head for the door."

"I can't just leave you behind."

"I'm not exactly bleeding out on a battlefield. Besides," he said, taking a drink of his Coke, "I'm not going to get caught."

"Neither am I," she said, bouncing her leg as the adrenaline began to flow. She felt like a sprinter poised in the starting blocks, waiting for the gun to go off.

He laid his hand on her leg for just a moment. "Easy there, grasshopper."

"I can't. I feel like Spy Girl. Tell me again why you don't like doing this?"

"Because it's not remotely as fun when your wife's not with you."

In the first-floor copy room, Kate snapped several pictures of the sensitive documents an employee tossed into the trash instead of the shredder.

Ian sent an employee into a full-blown panic attack after sitting down at a computer, cracking the password on the first try, and, upon the young man's sudden return, saying to him, "I'm not going to find any porn on this, am I?"

Between them, they collected the badges of seven employees who'd left them on their desks where anyone could swipe them, and Kate took photos of the proprietary information people left in full view on their monitors after they walked away without locking down their computers.

They were walking down the aisle of a long row of cubicles when Ian stopped at the desk of a female sales manager and sat down on the edge of it. "I'm Todd Smith from the help desk. Can I borrow your computer?"

She looked him up and down. "Sure," she said, getting up with no questions asked.

"You should really say no," Kate said, leaning against the wall of the manager's cubicle.

"He's from the help desk," she said, barely glancing at Kate and acting as if her concern was totally unnecessary.

Ian sat down in her chair, held her gaze for a slightly inappropriate amount of time, and asked for her user name and password.

"Don't give it to him," Kate said.

"Who are you?" the manager asked in a completely different tone, one that definitely wasn't as nice.

"Jeannine. *From Legal.* Urging you to use caution."

"It's okay," Ian purred. "I'm not going to steal *all* your secrets."

The manager giggled. "Of course not." She gave him the information and settled on the edge of the desk, running her fingers through her hair and smiling as Ian typed in the commands to access her confidential files and send them to his laptop in the conference room. When he'd taken everything he wanted, he stood and pulled the chair out for her.

She appeared to be in some kind of trance when she sat down, and he pushed her chair back in as if they were in a restaurant getting ready to have dinner together. "Come back if you need anything else. I'll be here until six."

"Thanks. I might do that."

Kate pulled him into an empty hallway near the break room. "Wait a minute. I can't use my boobs to get what I want, but you can bend people to your will with your stunning good looks and charm?"

He feigned innocence. "Did I do that?"

"You glamoured her like some kind of hacker-vampire."

"Being a hacker-vampire would be *so cool.*"

She laughed. "Bite me, Todd."

"I can make that happen when we get home, Jeannine."

They split up, and Kate made another round of the third and fourth floors. She was strolling down the aisle where the customer service reps sat when an employee whose name plate read Connor popped out of his cube and startled her.

"Hey, uh, Jeannine?"

"How do you know my name?"

"Todd told me. He's looking for you. He described what you were wearing and said to keep my eyes open for a hot blonde with long legs. Those were his words, not mine. I don't think we're supposed to say things like that."

"Which one is Todd again?"

"Uh, that really tall guy. His hair's a little long. Not sure what his job title is, but he fixed my computer and it's working much better now."

"I bet," she said.

"There he is," Connor said pointing over her shoulder.

Kate turned around.

"How's it going?" Ian asked pointedly.

Wait. Was she supposed to say great or couldn't be better? She had no reason to believe Connor suspected either one of them. "Great."

Ian nodded. "Excellent."

Connor's eyes narrowed as he scrutinized Ian. "Where did you say you came from again?"

Okay, maybe he suspected them a little bit.

"Consulting firm."

He turned toward Kate. "And you?"

"Temp agency."

"Do you have desks?"

"Yes, but I don't like to sit for too long," Kate said.

"Me neither," Ian said.

"Feel like taking a walk?" Kate asked.

"Let's," Ian said.

Kate looked over her shoulder as they moved into the aisle. "See you later, Connor."

At four thirty, Ian wanted to attempt entering the server room. He'd said the employees would be less vigilant at the end of the day, and hopefully some of them had already left.

"Here's what we're going to do. I'm going to station you near the desk of the guy whose job it is to keep an eye on the server room. You'll be able to see me walk toward the door. I want you to distract him so I have time to fish my wire under the door and trigger the heat sensor. Engage him in friendly conversation until you see me come back out. Then meet me in the conference room."

"I'm ready."

"Hey, Todd," someone yelled as they were walking toward the server room.

"Shit," Ian muttered.

They turned around.

"Connor said I could probably find you down here. Do you think you can help me for a minute? My computer's doing something weird."

"Sure. As he turned to follow the guy, he nonchalantly handed Kate the folder. "Give it a whirl, sweetness. No pressure. If you can't get in, we'll come back tomorrow." Kate took the folder, clasped it tightly to her chest, and kept walking.

When Kate reached the server room, the employee monitoring it gave her a cursory glance and then turned her attention back to something on his desk. She waited until there were no other employees in the area and extended the wire in a way that wouldn't draw attention to the fact that she'd just pulled something that resembled a bent-in-thirds coat hanger with a hand warmer taped to the end out of her folder.

I can do this, she told herself. *I have a get-out-of-jail-free letter and nothing bad will actually happen to me if I'm caught.*

But she didn't want to get caught, because she was just as invested in gaining entry to that server room as Ian was.

Kate walked up to the server-room door, looked around one last time to make sure no one was watching, and bent down and slid the wire under it, angling it upward.

The tech whose cubicle was right outside the server room was in the middle of a wicked coughing attack. Ian waited until it had subsided and then materialized at his side. "You sound like you could use some water. Do you want me to keep an eye on things while you get a bottle from the break room?"

"No thanks, man. I'm good."

"Have you been to the doctor?"

"I'm going later today. Can't get in until five thirty, so I'm stuck here for a while longer." He started coughing again, barely covering his mouth, and Ian flinched.

"I'm not a doctor, but that sounds like an upper respiratory tract infection. Cough, congestion, chills. Maybe a fever, although it probably won't get too high. Of course, it could be the flu."

"God, I hope not. I had it last year. I was sicker than a dog."

Over the man's shoulder, Ian caught a glimpse of Kate near the server-room door, and then her head ducked out of sight. He anticipated she would need five to ten seconds to slip the wire under the door and trigger the sensor.

All he had to do was keep this guy talking.

Nothing happened when Kate waved the hand warmer in what she thought would be the vicinity of the sensor. There was no audible click to let her know it had been tripped. She twisted her elbow, attempting to slide it farther under the door so she could get the wire up higher. The sound of voices reached her ears, and two people engrossed in conversation rounded the corner at the far end of the hall. She flung the wire under the door and listened as it skittered across the server-room floor and hit something with a thud. With her heart pounding and only moments to spare, she stood and pushed on the door handle. Maybe she hadn't heard the click over the whirring of the machinery, but the door opened and Kate slipped inside.

Ian sat down on the edge of the tech's desk. "Have your symptoms worsened in the past twenty-four hours? Are you having trouble breathing?"

"What?" He seemed irritated by the questions. "No."

"I never get sick. I'm impervious to germs."

"Good for you. That must be nice."

"Oh, it is."

"Is there something you need?"

The server door opened and he caught a glimpse of the back of Kate's head as she disappeared inside, pulling the door closed behind her. *That's my girl.*

"Yes. I wanted to let you know tech support will be doing a company-wide update overnight. I'm just helping to spread the word in case you didn't get the e-mail. If you could log off before you leave, that would be great."

"Sure, whatever." A sheen of sweat coated the guy's brow.

Ian's heart rate quickened when two men walking side-by-side, one of whom he recognized as the assistant IT manager, stopped in front of the server room. The assistant manager swiped his badge and they went inside.

Kate worked quickly, moving down the rows of servers, opening the glass-front doors and wedging Ian's business cards into the corner of the racks holding the equipment. She took several pictures of herself standing in various parts of the room in front of the servers. Her mission was nearly complete when she heard the door open and the sound of people talking. Kate froze when the two men came into view. Trying to slow her galloping heart rate, she ignored them as she walked past with her head down, folder held open, pointing at invisible items as if she were going through a checklist.

"Excuse me?" one of them said when she had almost reached the door.

She turned around, acting as if she was surprised to see them there. "Yes?"

"What department are you from?" He looked older than the employee who was standing next to him, and he was wearing dress pants and a shirt and tie.

"Legal. I'm conducting an audit."

"My boss didn't say anything about an audit." *He would have if he'd known about it,* she thought.

She looked at him pointedly. "I'm sure he didn't."

"What kind of an audit is it?"

She appeared thoughtful and confident. "I can't divulge that, but you'll be happy to know you passed with flying colors. Your boss will be so pleased. Keep up the good work."

Their expressions softened, and the man in the tie even smiled. The first step in manipulating people was to tell them they were doing a good job. All anyone wanted to hear was how much value they brought to an organization. If the men didn't push back too hard, maybe their boss would have some glowing praise for them in the morning.

Kate smiled back and walked out.

The door to the server room opened, and Ian watched Kate emerge and walk toward the stairwell.

"Well, hey. I hope you feel better. You should stay home tomorrow." He had to raise his voice in order to be heard above the man's coughing attack.

The man waved him away. "Yeah, maybe I'll do that."

She was waiting for him in the conference room, and she was on fire. She flew into his arms and said, "Holy crap, that was intense. I'm still waiting for my heart to stop ping-ponging around in my chest."

"Excellent job, Jeannine. You've earned your Spy Girl title."

"I took a bunch of pictures and planted the business cards, but I got stopped on the way out."

"That's okay. I'll admit to being a bit concerned when the assistant manager joined you, but the important thing is you got *in*."

"That was the assistant manager?"

"Not just any assistant manager. The assistant *IT* manager."

"Oh my God."

"And no other firm has been able to penetrate that server room. They're supposedly guarding it like a hawk and claim it can't be done. The CIO told me that himself."

"And you didn't mention this before, why?"

"Didn't want you to think we couldn't do it. And see? It worked."

She handed him her phone, and he scrolled through the pictures she'd taken. Then he set it on the table and put his arms around her. "Sweetness, I have a question for you. If someone asked you if our life together was boring or exciting, what would you say?"

"I'd say that so far, it's every bit the adventure I hoped it would be."

"I know it's been a long day, but I need to see you in the conference room. We have some unfinished business to take care of," Ian said when they got home.

She set down her purse and kicked off her shoes. "Of course. I'll be there in five minutes."

He was sitting at his desk when she walked in. She'd played it so straight he wasn't positive she'd understood, but she'd changed out of the sedate clothes she'd worn that day into a short black skirt, a white silk blouse open far enough that he could see the top of her black bra, sheer stockings, and extremely high heels. He suppressed a smile because the glasses and ponytail were back.

This is what he'd been talking about when he said they didn't need any extra spice.

He'd bet money they never would.

She sat down on the couch. He had difficulty taking his eyes off her legs and she recrossed them slowly, as if she knew that.

"Are you ready to begin?" she asked.

"Yes. I'd like to start outlining my report tonight, so we'll need to recap the many ways in which we were successful in our penetration methods."

"I'll write them down for you," she said, opening the notepad and clicking open the pen she'd brought.

He put on his glasses. "Technical penetration was successfully executed externally, internally, and wirelessly. Entrance to the building requires a badge, yet we circumvented the building's physical security three times each for a total of six breaches. We were never stopped or questioned. Over the course of three days, we entered the office of the CEO, installed a keylogger, raised our profile to the extent that our presence should have raised a red flag, and penetrated the server room. Did I forget anything?"

She finished writing down their accomplishments and looked up. "I think that's everything."

"Well done, Jeannine. Especially the server room."

"Thank you. I look forward to doing it again."

He leaned back in his chair and steepled his fingers. "Why don't you come over here?"

She walked over to his desk and perched on the corner, just out of reach. In the black stilettos and sheer stockings, her legs seemed to go on for miles.

"That skirt is a bit short for the workplace, don't you think?"

Her face was flushed, not pink like when she was embarrassed, but rosy, a color he'd come to recognize as the by-product of desire, as if her core temperature had slowly been heating her from within.

"You don't like it?" she asked.

He pushed in the keyboard tray and reached for her, placing his hands on her hips and dragging her over a bit so she was sitting on the desk directly in front of him. He positioned her feet so they rested on the tops of his thighs, which gave him a nice view of her stockings attached to her garter belt. "I only said it was short. I never said I didn't like it." He took off her shoes and they landed on the carpet with a soft thud.

Her chest rose and fell as he stared at the buttons of her blouse and observed the increase in the tempo of her breathing. After leaning forward and pulling the hem of her blouse from the waistband of her skirt, he began unbuttoning it from the bottom. When the buttons were undone, he stood and stripped her of it. The bra was black with a purple lace overlay. He'd bought it about a month ago, and he'd tucked it into her lingerie drawer with the other pieces that made up the set. He'd been waiting patiently because part of the allure was not knowing when Kate would wear it. She often wore the lingerie he bought her under her oldest pair of jeans and her plainest T-shirts. He was always pleasantly surprised to encounter silk and lace when he'd been expecting cotton, and he swore she did it on purpose just to keep him guessing.

"Are you aroused, Jeannine? I know what a good hack does to you."

"You tell me, Todd."

Tracing his fingers along her bra, he reached behind her and unhooked it, and it sailed onto the floor and landed next to one of her shoes. Though her skin was warm, she shivered when he skimmed his palms over her breasts.

142

"You're breathtaking." He cupped her jaw and kissed her because he couldn't wait any longer.

She grabbed his biceps and squeezed, kissing him back just as heatedly. It required a bit of maneuvering to remove the skirt while she was still in a sitting position.

"Lift," he said once he'd reached behind her and unzipped it. When she complied, he eased it past her hips and down her legs and let it fall to the floor.

She preferred wearing the thong under the garter belt instead of over it because she thought it looked better, but that required unfastening the stockings in order to slip it off if he wanted to leave the garter belt on, and he always did. He didn't mind, but it did slow down the process a bit. This time, he'd circumvented the issue by choosing a thong that tied on each side. Now he yanked on the strings and pulled it right off her, leaving the garter belt in place. He smiled because he always took satisfaction in coming up with a successful work-around. Then he smiled and took a good long look at his wife sitting almost naked on his desk.

Gently, he lowered her so she was lying flat on her back facing him, pushing his computer monitors out of the way so there was room for her head. He spread her legs and stroked her softly, gently, just the way she liked it. "I was right about the arousal. What I'm doing feels good, doesn't it? I don't even really need to ask, because you've closed your eyes and you just made one of those little sounds you always make when you're turned on. But you have to be quiet. We don't want anyone at this company to hear us. Can you do that? Better decide quickly, because I'm about to slide my finger inside you and we both know what that's going to do."

Her breath hitched and she let out a soft moan, nodding, her breathing sounding ragged. She kept her word even when she exploded under his touch moments later, arching up off the surface of his desk.

He loved watching her come undone like that. "Such a good girl."

He took off his polo and the white T-shirt he wore underneath it. After he unbuttoned his khakis and lowered the zipper, he quickly removed his shoes and socks and shrugged out of his pants and boxer briefs, kicking them toward the growing pile on the floor. Stifling a groan, he entered her, loving the view as he watched himself slide in and out. Kate wrapped her ankles around his lower back, and the sound of their breathing filled the room. From now on, getting any work done in his office would be a challenge because he would always have the memory of the way Kate looked spread out on his desk.

He was close, but she was close again too. He could see it on her face, hear it in her whimpering and the sounds she was no longer even trying to suppress.

"Ian. Oh God. Don't stop. Don't stop."

"I hear footsteps, Kate. They're going to discover us if you can't be quiet." He slid his hand over her mouth, pressing hard and continuing to thrust, and seconds later she screamed, the sound muffled by his palm. He came hard then, and the sensations seemed to go on forever.

Afterward they moved to the couch. Ian wrapped his arms around Kate and they kissed and cuddled, both of them spent. If he wasn't so hungry, he could have fallen asleep.

"Let's go pick up a pizza," he said. "Then let's eat it in bed and not get up for the rest of the night."

"You always have the best ideas."

"We've worked hard these last three days. Time for a little rest and relaxation."

"I'm almost sad we're not going back there tomorrow. Plus I'm dying to know if Tristan asked Ashley out."

"You know who's going to be even sadder? Those tech support guys. They were really looking forward to my cheese dip."

CHAPTER SIXTEEN

THE NEXT DAY WHEN SHE returned home after running errands, Kate stuck her head into Ian's office, but it was empty. He wasn't in the kitchen or downstairs working out in their home gym, either. She finally found him in their bedroom, lying on the couch under a blanket, watching TV.

She sat down on the edge near his head. "Hey. I didn't expect to find you here."

"I felt kind of tired." He sounded congested, and as soon as the words were out of his mouth, he started coughing.

"Honey." Kate felt his forehead, and his skin was warm against her fingers. "Are you feeling okay?"

"I think that guy who sits by the server room gave me his germs. His desk was a giant hot zone."

"Come here," she said, pulling gently on his arm until he rose. "You need to get in bed and let me take care of you." She stripped off his T-shirt and helped him out of his jeans.

"Will you rub Vicks on my chest?" he asked as she tucked him under the covers.

"Absolutely."

"What will you be wearing?"

She smiled and ruffled his hair. Clearly he wasn't *that* sick. "I don't own a nurse's outfit, but how about a tank top and those new boy shorts you bought me?"

"Without a bra?"

Kate laughed. "If it helps, yes."

"It will."

"Okay. I'll be right back."

When she walked into the room in the appointed outfit, he raised himself on his elbows.

"Do you want me to stroke your head?" she asked after she set a box of Kleenex, a glass of water, and a selection of pill bottles on the nightstand.

He looked confused. "Isn't the answer to that question always yes?"

"This head," she said, sitting down on the bed and tapping his temple lightly.

"Oh. I thought you meant the other one. I bet I can still get hard." Two seconds later he had a coughing attack, flopped back onto the pillow, and groaned. "No I can't. Oh my God, *what's happening?*"

"Easy, lover. No need to panic. You'll be back to normal in a few days."

"This is why I became a hacker."

"Avoiding workplace illness is the reason you became a hacker?"

"There were a few other reasons."

"Okay," Kate said soothingly. "Let's just consider your man cold the occasional collateral damage."

"It's tuberculosis. I looked it up."

"It's not tuberculosis. Trust me on this." She picked up the ear thermometer and gently inserted it. When it beeped she checked the reading. "One hundred point five. I think you'll live. Have you taken anything yet?"

"No."

She shook some cold medicine that would make him drowsy into her hand, put the capsules in his mouth, and held a glass of water to his lips. Then she opened the Vicks and began rubbing his chest. "Remember when I was sick and you took care of me?"

He smiled. "You wouldn't let me rub Vicks on your chest."

"That's because I didn't know you very well. Did you really think I was going to unbutton my pajama top and let you rub me?"

"I didn't think so, but I was still hoping."

She rubbed his chest until his skin had absorbed the Vicks and then slipped his T-shirt back on so the ointment wouldn't get all over the sheets. "Are you hungry?"

"Not really."

"You want to just chill for the rest of the day? I can find something for us to watch."

"Yeah."

She got under the covers with him, pulled his head onto her chest, and stroked it while they watched a movie.

"That feels good. I like it almost as much as when you stroke the other one." He sounded drowsy, and Kate didn't think it would be long before he fell asleep.

"Why don't you close those gorgeous green eyes of yours and take a nap?" She eased herself out from under him, kissed his forehead, and pulled the sheet up around his shoulders. "Nurse Kate will be back to check on you in a little while."

The next morning when Kate opened her eyes, the tickle in the back of her sore throat and her aching head told her that whatever illness Ian had come down with had made its way to her. *Of course it did*, she thought.

Unfortunately, Ian was in no shape to attend to her. He'd been up half the night coughing and hadn't gotten back to sleep until almost four a.m.

"Will you hand me some more of that cold medicine?" he asked. He was spooning her, and it felt like his body was made of hot, molten lava.

"It's all gone." Kate had discovered that when she'd taken the last two capsules around seven. "I might have some Motrin in my purse."

"Are you sick too?"

"Yes."

"I'm sorry."

"It's okay." Truthfully, Kate didn't really mind that she'd come down with whatever he had. It's not like it was the first time she'd ever been sick, and it certainly wouldn't be the last. He sounded miserable, and Kate knew the way he felt was a pretty good preview of how she'd likely feel tomorrow when her illness progressed. The second day was always the worst. "I'll be right back." She went into the kitchen to get her purse, relieved to find that she did in fact have a half-full bottle of Motrin in it. She filled two tall glasses with ice water and grabbed another box of Kleenex on her way back to their bedroom.

"I love you, sweetness," Ian said after he took the Motrin and drained his glass.

"I love you too."

They were lying in bed, wallowing in their individual misery, when Kate heard a series of light taps on the door. "Diane? Is everything okay? Mr. Smith isn't in his office."

"Oh thank God, Renee is here," Ian said.

They'd thrown back the covers and neither of them were wearing clothes, not because they were feeling the slightest bit amorous, but because they were generating a significant amount of body heat.

"Hi, Renee. Will's in here with me. We seem to have come down with a little something and we could use a few things if it's not too much trouble."

"Is it okay if I come in?" she asked.

"We have to get back under the covers," Kate whispered. "Her job duties do not include seeing us naked."

"Technically, she's already seen me naked."

"Go ahead, Renee. It's unlocked," Kate said once they were fully covered. "Don't come too close. I'd feel horrible if you came down with this."

"We have tuberculosis," Ian added. "It's wildly contagious."

"We do not have tuberculosis. We have mild upper respiratory infections, and we're both going to live."

Ian experienced a rather sudden and violent coughing attack. "Mild?"

"Hush," she said placing a hand over his mouth.

"Let me grab a pen and some paper so I can write down what you need."

They finished giving Renee their list, and she left for the store. Ian leaned over and pulled back the sheet, exposing Kate's naked body from the waist up.

"What are you doing?" she asked.

"I don't care how horrible I feel. I'm rubbing Vicks on your chest."

Renee checked on them before she went home for the day and asked if there was anything they needed.

"I think we're good for now," Kate said. "Thank you so much."

"Call me if there's anything you need, and I'll be happy to bring it by. I hope you feel better soon."

Kate had told Ian that rest was the thing they needed most as they waited for the illness to run its course, so they spent most of the day in bed, sleeping or watching TV.

After waking up from one of their many naps, Ian reached for his phone to check his e-mail. "Oh, you're going to love this, sweetness. It's from the CIO regarding my report on the findings of our joint social engineering assignment."

"I imagine he had plenty to say."

"Judging by the length of this e-mail, it appears he did." A coughing attack prevented him from reading the words, and when it finally subsided, he rubbed his chest. "Damn, that hurts. Okay, listen to this. 'Dear Mr. Smith. I'm extremely disappointed that our agreed-upon terms for the security audit were so blatantly disregarded by your firm.'"

Kate laughed. "He's clearly unaware of your shortcomings when it comes to following the rules."

"I can really only get away with it once. They start to wise up after that." He scrolled through the message and continued reading. "'I find your unauthorized attendance at the IT staff meeting especially brazen.'"

"It's like he doesn't know you at all."

"Four paragraphs in and he's still complaining. Maybe I'll just skip to the part where he acknowledges our hard work."

"Assuming he does."

"'However, your firm has shed light on the many security deficiencies of this organization, and the suggestions you've outlined will be implemented immediately.'" Ian shot her a smug look. "Did I call this, or what?"

"You did."

Ian scanned the rest of the e-mail. "'I will remind you, however, that per your offer there will be no monetary compensation.'"

He started typing, saying the words aloud as he composed his reply. "As promised, there will be no invoice issued for our services. In lieu of payment, please send along a written referral as I'm sure you have plenty of colleagues who would also benefit from our expertise. And if it's not too much trouble, I'd really appreciate it if you could write a short recommendation for my testimonials page. A paragraph or two is plenty."

Later that evening, Kate filled the tub and convinced Ian a hot bath would do wonders for his aching body.

"Come on," she said. "You can even be in front."

He lowered himself into the tub and leaned back against Kate's chest. She scooped handfuls of warm water onto his head, and when his hair was wet, she massaged the shampoo into his scalp with her fingers.

He groaned softly. "Tuberculosis isn't *completely* horrible."

"That's the spirit," she said, rinsing the shampoo with handfuls of water.

"There's no one else I'd rather be sick with. There's no one else I'd rather be healthy with either." His voice sounded congested and hoarse, and yet there was no mistaking the conviction in it.

She kissed his wet head. "Me too." It didn't matter that their noses were red and both of them looked pretty rough. All that mattered to Kate was that they were together.

She became engulfed in a coughing attack followed by a giant sneeze.

"Did you just sneeze on my head?" he asked.

"No way. That would be gross."

He laughed when she reached for the shampoo and washed his hair again.

A day and a half later, they were both feeling much better. Kate seemed to have bounced back a bit faster than Ian, but her immune system was probably stronger considering she came into contact with germs more frequently than he did. She was going stir-crazy after lying in bed for so long and felt desperate to leave the house. After taking a hot shower, she pulled on some clothes while Ian lounged in bed, scrolling through the TV channels.

"I'm going to the store. I'm tired of soup and feel like cooking something that requires a knife and fork to eat."

"Can't Renee go for you?"

"She's not coming today. She went to visit her daughter and son-in-law. I can pick up the groceries. I'm not feeling too bad."

"How can you not be?"

Kate laughed to herself. Her hacker husband might be invincible in most scenarios, but he was a typical man when it came to being sick. *And this is why women have the babies.* "Take a hot shower. I guarantee you'll feel better." She kissed him good-bye. "Back soon."

Kate usually drove the Tahoe when she went on a grocery run, but that day she chose the Porsche. It was almost Thanksgiving and the weather would be turning soon, which meant she'd have to park the sports car until spring. She decided to take a nice long drive and then pop into Safeway on her way back through town.

She hadn't driven the Spyder since she'd started working for Ian, and it felt good to be behind the wheel again. Her familiar route beckoned, and on a long and fairly deserted stretch of the highway, she cranked up the stereo and tapped the shift paddle in time to the music as the car zoomed along. Her mind wandered as she thought about the upcoming holidays and Chad and Kristin's wedding. There were more social engineering strategies to plan, and Ian had promised to start teaching her phishing techniques she could implement from her home computer. She looked forward to seeing if she could convince people to click on the links she sent them, which would give her access to their networks.

She was so wrapped up in her thoughts and the music that at first she didn't realize the car had begun to lose speed. She turned down the stereo so she could listen for any troubling engine sounds and was alarmed to discover she couldn't hear the engine at all. The speedometer reading fell rapidly, and she pulled over to the shoulder as the car coasted to a gentle stop. It seemed odd that such a new and expensive vehicle would be having mechanical problems already.

She was about to call Ian when her phone rang and his name flashed onto the touch screen. She hit the hands-free button on the steering wheel. "Hey. I was just going to call you."

"One hundred and two miles an hour? Seriously, Kate?"

It wasn't a mechanical problem at all.

It was her husband.

"Oh my God, you did *not* hack my car."

"Yes I did."

"Does that special app of yours track my every move?"

"Technically, yes. But I wasn't spying on you. I wrote a program to monitor your speed, and it sends an alert anytime you exceed one hundred miles per hour. Imagine my surprise when the most annoying beeping interrupted my nice hot shower."

"One hundred? That's it?"

"One hundred miles per hour is quite generous."

"So then you just... killed the engine? You don't think that was a bit heavy-handed?"

"How so?"

"You could have called me and told me to slow down."

"I had to act quickly. Cutting the engine and bringing your car to a nice, gradual stop is highly preferable to the jarring and abrupt stop that would have occurred had you hit a tree or other inanimate object."

"You hacked my *car.*" It shouldn't have surprised her because clearly the man could hack anything.

"I thought we'd already determined that."

"You're the one who bought it for me. You said you wanted me to have fun with it. I was having fun."

"Yes, but if I'd known you had a death wish, I would have bought you something slower. Like a Ford Focus."

"Turn my car back on," she said as sternly as she could.

The engine purred to life. "Carry on, sweetness, but please drive safely. I'll be waiting for you at home."

She went into Safeway and filled her cart with enough groceries to make dinner for the next several days and pushed it out to the car. She reached into her purse for her key fob, but it wasn't there. She specifically remembered locking the car and throwing the fob into the inside pocket of her bag, where she always kept it. Maybe she'd missed the pocket and the fob had settled among the contents at the bottom of her purse. After sifting through everything twice, she shook her head in confusion.

Oh, *goddamn*. Had she dropped it on the ground by mistake? She retraced her steps but didn't find it. Inside the store she spoke to an employee who promised to keep an eye out for it and call her if anyone found it.

Back outside, she leaned against the car and pulled her phone out of her purse.

Kate: I have apparently lost my key.

Fifteen seconds later, the locks of the car popped up with a loud click. Five seconds after settling herself behind the wheel, the engine turned on.

Ian: *Is there anything else I can help you with, sweetness?*
Kate: *No thank you. I'm sure I can handle it from here.*

Ian was lounging in their bed when she got home, shower fresh, with wet hair and his naked chest on full display. A sheet covered him below the waist, but Kate could almost guarantee his upper body wasn't the only part of him that lacked clothing. The detritus of their illness—the crumpled Kleenexes, the water glasses, the Vicks and the cold medicine—had all been cleared away. She stood in the doorway, leaning against it with her arms crossed in front of her.

He stretched, shooting her a calculated smile in the process. "You were right about the shower. I'm feeling so much better."

"Is there *anything* you won't hack?"

"I put fresh sheets on the bed and everything."

"I'm driving along and the engine just… cuts out," Kate said.

"I lit that candle you like. Can you smell it?"

She inhaled the mix of sandalwood and vanilla. "How is it even possible to hack a car?"

He scoffed. "That car is nothing but a smart phone on wheels. If it's connected to a network, I can hack it. First I— Well, I can tell by your expression you don't want to hear exactly how I did it."

"No, I don't." *Well, maybe a little.* The fact that he could hack a moving vehicle fascinated her, but his continued disregard for boundaries frustrated her enough that she would postpone asking him to explain it.

"You risked your safety after promising me you wouldn't drive so fast. So really I'm the one who should be mad."

"Why was it okay when I drove a hundred and ten miles an hour in the Shelby?" Ha! She had him there.

"Because I was in the car with you, and I hadn't yet made you my wife. I wouldn't have wanted any harm to come to you back then, but I really can't handle the thought of something happening to you now. It would end me."

It was really hard to stay mad at him when he said things like that.

Something unspoken passed between them, and her expression softened. Her need for boundaries and his need for freedom would always be at war, and that would never change. His methods might have been heavy-handed, but his heart was in the right place. He'd come a long way, but she doubted he would ever completely lose his impulsive, free-spirited ways and there would probably always be a wild-card component to his behavior. He'd tried to temper it for her, but it was like trying to keep air from escaping a balloon that had a tiny hole in it. Eventually it was going to leak out.

She pictured herself nuzzling her face in his neck and catching a whiff of soap on his clean skin.

He looked at her as if he knew exactly what she was thinking. "Why don't you come over here?"

"We both know what will happen if I do." Ian's sex appeal would always be his mightiest superpower.

"Exactly. Please hurry."

"I have groceries to put away."

"I'll put them away for you. Afterward. It's been three days. We'll barely need any time at all."

She walked toward him but stopped halfway.

"Aw, sweetness. You're going to make me work for it, aren't you? Come closer. I just want to kiss you."

She was trying hard not to smile because she wanted him as much as he wanted her, and it was only her lingering obstinacy that stood between them.

"Right here," he said, patting the bed beside him.

She sat down and he slid his hand up the back of her shirt, pulling her closer so that their mouths were only inches apart. Kate's body buzzed with desire as their lips danced, almost touching, each of them withholding their full commitment to the kiss as they waited for the other to give in. He might have coaxed her back into their bed, but she would not give him the satisfaction of surrendering first. His hand slid under her jaw and he closed his eyes. So did she. Then he brushed her lips with his and pulled away. She opened her mouth slightly, searching. It would feel so good to let him in, to kiss him deeply. He brushed her lips again and she felt just the tip of his tongue. Expecting him to do it again, she was surprised when he used his teeth to gently bite her bottom lip. She wouldn't be able to hold on much longer, especially if he did that again, and seconds before her resolve crumbled for good, he broke.

He opened his mouth and wound his fingers tightly in her hair to hold her in place as he kissed her roughly, with abandon. There was something primal and barely contained in the way neither of them could stop kissing the other, and it seemed to go on for hours. He reached for her hands when they finally came up for air and interlocked their fingers.

"I won," she said, her chest rising and falling.

"Did you? Because I'm about to take off all your clothes. If that's losing, you can win every time."

"You kissed me first."

"And that kiss definitely needs a number."

"Nine."

"Or we can just call it the 'I'm sorry' kiss."

"I'm not sorry."

"You don't have to be sorry, but you do have to slow down, Katherine Bradshaw," he said in a whisper that tickled her ear. He kissed her again, and then he took off her clothes and she forgot all about the groceries.

Like he said, it *had* been three days.

CHAPTER SEVENTEEN

"DO YOU WANT TO go out for coffee with us?" one of the women in her Pilates class asked as Kate hung up her jacket and stowed her purse in a locker, shaking raindrops from her hair. The temperature had dropped and it had been raining off and on for the past two days.

"Sure." Despite the gloomy weather, her mood brightened considerably at the thought of going out for coffee. Though Kate kept plenty busy working for Ian, she still longed to make friends. She'd made some strides with the women, as they were now regularly returning her greetings, but she hadn't attempted any further engagement and, until this morning, neither had they.

"We always go to Common Grounds after class," the woman said. "We can all walk together."

"Great."

When the class ended, they filed into the locker room to shower and change. No one seemed to be in a hurry and no one seemed to own a robe either, maybe because some of the best bodies Kate had ever seen all seemed to be congregated in this room. There was also a lot of stretching and bending. She'd noticed this before, and while she herself wasn't the least bit modest, she had no desire to put on a show for the others and found their posturing strange.

Kate was standing in her underwear about to reach for her bra when one of the women in the group walked over, pointed at her breasts and said, "Who did those?"

"Um, they're factory originals."

The woman put both hands on Kate's breasts and squeezed them gently, one at a time, as if she were comparing melons at the grocery store.

Kate removed the groping hands from her boobs. "No touching," she said with a smile.

"They really turned out great."

"Well, like I said, I was born with them, so I guess I got lucky." She finished getting dressed, closed her locker, and followed the others out the door. The coffee shop was a few doors down from the Pilates studio, and since her Tahoe was parked at one of the meters in front of the building, she paused to throw her bag in the backseat. One of the women glanced at her car with something that looked an awful lot like disdain.

"You're Diane, right?" one of them asked after they received their drink orders and carried them to a nearby table.

"Yes."

There were five of them, and a woman named Wendy went around the table making introductions as Kate did her best to commit their names to memory. "We attend the Monday, Wednesday, and Friday class."

"Me too," Kate said. "Unless I have to work."

The conversation screeched to a halt. All of them looked at Kate like she had horns growing out of her head.

"You work?"

"I work for my husband. He owns his own company."

"Like, doing the books?" a woman named Nina asked. The center stone on her wedding ring had to be at least five carats. Wasn't she worried about being mugged?

"Something like that," Kate said.

"Does he make you?"

"Oh, no. I want to work. I told him there was only so much time I could fill cooking and exercising."

"You cook?" Wendy asked.

Blank looks, all around.

"Only when we feel like eating," Kate said lightly.

"You don't have a staff? Someone to cook for you?" Kate was almost certain the woman's name was Kaitlin.

"I have a housekeeper but not a cook."

"Do you ride?" In Middleburg, that only meant one thing.

"No."

"You must be from out of town," Kaitlin said.

"We moved here in September. I'm originally from Indiana, but my husband and I were living in Minnesota."

"Is that in the Midwest?"

"Yes, it's north of Iowa."

"Is Iowa where they grow the potatoes?"

"No, that's Idaho. They grow corn in Iowa."

"What do they grow in Indiana?"

Kate smiled. "Smart women."

"Do you have kids?"

"Not yet."

"Are you trying?"

"Not at the moment."

"How old are you?"

"Thirty."

Suddenly none of them would look her in the eye.

"What?"

"It's just that you're starting pretty late."

Kate took a drink of her coffee. "You think so?"

"The clock started ticking at twenty-seven."

"Women are having babies much later now. I'm not worried. Hardly any of my friends have kids yet."

"Maybe you'll get pregnant right away. Then you won't have to work anymore."

"I like working. Do any of you work?"

"We stay at home with our kids. I have four," Wendy said.

"Oh," Kate said. "Where are they now?"

"They're with their nanny."

For the next five minutes, they passed Kate their phones so she could thumb through the pictures of their adorable and well-dressed offspring, whom they clearly doted on.

"Well, I should probably be on my way," Kate said when she'd finished her coffee. "It's getting close to lunchtime and I have some work to finish up this afternoon. Thank you so much for inviting me."

They gave her a warm send-off and told her they must do it again. Now that they'd welcomed her into their fold, they were quite friendly and it probably wouldn't be long before their lifestyles didn't seem so foreign. But she couldn't help but feel she'd failed their initiation in some way and that she'd always be the outsider for reasons that had nothing to do with how long she'd lived there.

When she got home, she walked into Ian's office, kissed him, and plopped down on the couch.

He pushed his chair back from the desk and smiled. "What's the scene, jelly bean?"

"Paninis. Your favorite. Are you hungry?"

"Yes. Thank God you returned to feed me. I could feel myself wasting away."

He followed her into the kitchen, and she began rummaging in the refrigerator for meat and cheese. "The women from Pilates finally asked me to go out for coffee with them."

"That's great. How did it go?"

She shook her head. "I don't fit in with them."

"I'm sure you do."

"They were very nice, but I have a job, I cook, I'm not a mom, and I don't ride horses. And you should see the diamonds. One of those girls is going to get rolled and stuffed in a trunk, and then she'll be sorry."

"Maybe you need to get to know them a little better."

Kate got out the panini maker and the cutting board. "Well, one of them already knows me *intimately*. She reached out and honked my boobs. Can you believe it? She put both hands on them and squeezed."

Ian gave her his undivided attention. "Okay, tell me again, but slower this time. Maybe you should demonstrate on yourself to make sure I understand."

Kate laughed. "Oh, you understand *perfectly*."

"Were you naked? Was she?"

"They were *all* naked. It's always this bizarre naked locker room parade. She swooped in when I was trying to put on my bra."

Ian licked his lips and swallowed. "Oh my God."

"Having your breasts groped by a bona fide Real Housewife is not as fun as you're making it sound."

He shook his head. "Of course not. Then what happened?"

"Well, this is where it gets really intense." Kate dropped her voice to a whisper. "After she finished with my boobs, her hands slid quite a bit lower and she touched me *down there.*"

He picked up Kate and threw her over his shoulder. "I don't even care that you're just messing with me now."

She shrieked and pounded on his back in mock outrage. "Put me down, you caveman!"

He laughed. "Shouldn't have yanked my chain, sweetness. I'm all fired up now."

"I have sandwiches to make. You said you were hungry."

"Maybe I can find something in the bedroom to tide me over for a little while."

"The *mouth* on you."

"I think you mean my mouth on *you.* And just so you know, I feel like doing all the really dirty stuff."

"What do you think this is, your birthday? A special occasion?"

"Stop being coy. You were the one who threw out that rule a long time ago."

Kate laughed. "Why are you walking so slowly?"

When they reached the bedroom, he tossed her onto the bed, and it was a good long while before they made it back to the kitchen.

CHAPTER EIGHTEEN

IAN WAS IN THE SHOWER when the disposable phone he only used for the task force rang.

Kate walked into the bathroom with it. "The supersecret Batphone is ringing. Do you want me to answer it? It says *C* on the screen."

He stuck his head out, wiping shampoo out of his eyes as the suds ran down his face. "That's Charlie. Can you grab it, sweetness? Tell him I'll be out in a minute."

Kate answered the phone. "Hey, Charlie. It's Kate."

"Well, well, well. It seems I got lucky with this call. I'd much rather talk to you than that husband of yours."

"Ian's taking a shower. He's almost done."

"How are you?" Charlie asked.

"Good. How are you?"

"Can't complain. What are you up to?"

"I'm meeting a friend for dinner."

After having coffee with the women from Pilates, Kate had called Jade. She'd mentioned to Ian how well she and the interior decorator had gotten along. "I like her. She seems really nice. Plus she's a working girl, so maybe we'll have more in common. I think I'll see if she wants to grab dinner or a drink or something." Jade had seemed happy to hear from Kate and she'd enthusiastically accepted her invitation to dinner.

"Where are you going?" Charlie asked.

"The French Hound."

"I ate there once. It's been a while though. Try the lobster risotto if they still have it. It was wonderful."

"Maybe I will. Thanks for the recommendation."

"What time are you meeting her? It can get pretty crowded."

"Seven o'clock. I made a reservation."

"Then you shouldn't have any problem."

Ian appeared in the doorway, naked. Kate motioned for him to turn in a circle and he happily obliged. She gave him a thumbs-up. "Here's Ian. It was nice talking to you, Charlie."

"You too, Kate. Have a great night."

Jade was sitting at the bar when Kate walked into the restaurant.

"I love your dress," Jade said after they hugged hello. "Where did you get it?"

"Anthropologie. Will bought it. He likes to shop for me."

"Now that is a rare quality to find in a man."

"Trust me. I know how lucky I am."

"The hostess said our table will be ready in a minute."

Kate sat down beside Jade and ordered a glass of wine. "I'm so happy you could make it tonight. I haven't met many people since we moved here."

"I was really glad you called. When I'm not at work, I tend to keep to myself. People don't mean to, but they sometimes act like your marital status is contagious or worry you might try to steal their husband."

"I'm not sure I understand." Though Jade had never mentioned a husband, Kate had assumed she was married because she wore a diamond ring and matching gold band on the ring finger of her left hand.

"My husband died in a car accident a couple of years ago. For some reason, I thought I'd already told you."

"No," Kate said. She covered her mouth with her hand as her eyes filled with tears. She felt like someone had knocked the wind out of her as it all came flooding back: The shock. The disbelief. The tears. For Jade, there had been no waking from the nightmare the way there had been for Kate. She grabbed Jade's hand and squeezed. "I'm so sorry."

"Thanks, Diane. I have my days, but I'm okay. Really."

"How long were you together?"

"Twelve years. We met when I was twenty-two and got married two years later."

"Kids?"

"Neither of us really felt a strong urge to have them. We mostly enjoyed each other. We ran the design firm together, and that's been one of the hardest adjustments. I no longer have a business partner. Now it's just me making the decisions."

The fact that Jade and her husband used to work together just like she and Ian did saddened her, and her tears threatened to return. Kate felt very undeserving of her good fortune and wondered if the universe would someday expect payment.

Jade laid her hand on Kate's arm. "Are you okay?"

"I'm sorry. I should be asking you that." Fearing her reaction would seem extreme, she scrambled to come up with a plausible reason for why the news had rattled her so. "A good friend of mine lost her husband not long ago, and it was so hard on her. She didn't think she'd ever get over it."

"You never really do. But in time it fades enough for you to put one foot in front of the other. The worst thing is how much I miss the little things like eating breakfast together or sitting on the couch holding hands and watching TV. Maybe I'll find someone to do those things with again someday."

"I know you will," Kate said. And she meant it.

The hostess approached them. "Please follow me. Your table is ready."

They found themselves tucked away at a table for two in the back corner. Kate opened her menu, and when their waiter arrived to take their orders, she ordered the lobster risotto.

"So what's your story?" Jade asked. "Linda told me you moved here from Minnesota and, I know Will owns his own company. What's your background?"

"I used to be an attorney."

"Wow, that's impressive."

"Well, I didn't stay in the profession. I left my law career to run a nonprofit food pantry, which I found very satisfying. Then we moved here, and now I help Will."

"Why this area?"

"A few of his clients are here, and it made sense to be closer to them."

"How are you settling in?"

"It's been slow going. To be honest, Will is kind of a private person, so we haven't met a lot of people."

"I'm sure you will eventually. It just takes time."

Their conversation flowed easily, and they never ran out of things to talk about. The lobster risotto was every bit as good as Charlie said it would be, and after she and Jade split a lemon tart for dessert, they lingered over another glass of wine. It was almost closing time when they finally left the restaurant.

"I'm parked on the street," Kate said.

"Me too," Jade said as they walked in the direction of their cars.

A thick fog had descended while they were inside the restaurant. The eerie glow of the gas-lamp-style streetlights and the cobblestone pavers under their feet reminded Kate of London circa Jack the Ripper.

"I'm glad I'm not walking to my car alone," she said.

"Me neither. It's quite spooky."

"I'd love to do this again," Kate said before they parted ways.

"Anytime," Jade said, reaching out to give her a quick hug. "Drive safe."

Kate headed for home. It was almost ten o'clock, and the roads were deserted except for the car that had been behind her for the past five minutes. It seemed to be following a bit closer than normal, its headlights illuminating the interior of her car. Or maybe the lights seemed brighter because of the fog and the clouds that obscured the moon, making the darkness more noticeable. The driver never got close enough to qualify as a tailgater, but they were near enough that it was hard to ignore their presence. Had someone taken notice of her and Jade as they'd stood in the parking lot chatting? If they'd watched her get into her car, they'd know she was alone.

She stayed on her route until she reached the turnoff that would take her the rest of the way home. Though it was open to the public, it was more like a narrow, private driveway than a road, and only someone who knew where it went would have a use for it.

The car turned too.

A prickle of unease wormed its way under her skin, and even though she told herself she was overreacting, she called Ian.

He was sitting on the couch with his laptop when his phone rang. "Hey, sweetness. How was dinner?"

"I think someone's following me."

He removed his feet from the ottoman and leaned forward, pressing the phone tighter to his ear. "What?"

"There's a car that's been behind me for a while. It's following awfully close. It's probably just a coincidence. Should I not pull into the driveway?"

"Kate. I want you to pull in." His tone left no room for debate.

"But if someone's following me, they'll know where we live."

It was a valid concern, but if someone was following her intentionally, the only thing he could think about was getting her safely on the other side of the gate. There was no reason to jump to any conclusions, at least not yet. Maybe someone had noticed Kate and Jade when they left the restaurant. Maybe they figured they'd follow her. See if she stopped somewhere on the way home. Someplace deserted and not well lit.

"I'm going to walk down to the gate."

"I'm still a few minutes out."

"I'll be waiting."

He hadn't realized it was so foggy, and when the gate swung open, he stayed in the shadows, watching as the car following close behind her continued on. It was a sedan, but it was too dark for him to determine the make or get a good look at the license plate. After Kate drove through, she stopped the car and he got in, hitting the button on her remote to close the gate.

He leaned over and kissed her. "Are you all right?"

"I'm better now that I'm home. I'm probably just being paranoid. It's dark and foggy and I let my mind play tricks on me." She drove up the driveway and parked the car in the garage.

"From now on, if you want to go out at night, I'll drive you." The dark tint on the Navigator's windows would make it difficult to see who was in the car.

"It's probably nothing," she said.

"Just as a precaution."

That night, when Kate was asleep in his arms, his mind conjured up various scenarios, none of them good. He'd always worried that someday whoever had doxed him would come looking for them, and no matter how well they hid, if someone wanted to find them badly enough, eventually they would succeed.

He tightened his hold on her, listening to the gentle sound of her breathing. But for him sleep did not come for a very long time.

CHAPTER NINETEEN

CHARLIE WAS THE FIRST MEMBER to arrive at the next task force meeting. Ian was the second.

"Hey," Ian said as they powered up their laptops. "Find anything interesting?"

"Found a chat transcript I want everyone to take a look at. You're going to find it especially noteworthy."

As point man on the task force, Charlie had immersed himself in his undercover role and was now spending ten to twelve hours a day monitoring the hacktivists' activity as they conversed online in an area of the Internet not indexed by search engines. Everyone—including Charlie—used software called the Onion Router, or Tor, to conceal their identity and hide their location from anyone who might be listening in or analyzing the traffic.

The remaining members of the task force filed into the room and took their seats.

"Okay, Charlie. Let's see it," Phillip said.

Charlie typed a command on his laptop, and the screenshots of several chat transcripts appeared on the screen on the wall. An Internet Relay Chat, or IRC, was a way to facilitate the exchange of messages in text form by more than two people at a time using a specific channel. Hackers utilized the channels to communicate anonymously on a wide scale, believing they were a reasonably safe place to conduct their conversations. Each chat log began with the time the message was written and the screen name of the participant.

Ian scanned the block of text, ignoring the posturing and profanity and focusing his attention on certain words and phrases.

01:12 <thehuntsman > they think u have no power
01:12 <nicklas > feds dark they have no power
01:12 <thehuntsman > silence is not power darkness is power
01:13 <Fox7825> power from spying feds
01:13<thehuntsman > priv8 no invites
01:13 <Fox7825> lulz in darkness

It appeared that prison had done very little to silence Joshua Morrison, and those he'd left behind were more than willing to take up the cause and act as his mouthpiece. Hacktivists functioned primarily as a loose collective, but one of their strengths was their ability to unite to promote a shared agenda, and they were quite capable of appointing new leaders who would ensure it was carried out.

Several lines in particular caught Ian's eye, and he realized immediately what Charlie had meant when he'd said they would interest him. Magician was the screen name he'd gone by during the time he'd been collecting the evidence that would send Joshua Morrison to prison.

01:33 <X2frr9> magician dead2me
01:33 <jojoju> magician dead not enough.
01:33 <nightrider> magician dead in crash
01:33 <boizz79> magician die
01:34 <boizz79> magician die snake

01:34 <nightrider> magician dead for realz
01:34 <X2frr9> magician idgaf burn burn burn
01:34 <nightrider> magician dead for realz dead crash
river
01:35 <jojoju> magician burn burn rat fink h8t snitch
burn in hell

"Greedy bastards," Ian said. "I'm dead and they're still not happy."

"At least they actually believe you're dead. You should celebrate. That's one less group of people who'd like to kill you."

"Your glass is always half full, isn't it Charlie?" Tom said.

"If you mean half full of whiskey, then yes."

The news *was* a cause for celebration. In all his years of undercover work, what he'd done to put Joshua behind bars worried him the most. Not because he felt he'd acted inappropriately or outside the law, but because hacktivists were well known for their staunch refusal to ever forgive or forget. They were largely nonviolent, but that didn't eliminate the possibility that one of them felt strongly enough about what had happened to become an outlier.

"Dark and darkness. What's that supposed to mean?" Pete said. The two words appeared over thirty times throughout the transcripts, and despite the garbled, disjointed nature of the conversations, it was hard to miss the battle cry of revenge that permeated their exchanges.

"Almost seems like a taunt," Charlie said. "Maybe a DDoS?" A Distributed Denial of Service attack involved sending an overabundance of traffic to a website until it crashed or went dark.

"Seems a little on the nose," Tom said.

"Even if they are planning a DDoS, why now?" Pete asked. The carding ring had been his first opportunity to work with the task force, so he wasn't aware of the history.

Ian leaned back in his chair. "Because Joshua was denied parole last summer."

"You're following his parole hearings?" Pete asked.

"When you send someone to prison, it makes sense to keep tabs on when they might get out, especially when they've made no secret of their hatred for you."

"Doesn't look like you have to worry about that anymore," Charlie said. "Being dead has its perks."

"We first became aware of the group's activity last summer," Phillip said. "Joshua has been a model prisoner, and everyone assumed parole would be granted. When that didn't happen, they began to mobilize."

"So we know they're planning some sort of retaliation for the denial of parole, but what we don't know is *how* they're going to do it," Tom said.

Phillip glanced at his watch and wrapped up the meeting. "We may not know their exact agenda, but hopefully Charlie will become privy to more of their plans. In the meantime, try to come up with ways they might carry this out so we can plan our defense accordingly. We'll meet again on Friday."

"How'd Kate like the French Hound?" Charlie asked. He seemed to be in no hurry to head back to his desk, probably because he'd been putting in more hours than all of them. Ian knew firsthand how brutal and exhausting that could be.

Ian zipped his laptop into its case. "How'd you know she went there?"

"She told me she was meeting a friend for dinner when she answered your phone the other day."

"She said it was good."

"I recommended the lobster risotto."

"That's what she ordered." His unease over Kate being followed had not faded despite trying to convince himself it had been nothing but a fluke. He refused to succumb to paranoia and had forced himself to stick to the facts: a car had been behind Kate on her way home. It didn't automatically mean someone was following her. But still, there was something—call it gut instinct—that prevented him from dismissing it entirely.

"Ian."

Charlie's raised voice shook him from his thoughts. "Sorry. Did you say something?"

"I said I need to get going."

"Sure. See you later." When Charlie had almost reached the door, Ian said, "Don't forget to sleep, okay? And go easy on the whiskey."

Charlie laughed and walked out.

CHAPTER TWENTY

KATE STOOD IN THE DOORWAY watching as the rental car appeared at the top of the driveway. A few snowflakes swirled through the air, but the forecast only called for flurries. Just moments before, Ian had buzzed her parents and Chad and Kristin through the gate, and Kate rose on the balls of her feet, practically bouncing in her excitement. She was so happy to see them that she threw her arms around her parents the minute they stepped over the threshold.

Diane reached out and slid a lock of Kate's hair through her fingers. "This is new."

"I always wondered what my hair would look like a little lighter. It's fun!"

Ian embraced Diane and held his hand out to Steve who shook it. Kate hugged Chad and Kristin and ushered everyone inside.

Chad and Ian shook hands. "I'll put your car in the garage," Ian said. "There's room for one more."

"Thanks," Chad said. "The keys are in it." He looked back and forth between Kate and Ian. "Were we supposed to change our hair? Because Mom didn't say anything about that."

"I felt like a change, and Ian's a little overdue for a haircut, that's all. He's been really busy."

Chad laughed and held up his hands. "I was just curious."

"I've never pictured you as a blonde, but I love it," Kristin said. "And somehow the length suits Ian. It fits his personality."

"It was longer than that when I first met him. But enough about our hair. I'm so happy to see you. I bet you're getting excited for the wedding. Is my mom driving you totally nuts?"

"It's more the combination of your mom and mine that's about to put me over the edge." Kristin looked around. "This house is amazing. I'll admit when Chad told me you and Ian had bought a horse farm, I didn't actually believe him. But you really do have a barn and a stable. What are you going to do with them?"

"I have no idea. The only thing I know for sure is there won't be any horses in them. Come with me. I'll give you the grand tour."

Kate had made an assortment of appetizers, and they spent the evening in the basement, eating and drinking and playing pool before turning in early. The next morning, Kate served breakfast.

"Did you make these?" Chad asked around a mouthful of cinnamon roll.

"I did."

"They're awesome." He reached for another and also helped himself to more bacon. "When did you start cooking?"

"Shortly after we moved in. I figured since we had this great kitchen, I should learn how to use it."

"It probably gives you something to do."

Kate knew he didn't mean anything by it because it was not in her brother's nature to be unkind, but she bristled at the assumption she had nothing better to do, even if that was exactly why she'd taught herself to cook in the first place. She kept plenty busy now, but she'd promised Ian she wouldn't say anything to her family about working for him.

After they cleared the breakfast dishes, Diane and Kate prepped the turkey and slid it into the oven.

"What do you want to do next?" her mother asked. "Casseroles? Salads?"

"I did everything yesterday," Kate said.

"Everything?"

"I told you I was going to."

"But now I don't know what to do with myself."

"Phillip and Susan won't be here until this afternoon, so I thought we could show Kristin some of the quaint little shops we visited when you came for my birthday."

"That sounds wonderful."

Chad and Ian walked into the kitchen with their coats on.

"Where are you two headed?" Kristin asked.

"I never got to drive the Shelby, so I'm taking Kate up on her offer to drive the Porsche before something tragic happens to it," Chad said.

"Chad!" Kate shot him a look. "I can't believe you just said that. *Nothing* is going to happen to it."

"I was just kidding."

"Bet you'll let him go over a hundred," she muttered when Ian bent down to give her a kiss."

He laughed. "Not quite ready to let go of that, are you?"

Kate parked the Tahoe at a meter on East Washington. She loved the historic feel of downtown Middleburg. The temperature was in the midforties and the air held a distinct chill, but it wasn't too cold to explore on foot.

"You have to see the Christmas Sleigh," Kate said, leading them toward a high-end store that sold holiday items year-round. The window displays were filled with nutcrackers and Christmas trees. "They have the most gorgeous decorations."

They went to Lou Lou, a women's clothing boutique where Kristin bought a scarf, and after making their way up and down both sides of the street, they went into Common Grounds to have coffee and warm up.

"This is such a cozy little place," Kristin said after they carried their coffee to the same small table by the window that Kate had sat at with the women from Pilates.

"It's great, isn't it?" Kate said. Maybe she'd see if Jade wanted to meet here for coffee sometime.

When they returned home, they put the rest of the food in the oven and retrieved a couple of bottles of chardonnay from the wine cellar.

Diane looked at the label. "Is this the one we liked so much on our tour?"

"Yes." She opened the wine and poured them all a glass. "I stopped by the winery last week and stocked up."

Ian walked into the kitchen. "Do you need help with anything?"

"Thanks, but we've got everything under control."

"And we have wine," Kristin said. She raised her glass to Kate and they clinked them together.

"I can't wait for your wedding," Kate said. "There's something so magical about getting married on New Year's Eve."

"I'm not the only bride who thinks so. I feel like we've been waiting forever for our turn at this venue. I never would have guessed that by the time we actually got married, you'd be married too."

"Things did move rather quickly for Ian and me."

"How are you going to explain to your extended family that you eloped over the summer?" Kristin asked.

"I think we're going to keep that news to ourselves for a while longer. We'll tell them eventually. I'd love for everyone to get to know Ian, and I think it's great Chad wanted to spend time with him today, even if it was under the pretense of driving the Porsche."

"Are you kidding me?" Kristin said. "Chad probably won't admit it, at least not to you, but Ian is the most exciting thing that's ever happened to him. You know the special phone Ian gave him before we left Roanoke Island after your wedding?"

Ian had given one to Steve and Diane too. "Yes."

"Chad keeps that phone with him at all times. It's always fully charged. If it ever actually rings, he'll probably be so startled that he'll drop it."

"Aw, that is so sweet." When Chad walked into the kitchen a few minutes later, Kate smiled at him. "I love you, Chad."

"How much wine have you had?"

"This isn't the wine talking. It's just sisterly love."

He looked at her like he didn't believe her. "I love you too, Kate."

Diane topped off their wineglasses and beamed. "Aren't the holidays wonderful?"

Phillip and Susan arrived at three bearing a pecan pie and apple pie, which Susan had told Kate were Ian's favorites. Kate couldn't help but smile when Susan embraced Ian as soon as her hands were free. It must have been hard for her to let go of him again after they moved out of the guesthouse, but Kate thought she likely took comfort in the fact that he would no longer be moving from place to place.

They sat down to dinner half an hour later.

"Now that Kate's finished redecorating the house, wouldn't it be amazing if there was a baby on the way next year at Thanksgiving?" Diane said.

"Oh, I love babies," Susan said.

Diane took a drink of her wine. "I feel like I've been waiting such a long time to become a grandmother."

"We don't have any children of our own," Susan said. "But Ian is like a son to us."

Ian took a bite of his turkey to hide his grin. A family was something he and Kate both wanted, but he'd decided to leave the timing up to her since she was the one who had to do all the hard parts.

"How long have you been working with Phillip, Ian?" Diane asked. "I don't think Kate ever told me."

"Since he arrested me."

Steve put down his fork. "You've been arrested?"

"Just the one time."

"What did he do?" Steve asked, directing his question to Phillip.

"He hacked the Pentagon."

"Only to see if I could," Ian said. "I didn't mean any harm."

Susan smiled and looked around the table. "Boys."

"He was only twenty," Phillip said. "Haven't had any problems with him since."

A slightly awkward silence followed as everyone turned their attention back to their plates.

"So, have you met any of the other Real Housewives?" Chad asked. Kristin shot him a look. "I'm just asking."

"Oh, Kate tried," Ian said. "It wasn't a good fit."

"I bet the shopping in DC is to die for," Kristin said. "Have you been to the Galleria?"

"Not yet. I'm not really a mall person. Ian does most of my shopping. He's better at it than I am."

"It's true," Ian said spearing a green bean. "I'm an expert as long as I don't have to leave the house."

"Maybe you should take up a hobby," Chad said.

"She did," Diane said. "She started cooking. And judging by how wonderful this meal tastes, I'd say she's been very successful at it."

"Maybe there's a law firm in DC that could use some part-time help," Steve said.

"There's nothing wrong with being a homemaker," Diane said.

"There's nothing wrong with using her education, either," Steve said.

The suggestions were good-natured because the Watts family liked each other too much to be deliberately hurtful. Kate might have been smiling on the outside, but Ian could tell it bothered her that everyone assumed she had nothing better to do than cook or shop now that the house had been redecorated.

"Kate's pretty busy these days," Ian said. "I hired her and put her in charge of the social engineering for my company. She's a natural."

"What is social engineering? What does that mean?" Diane asked.

"Tell me you did not turn my daughter into a hacker," Steve said.

"Tell me what that is, Steve!" Diane said.

"I did not turn her into a hacker," Ian said. "Actually, that's not true. I did. But social engineering is human hacking. I taught her how to manipulate people so they'll do what she tells them to do. Then I hack them."

Chad started laughing. "This is awesome. I love how this family has been shaken up over the past year. Our street cred just keeps getting better and better."

"Kate's been instrumental in helping me get my company off the ground again. She's smart, confident, and fearless."

"She really is a natural," Phillip said.

"You're okay with this?" Steve asked.

"It was actually his idea," Ian said. It wasn't that he was trying to make Phillip the heavy, but he'd learned over the years that while he usually succeeded in riling people up, Phillip had a knack for calming them back down.

"Who needs more wine?" Kristin asked.

Chad reached for his mother's glass and Kristin refilled it.

"I simply pointed out that women make fantastic social engineers," Phillip said. "Ian needed someone to handle that aspect of his business, and Kate seemed like a logical choice."

"I still don't understand what it means," Diane said.

"Let me give you an overview that I'm sure will put you both at ease." Phillip gave Kate's parents a detailed explanation of the social engineering portion of penetration testing. He was still answering their questions when the meal ended and the plates had been cleared, but they both seemed a lot calmer.

"Ian? Can I talk to you for a second?"

He thought she'd pull him into the kitchen, but she didn't stop walking and he followed her all the way to their bedroom. Oh, shit. She must be really mad if she wanted to talk to him in private.

"I had to say something, Kate. I could tell their comments were bothering you. And I was the one who told you to keep it quiet, so it was only fair that I be the one to break the news."

Kate led him over to the couch. "Sit down. We don't have much time."

When he complied, she dropped to her knees in front of him and unbuttoned his pants.

He blinked because he couldn't believe what he was seeing. "You're... not mad."

Kate looked at him with love and adoration. "I'm not mad." She lowered his zipper and tugged on his boxer briefs, freeing his rapidly growing erection. "Do you know how awesome it was watching you jump in to support me like that?"

"I know how awesome this is going to be."

"I hate to rush you because you deserve nothing less than my best to thank you for what you did out there, but would it be possible for you to kind of hurry?"

"I can do that, and news flash: every time you put your mouth on me, it feels incredible." Maybe he should have been concerned with the fact that Kate's entire family was waiting for them in the dining room, but it was hard of think of anything other than his wife's hot mouth and what she was doing with it. He brushed her hair out of the way so he could get a better view. "That feels so good."

He no longer cared that everyone might be wondering what he and Kate were doing, and he was reasonably certain no one could hear the sounds he'd started to make. She needn't have worried about him being able to hurry because her obvious enthusiasm, which she conveyed to him via eye contact and murmured declarations of how much she loved doing that, got him close to the finish in no time.

He put his hands on her head as his orgasm began to build. "Sweetness, you've got about five seconds before I come."

She didn't stop, and she made sure cleanup was a breeze too.

"Okay," Kate said, smiling as she zipped him up. "I'll be out in a minute. Make something up."

"Where is everyone?" Kate asked when she walked back into the dining room. Her dad was sitting at the table by himself.

"Ian took dessert down to the basement. Your mom and Susan are helping him serve."

Kate spied an untouched pumpkin pie on the sideboard along with a bowl of whipped cream.

"They left that behind for us so we could continue our tradition," her dad said.

"I'm glad they did." Kate dished up the pie and took a seat across from him.

"Are you sure you're feeling well enough to eat that?"

"What do you mean?" Kate asked. She forked in a big mouthful and groaned. She'd made the pie herself, and it pleased her to discover it tasted as good as it looked.

"Ian said you were having some stomach trouble."

"What?" Kate said around a mouthful of pie and whipped cream as suddenly the realization of the excuse Ian had given for their absence dawned on her. *I am going to kill him.* She swallowed. "I'm fine. Totally fine. Just a passing... I'm fine."

They both got very interested in their pie and the awkward silence seemed to go on forever.

"So, Phillip told us all about this thing you're doing for Ian's company."

"Did he tell you the part where Ian totally shot me down when I asked if I could do it?"

"Yes."

"And how I had to convince him to give me a chance?"

"He said that Ian eventually changed his mind."

"We compromised," Kate said. "Both of us just want the other to be happy." Ian could tell her dad about his return to the task force if he wanted to. Kate wasn't going to touch that topic with a ten-foot pole.

She walked her dad through each of her completed assignments, explaining how they'd worked and what she'd accomplished with each one. She watched his expression change from mild interest to admiration when he learned how well she'd planned and executed the hacks.

"People hear the word hacker, and they immediately associate it with bad things. But white hat firms are all about protecting people. Ian spent ten years building his first company, and it was hard on him when he threw it away. I love that his new company is something I can be a part of. I know I'm not using my law degree, and I'm no longer running the food pantry either. But I'm using my brain and I like the work."

They finished their pie and carried their plates into the kitchen. "Are you happy?" Steve asked. "With everything?"

Kate thought what he really meant was *Are you happy with this life you've chosen? Was he worth it?*

"I'm very happy. With Ian, our lives together. Everything."

He smiled. "Okay. That's all any parent wants for their child, Katydid."

Kate and Steve joined the others downstairs. Her mother and Susan were clearing plates and refilling coffee while Ian talked to Chad and Kristin.

"Ian? Can I talk to you for a second?"

He grinned and followed her into the hallway. "Kate, what's gotten into you?" He lowered his voice. "I don't know if I can go again so soon." He chuckled like he couldn't believe what he'd just said. "Wait a minute. Of course I can. I totally can."

"Did you tell everyone I was suffering from some kind of"—she made air quotes—"gastrointestinal distress?"

His eyes narrowed and he looked at her worriedly. "Maybe?"

"Ian!"

"I'm sorry. They were all staring at me when I walked back into the dining room. I think we were gone longer than we thought."

"Oh my God."

"I couldn't exactly tell them you were on your knees, now could I?"

Kate raised her hands, palms up as if she were weighing one side against the other. "Those were the only two choices?"

"Well, there aren't a lot of things to choose from when a man and woman disappear for a while. Trust me. Nobody ever questions stomach problems."

"The supreme court justice did. And thanks to my being caught completely off guard, I don't think he bought my fumbling explanation. The only thing that saved me from cross-examination is that he probably knew what we were doing in there and would rather shove a hot poker in his eye than hear anything more about it."

Chad passed them as he walked down the hall. Before he reached the bathroom door, he turned around and started laughing. "I'm sorry. Do you need to get in here again, Kate?"

"You're hysterical, Chad. And there's nothing wrong with my stomach."

He didn't say anything for a second, and then he groaned. "Oh, Jesus, I just realized what you two were really doing."

"Yeah, well, we're newlyweds, so deal with it." She turned back to Ian. "I won't be able to look Phillip and Susan in the eye. I'm too embarrassed."

"Eh, shit happens, Katie."

She laughed and grabbed him by the shoulders. "Oh my God, *stop*."

He slid his hands underneath her jaw and kissed her. "Mmmm. Minty."

She pinched his ass—hard—as they walked down the hallway on their way back to join the others.

"You know what? You're a pincher. I'm going to pay you back for that later. You can count on it."

The women went into the theater room to watch a movie while the men opted for whiskey and pool. Steve and Phillip sat down with their drinks while Ian racked the balls.

"Go ahead and break," he said to Chad.

"So Kate's really good at this—what do you call it again?" Chad asked as he sank two balls in the left corner pocket. He knocked two more in on his second shot, but on the third the ball banked off the side and rolled just short of its goal.

Ian lined up his shot, aimed, and knocked his first ball into the pocket with ease. "Social engineering, and she's phenomenal. She's smart and she can think on her feet. Plus she's likeable and people trust her. The truth is, she *was* bored and she was never going to be satisfied without something more stimulating to fill her days. She's much happier now."

"My sister has always succeeded at anything she put her mind to," Chad said, and there was no mistaking the admiration in his tone.

"You know what else she's really good at? Pool. We play a lot, so if she challenges you to a game, don't assume you'll beat her. There's a good chance she'll wipe the floor with you." Ian sank his second, third, and fourth shots before missing.

"Thanks for the heads-up." Chad made his next shot but missed the one after that, a rather tricky bank shot. "You seriously hacked the Pentagon?"

"It was just so damn tempting. I was young and thought I was invincible."

"That's cool that you and Phillip are so close now. I'd wager not many long-term friendships begin with an arrest."

"He thought I needed some guidance, and he was right. He's been a great mentor."

When they finished their game, they joined Phillip and Steve. Ian fetched the bottle of bourbon, and Phillip poured two more, sliding one across the table to Chad.

"How long have you worked for the FBI?" Chad asked Phillip.

"Almost thirty years."

"Have you always worked in the cyber division?"

"I have for the past twenty. Been leading task forces for almost fifteen."

"I bet that's been interesting," Chad said.

"Technology is constantly evolving, so we always have a wide range of cyberthreats to address and eradicate. The task force recently brought down a large carding ring responsible for bilking consumers out of millions of dollars, but fraud and theft will always be an ongoing battle. Hacktivism activity and cyberterrorism are our biggest concerns right now."

"What's the difference, exactly?" Chad asked.

"Hacktivists are driven by ideology, and the end result is often more disruptive than damaging. A hacktivist group might protest outside a church whose beliefs they don't agree with, but they're just as likely to bring down a ring of pedophiles because they hate anyone who would harm others, especially children. They don't believe in suppressing information, and they definitely don't want to be silenced, so their first objective might be to steal data before proceeding to a denial of service or destruction of data attack. Hacktivism is something we were battling long before the Sony hack drew the attention of the mainstream media."

Phillip took a sip of his whiskey. "Then there's cyberterrorism, which is our biggest concern of all. Attacks are often politically motivated, and the intent is to do great damage, including loss of life. Traditional terrorists are not as technically savvy as cyberterrorists, and they're more likely to rely on time-honored methods such as bombs. But it would be naïve of us to think they're not working to combat that. Terrorists taught themselves to fly planes. There's no reason to believe they're not honing their computer skills right now, or aligning with hackers who have a vendetta against the US government. Any hacker who's capable of exploiting the technical vulnerabilities of our computer-supported infrastructures is a threat to us, whether it's the disruption of our electricity, the pipelines that deliver our natural gas, or the systems that ensure our cities have clean drinking water."

"What about nuclear weapons?" Chad asked. "Do you think anyone will ever have the ability to control or override them?"

"They already have," Phillip said. "In 2009, a computer worm called Stuxnet caused the centrifuges that separate nuclear material to spin out of control at an Iranian nuclear power plant via its control system. You can read about it online."

"This is some seriously alarming stuff," Chad said a few minutes later, looking up from his phone. "Is this the kind of thing your task force is involved with?"

"Not yet. The issues we're trying to combat are domestic, and we have plenty of help. But we're definitely an exclusive task force, and the threats we deal with are of a certain nature."

"I'm not sure when would be the *ideal* time to break this news, but before this discussion goes any further, I think you should know I'm working with the task force again," Ian said to Steve.

Steve remained silent as he processed Ian's statement. "Does Kate know?"

"She's the one who encouraged me to return."

Steve rubbed his temples. "Of course she did."

Did Steve regret the day Ian came into his daughter's life? Probably. But the closeness of this family was the one thing working in his favor. They might still be a bit unsure about him, but they loved Kate, and if they hadn't completely accepted her decision to stand by him no matter how much havoc he'd already wreaked on their family, he hoped they soon would. The Watts family was a stoic bunch, and Kate came by her roll-with-the punches attitude naturally. Diane especially seemed to want to embrace Ian unconditionally the way she did

Kate and Chad. She was simply too kind, too genuinely interested in the well-being of others, to shut him out.

"I was under the impression that working undercover was a risk you were no longer willing to take."

Ian had a pretty good idea of the thoughts that were probably swirling in Steve's head. *Especially since you dragged my daughter along with you.*

"I'm not in an undercover role this time. I'm simply there to help."

Phillip chimed in. "We're facing some difficult challenges, and Ian's had extensive interactions with this particular group. His prior experience is invaluable."

"What about the person who might be looking for you?" Steve asked. "Do you think that threat has passed?"

Guilt consumed him as he answered Steve. "I'd like to think so." Before someone had followed his wife home, he would have been telling the truth. But now Ian wasn't sure, and he worried it might be just the beginning.

Steve's glass was empty, and Ian poured him another because after everything Steve had learned that night, he was pretty sure his father-in-law needed one.

Ian topped off his own glass too because there was no question at all whether or not he did.

Later, after everyone had retired to their rooms, Kate changed into her pajamas. Ian was still buying them for her. She would go to put clothes away in the dresser and there they'd be. They mostly ended up on the floor next to the bed, but at least she had something comfortable to lounge around in while they were watching TV.

Kate crawled under the covers, and Ian turned off the lamp on his nightstand and joined her, pulling her into his arms and settling her head onto his chest.

"It seems my mother and Susan have come down with a raging case of baby fever," she said. "I bet if we listen closely, we'll be able to hear my mother's clock ticking all the way in Indiana."

"I noticed that. They weren't exactly subtle about it, were they?"

She laughed. "No, they were not. The women at Pilates were every bit as forthcoming with their opinions."

"Is having a baby something you've been thinking about?"

"I started thinking about having your babies when we were still in Minneapolis," she said. "But maybe it's not a good time."

"We could wait. We could put everything on hold until we think enough time has passed. If it would ease your mind, then that's what we should do."

But how would they know when they'd waited long enough? Should they wait six months? A year? Three? Kate didn't want to do anything foolish, but she didn't like giving an outside force the power to make a decision that should only be made by the two of them. "I don't think my clock is ticking quite as loudly as my mother's, but I'd like to start trying soon. See what happens. What about you?" She remembered how adorably happy he'd looked when she pretended to have morning sickness. "Is your clock ticking?"

Her head was still resting on his chest, and he ran his fingers idly through her hair. "I'll be really happy when it happens, but it's your decision. You're the one who has to do all the hard stuff. All I have to do is have an orgasm, after I've given you one, of course."

"Naturally," Kate said.

"I think we should practice right now."

As he kissed her, he slowly unbuttoned her pajama top and slipped it off her shoulders. His hands caressed her breasts, his touch gradually growing rougher until Kate ached for him to replace his fingers with his mouth, which he did as if he could read her mind.

He kissed his way south, stopping briefly when his lips reached her lower abdomen. "How's your stomach? Has everything calmed down in there now?"

She laughed. "There was never anything wrong with my stomach, and you know it."

She'd saved him the hassle of removing her pajama pants by not wearing them to bed in the first place. He knelt between her legs, skimmed his hands along her hips to pull down her underwear, and then threw them on the floor. He continued the path he'd been on until all his kisses were landing between Kate's legs.

"You do know that's not how you make a baby, right?"

He lifted his head, his warm hand resting on the inside of Kate's thigh. "It's not? I guess that means I'm going to need a lot more practice."

"Less talking, more of what you were doing," Kate said as she twisted her fingers in his hair and moaned when he obliged. Linda had been right: the lower level was perfect for guests, especially if you didn't want them to hear you making noise while you practiced trying to get pregnant and you'd already used up your holiday allotment of sexual escapades. After all, there was only so much she and Ian could blame on their newlywed status before they started to seem like horny teenagers who lacked any kind of self-control.

As soon as Kate cried out, Ian slid slowly and deliciously into her.

"How am I doing now?" he asked.

"Perfect. Everything's right where it's supposed to be."

"I have a feeling we're going to make beautiful babies, sweetness. And I hope Shelby looks exactly like her mother."

CHAPTER TWENTY-ONE

KATE WAS SITTING AT HER desk in her office, soft music coming from the computer's speakers. She'd tried sitting with her laptop on the couch in Ian's office so they could work in the same room together, but he was easily distracted and often suggested other, more satisfying, uses for the couch and desk. Her output had suffered because it took very little convincing before they were using his office furniture in ways it was not intended. The only way to maintain productivity was if they remained in their respective offices.

Ian was the best kind of boss because he didn't micromanage and he let Kate make the decisions regarding the attack vectors she wanted to use for her social engineering assignments. She'd just finished setting up a fake website the way Ian had shown her. Crossing her fingers that it would work, she sent a phishing e-mail to her target with a link to the site. When opened, it would upload malware to the target, which would allow her to leave behind a backdoor for easy, continuous access to the client's network.

While she waited, she decided to work on their holiday cards. The list of people she could send them to would be extremely short—Phillip and Susan, Kate's family, Jade, and Renee—but she really wanted to send them, and it would be a wonderful keepsake of their first Christmas as husband and wife. She scrolled through the photos on her computer and selected one from their wedding reception. Ian was holding her on his lap, and the look on his face—like he was the happiest man in the world—made her heart swell. She dragged it into the Christmas card template, and after selecting a font for the text, she reached for her phone.

Kate: *I'm designing our Christmas card. How do you feel about Happy Holidays from the Bradshaws?*

Kate: *Wait. Scratch that. How about Happy Holidays from the Merricks!*

Kate: *Damn. Happy Holidays from the Smiths!*

Kate: *I've got it. Happy Holidays from Kate and Ian!*

Kate: *Shit. Happy Holidays from Will and Diane!*

Kate: *Happy Holidays—you'll just have to guess who this card is from!*

Ian: *I'm glad you find this amusing.*

Kate: *I've embraced our anonymity. We can be anyone.*

Ian: *Now all I can think about is role-playing.*

She heard the chime indicating a new e-mail and smiled when she opened the response from her target thanking her for sending the link and telling her he'd already clicked on it.

Kate: *Phishing e-mail worked! No wonder you love going in the backdoor. The rush is incredible!*

Ian: *You just shattered my concentration in the best possible way. We should take a break. Seriously, like right now.*

Kate: *Can't. I'm very busy. I had to beg my boss for this job and I don't want to let him down.*

Ian: *Trust me. No part of your boss is "down" right now, and he's totally cool with you taking a break.*

Kate: *Are you sexually harassing me?*

Ian: *I'M TRYING TO.*

Kate: *Get back to work.*

Ian: *Come to my office. I have something to discuss with you.*

Kate: *Sure you do.*

Ian: *It's very important.*

Kate: *Maybe it can wait until lunch.*

Her e-mail chimed again, but it wasn't another message from her client. Ian had sent a meeting request via their calendar software.

SUBJECT: Lunch.

WHERE: My couch. Bent over my desk. In my chair. I'm not picky.

WHEN: As soon as you can get in here.

She clicked on Decline but added a note: *It's only 10:28 a.m. A little early for lunch, don't you think?*

She turned her attention back to her computer, but her cursor seemed frozen, so she wiggled her mouse. She turned it off and then switched it back on. Finally she pulled the batteries and replaced them. Still nothing. She was about to ask Ian to come in and take a look when she had a sudden thought.

Kate: *Fix my mouse!*

Her mouse started working again, but then "One Week" by the Barenaked Ladies blasted forth from her computer's speakers and startled her so completely she almost fell off her chair.

She got up, opened her office door, and yelled down the hall. "Stop hacking me!"

When she sat back down, the light of her webcam blinked on, and she grabbed a Post-it note and covered up the camera.

A few minutes later a notepad popped up on her computer screen. As if an invisible hand was typing, the words I AM IN CONTROL appeared.

He gave her a triumphant smile when she appeared in the doorway of his office.

"I forgot how frustratingly persistent you can be," she said.

He pushed his chair back and waved her over. After she sat down on his lap, he said, "Now that you're here, we can have lunch." He kissed her but then pulled back abruptly. "You know what I mean when I say lunch, right?"

She laughed. "Ian, when you say things like that, I always know what you mean."

CHAPTER TWENTY-TWO

KATE AND IAN FLEW OUT of DC early on the morning of December thirtieth. There had been talk on the news of an approaching winter storm, and Diane would not breathe easy—or be able to immerse herself in Chad and Kristin's wedding festivities—until they were on the ground in Indiana. Kate had promised her mother they would be there by noon, and their chartered plane touched down with an hour to spare.

Because they were traveling to Indiana for Chad and Kristin's wedding, she and Ian had stayed home for Christmas. They spent Christmas Eve alone, eating dinner by candlelight and cuddling in the glow of the lights from their nine-foot Christmas tree, which was exactly what they wanted. On Christmas Day, they joined Phillip and Susan for dinner. Kate loved the way Ian and Phillip put their work aside and enjoyed the holiday in a more familial way while Susan fussed over all of them. Kate had sent Ian's mom a holiday card, but Ian told her he didn't expect to receive one in return.

Kate checked their post office box every day, and it saddened her to discover that he'd been right.

"The decorations look beautiful," Kate said as she stood with her mom, sipping a glass of champagne. Her parents had rented out the spacious back room of Diane's favorite Italian restaurant for Chad and Kristin's rehearsal dinner. Twig trees wrapped in fairy lights were scattered throughout the room, casting everything in a romantic glow. Candles flickered on the tables, and flowers—lavender and cream roses in crystal vases—covered every flat surface. Ian stood at the makeshift bar talking to Chad and a few of his groomsmen while Kristin and her mother visited with the rest of the wedding party.

Diane leaned back in her chair and sighed. "I can't believe it. It seems like just yesterday you and your brother were toddling around the house. After tomorrow, both of my children will be married, and someday you'll have families of your own."

"Speaking of families, I didn't refill my birth control pills this month."

Diane reached for Kate's hand, clasping it in her own. "Oh, Kate."

"Don't get too excited. Nature still has to take its course. It could take a while."

"What does Ian think about this?"

"He tried to play it cool, but I think he wants a baby almost as much as you do." Kate fiddled with the stem of her champagne glass. "I said I wasn't sure if it was a good time and that maybe we shouldn't be thinking about taking this step until… things were more resolved. He said if I wanted to wait then that's what we should do, but he left the decision up to me."

"Your dad thinks I'm being naïve, but I choose to believe that everything will blow over. Do you think it will?" Diane had accepted her daughter's unorthodox lifestyle better than her father had, but that didn't mean she didn't worry.

Kate thought of the car that had followed her home. *There's nothing to worry about. It was probably just a coincidence.*

"I hope so. Ian's been in these situations before."

"And what happened?"

"They've blown over. Just like you said this one will."

During the wedding ceremony, Ian never took his eyes off Kate. She held a bridesmaid's bouquet of lavender and cream-colored roses, and she looked stunning in a long, flowing dress in deep purple shot through with glittering metallic strands. He wished there was some way to let her extended family know she was doing fine and that he was the luckiest man in the world because he would be spending the rest of his life with her.

Later, at the reception while he was at the bar getting a drink, an elderly woman elbowed her way in next to him. "Get me a whiskey sour," she barked. She had to be ninety if she was a day, and he found her direct approach amusing. When he handed her the drink, she took a sip, peered at him, and said, "I'm Doris. Who are you?"

"I'm Will. I'm here with Chad's sister, Kate."

"Oh, you're the plumber. You're Katie's new boyfriend."

He set his drink down on the bar. "Excuse me?"

"Stevie is my nephew. He told me Katie had a new beau named Will who is a very successful plumber." She appraised him like he was a piece of meat. "You are a fine-looking man, but your hair's a little long."

"Kate likes it this way." He'd thought about cutting it for the wedding, but since he wasn't the one getting married, he decided to skip it.

"Katie's last boyfriend died. I feel like I should tell you in case there's a curse or something."

He stifled his laugh behind his fist. "Thanks for letting me know, but I'm not worried."

"Before the one who died, Katie lived in sin with Stuart. I don't know what happened to him. He seemed like a very nice boy, but he was awfully beige. Do you know what I mean by that?"

"I do, Doris." He leaned against the bar, thoroughly entertained.

"You, on the other hand, seem very colorful. Like a peacock. Bet it drives Stevie crazy."

He outright laughed then. "You... really have no idea."

"Don't string Katie along. She's not getting any younger."

"She's only thirty. Women are getting married later in life now."

She made a face and waved her hand at him as if to say *what do you know?* "I was seventeen when I got married. My husband Tony, God rest his soul, was barely eighteen. How old are you?"

"Thirty-three."

"Have you ever been married?"

He shook his head. "No."

"Why, what's wrong with you?"

"Haven't found the right girl, I guess."

"Stop being so picky. Katie would make a fine wife. If you expect me to come to your wedding, you better hurry up. I'm not gonna live forever."

The DJ announced that Kristin was ready to throw the bouquet. "All you single ladies, please make your way to the dance floor. If you're not married, we need you out here right away." Someone pulled Kate onto the dance floor. From her pinched expression, Ian guessed she was not as excited about the bouquet toss as some of the other wedding guests, who were angling for a prime spot in the middle.

"Everyone get out of the way and let Katie catch it! She needs all the help she can get," Doris yelled.

Kristin threw the bouquet, but Kate ignored it, her feet remaining planted on the floor as it sailed through the air. A young woman almost took out three others as she swooped in, caught it, and held it over her head triumphantly.

Doris shook her head and sighed. "It's like she's not even trying."

Kate exited the dance floor and made a beeline for Ian. He caught the bartender's attention and motioned for a glass of wine, which he handed to Kate the second she reached him. She took a giant gulp and then bent down to hug her aunt. "Hi, Aunt Doris. It's so nice to see you."

"I like your fella. I'm trying to convince him to marry you, but if you keep giving the milk away for free, it makes things a lot harder."

"Well, that's… something to keep in mind," Kate said.

"I have to go to the ladies' room. That whiskey sour went straight through me and my bladder control is very iffy."

They watched her stride off with more speed than Ian would have thought possible.

"I'm sorry. She has no filter left," Kate said.

"No, she does not. But I like her a lot."

"When I'm ninety, I'm going to start saying whatever I want. I bet it's very liberating."

"Why wait until you're ninety? I've been saying whatever I want for years."

"You certainly have."

"Did you know your dad's telling everyone I'm a plumber?"

Kate burst out laughing. "He is?" She composed herself quickly, and her tone was decidedly more somber when she said, "I mean, you *have* made introductions rather tricky."

"I'm sorry about that, sweetness. I wish you could tell everyone how happy we are."

"That's okay. We know, and that's all that matters." The DJ started playing a slow song. "Do you think Will the plumber could take Katie the old maid for a spin on the dance floor?"

"He'd love to. And I want you to know that I would marry the crap out of you if I wasn't already married to you."

"You say the sweetest things. But just so we're clear, when Chad throws the garter, you're going to be out on that dance floor with all the other single men."

Not only was he on the dance floor, he caught the garter.

The next morning, Chad and Kristin managed to board their flight and leave for their honeymoon ahead of the big winter storm that had picked up a giant head of steam overnight as it bore down on the Midwest. Steve Watts had been looking forward to putting all the wedding festivities behind him and settling in with six solid hours of football on New Year's Day, but the snow continued to fall, and by late that afternoon, Zionsville had received nine inches. The Wattses' satellite dish was completely buried and unable to receive a signal. Steve was not the kind of fan who enjoyed watching bowl games in a sports bar; he wanted to watch them in his own living room with a beer and a bowl of snacks close at hand.

"I can climb up on the roof and brush off the snow," Ian said.

"No," Kate and Diane said simultaneously. Kate was lying on the couch with her feet in Ian's lap, reading a book. "This is why women live longer. We have no desire to climb up on roofs."

"You can stream most games to the TV from a computer," Ian said. "It doesn't require hacking. It's not even *illegal*."

"Who cares about football," Diane said. "They're still showing *It's a Wonderful Life*. I'll make some snacks."

Steve glanced at Ian, sending a silent plea.

"Oh, you want the plumber to do it?" He walked over to the TV and looked at the back. After finding the correct cable and plugging it in to his laptop, he typed a series of commands and the game appeared on the TV a few minutes later as if by magic.

"How'd you do that?" Steve asked.

Kate smiled as Ian explained it to her dad, walking him through the steps.

"Well, isn't that the greatest thing. Thank you, Ian," Steve said, settling back in his chair. He reached for his beer and grabbed a handful of popcorn from the holiday tin on the coffee table.

Ian sat down and Kate put her feet back in his lap, anticipating a nice long nap because nothing put her to sleep quite like football.

Zionsville had almost managed to dig itself out by the time Kate's parents drove Kate and Ian to the airport two days later. They could see their breath in the bitterly cold air when they got out of the car and said their good-byes.

Diane hugged Kate. "I love you, honey. Stay warm."

Her dad pulled her into his warm embrace. "Come back soon, Katydid. Bring that husband of yours with you."

"Sure, Dad. I'll miss you."

"I'll miss you too."

Diane hugged Ian, and when Steve shook his hand, Kate couldn't help but notice they both smiled.

"Shouldn't we be descending by now?" Kate asked after they'd been in the air for a couple of hours. The plane came equipped with a comfy leather couch, and they'd been lounging on it for the better part of the trip.

"We would if we were going home, but we're flying to Costa Rica."

She sat up. "What? Really?" She threw her arms around him.

"Surprise," he said with a big grin. "I told you I'd be ready to go someplace tropical by January."

"I've always wanted to visit Costa Rica. But I don't have the right clothes. Winter in Indiana is sort of the polar opposite of what one should bring to the jungles of South America."

"I packed for you."

She inhaled sharply. "Oh God."

He waved his hand in the air. "I call it Kate's Costa Rica wardrobe!"

"Did you pack actual clothes? A pair of shorts, maybe a sundress or two?"

"It's very hot and humid there, so I mostly chose lingerie and swimsuits. We have our own private pool, so I almost didn't bother with the bikinis. But then at the last minute I thought, better throw them in just to be safe."

She kissed him long and hard. "You think of everything, don't you?"

"Always."

A car was waiting for them when they landed at the Tambor Airport, and from there it was a little over an hour's drive to Santa Teresa and their accommodations for the next seven days. Nestled inside a lush, tropical jungle, the five-star resort offered luxury amenities and close proximity to the pristine beaches of the Nicoya Peninsula.

A uniformed bellhop opened the door. "Good afternoon, Mr. and Mrs. Smith. We've been awaiting your arrival."

Staff members quickly retrieved their luggage from the trunk as they stepped out of the car. Birdsong and the low, deep trill of tree frogs filled the air. A monkey howled intermittently in the distance as the concierge led them to their private beachfront lodgings.

"Welcome to your villa."

Kate looked around in amazement. A perfect blend of outdoor and indoor living, the main open-air room led to a terrace upon which sat a hammock big enough for two.

"You will find an assortment of cold drinks and sliced fresh fruit in the refrigerator," he said as they passed through the kitchen.

The opulent bathroom was also open-air and included a deep tub and outdoor shower that would make it feel as if they were standing in the rain in the jungle. The luxurious bedroom included a king-size four-poster bed with a flowing white canopy and curtains tied back with ribbons. Just off the bedroom sat a small pool and hot tub completely surrounded by flowers and jungle foliage.

"This is absolutely beautiful," Kate said.

"Please let us know if there's anything you need," the concierge said. "Enjoy your stay."

Another member of the staff had placed their luggage in the bedroom while they were touring the villa.

"I think I'll go put on one of those bikinis," Kate said.

Ian grinned and helped himself to a beer from the fridge. "Or not. That pool looks very private."

When Kate returned wearing a bikini, she was laughing and twirling a pair of underwear around on her finger. "What are *these*?"

"Vacation underwear."

She held on to the sides, stretching them out in order to get a better look. "Why's the crotch missing?"

He grinned. "Because they're awesome."

"I'm pretty sure you didn't buy these at La Perla."

"Nah. They're special. You should go put them on."

They spent the next seven days enjoying their utopian paradise. Phillip had promised not to call unless something extremely earth-shattering transpired, and Ian's laptop remained in its case. He only checked his phone a few times throughout the day; otherwise it remained locked in the safe in their bedroom.

Kate had never felt so calm or so peaceful. They began their day with breakfast on the terrace, and then she attended a Pilates class while Ian worked out in the resort's state-of-the-art fitness center, followed by a couples' massage. Ian went on several fishing excursions in a nearby town. Then the chef would prepare what he'd caught—tuna, mahimahi, snapper and grouper—and serve it to them in their villa. They spent hours lying on the beach and walking hand in hand along the water's edge.

"I could live here," Kate said one evening when they were lying together in the darkened bedroom among the twisted sheets, listening to the soothing sounds of the jungle. Ian was playing with her hands, rubbing her palms and interlocking their fingers.

"Say the word, sweetness. I'll make it happen."

But would he? If she looked him in the eye and said, "I want to spend the rest of our lives here, hidden away from everyone," would he do it? And would he be happy if they did? If she'd learned anything in the preceding months, it was that he wasn't ready for that. If she was honest with herself, she wasn't either.

She leaned over and pressed her lips softly to his. "Maybe someday I will."

CHAPTER TWENTY-THREE

THE SUN WOULDN'T RISE FOR another hour, and Kate and Ian were fast asleep in the quiet darkness of their own bedroom back in Virginia when the security system shrieked out its warning. Instantly awake, Kate shot up, heart pounding as she fumbled for the switch to turn on the bedside lamp and Ian threw back the covers and leaped from the bed. Struggling into a pair of jeans that had been draped across the arm of the couch, he scooped his phone off the nightstand and shoved it into his pocket.

"Get dressed. Lock the bedroom door behind me, and then go into the bathroom and lock that door too. Stay there until I come back. Do not come out." He had to shout over the earsplitting sound of the alarm as he ran out of the room.

As soon as she locked the door behind him, she plucked her pajamas off the floor and hurried to the bathroom, shutting and locking that door too. She dressed quickly, her body vibrating with fear. As the minutes passed, she grew more afraid until suddenly the alarm stopped shrieking. She breathed a sigh of relief when her phone rang and Ian's number flashed on the screen.

"Where are you? Are you okay?"

"I'm back inside. The police are on their way. I'm walking toward the bedroom now."

She came out of the bathroom, and by the time she reached the bedroom door, he was there.

"It's okay. Everything's okay," he said when she gathered him into her arms.

He'd run out into the cold winter air without a shirt, and his bare skin felt ice-cold under her fingers. "You're freezing." She left him to grab a sweatshirt from the closet.

"Whoever it was is gone now," he said, pulling the sweatshirt over his head.

"Maybe it was a false alarm," she said.

"Yeah. That's probably all it was."

But Kate noticed he didn't look at her when he said it.

Ian and two police officers walked the grounds, examining the perimeter of the house and checking windows and doors for any sign of attempted entry. A light snow had fallen the day before, but their search didn't turn up any footprints that would indicate an intruder had been responsible for tripping the alarm. After the police had gone and they'd showered and eaten breakfast, Ian disappeared into his office. Kate checked on him an hour later, and he looked up when she walked into the room, worry creasing his forehead.

"I was just about to come find you," he said. "We have a problem."

She sat down on the couch. She'd hoped he wouldn't find anything, but the minute he'd gone into his office, she knew he would.

"Someone hacked our security system. They tried to cover their tracks, but they didn't do a good enough job. I modified the system after we moved in so if anyone ever hacked us, they'd leave with enough malware to make them think twice about another attempt. I don't think they'll be back."

"Good."

"They hacked the camera in the garage. They were probably trying to figure out the cars we owned to make it easier to follow us." He rubbed his temples as if he was trying to stave off a headache building behind his eyes.

"Are you okay?" She walked over to him, and he pulled her onto his lap.

"Everything I've done to you. Everything I've already put you through was for nothing. There's no way that someone following you and our security system being hacked aren't related. Someone knows we're here."

She'd never seen him look so defeated.

"Maybe you should go home for a while," he said.

"I am home."

He looked at Kate. "Sometimes I feel like there's the two of us, and then there's the rest of the world. Do you ever feel like that?"

"All the time."

She smiled and brushed back the hair that had fallen over one of his eyes. "You told me once nothing would ever do it for you quite like a smart, fearless woman."

"I also said beautiful."

"I signed on for this, and I knew exactly what I was getting into."

"I don't know what I did to deserve you."

"I could say the same about you." She climbed off his lap. "Come on. We need something to take our minds off this. We could watch a movie. We could play strip pool. I know how much you enjoy that. We could build a big fire and take a nap in front of it. You know what I mean when I say nap, right?"

He no longer looked quite so defeated, and a smile played at the corners of his mouth. "I love you, sweetness. I've made some mistakes in my life, but you will never, ever, infinity, be one of them."

CHAPTER TWENTY-FOUR

THE IMAGES ON THE VIDEO surveillance screen for the front gate caught Kate's eye as she passed in front of it on her way to the fridge for some milk. Two men were stacking a large pile of lumber next to the gate while a third unloaded power tools from the bed of a pickup truck.

There were two other cameras connected to their security system: the one located in the garage and one that captured and recorded anyone going in or out of the front door, but those screens were dark because Ian had disconnected the cameras after discovering they'd been hacked. Though he felt strongly that the malware he'd used to strengthen their security system would deter someone from attempting another intrusion, he told Kate he wasn't going to give anyone the opportunity to obtain footage of them.

"What's going on down at the gate?" Kate asked when Ian walked into the kitchen for another cup of coffee.

"They're building a guard shack. We're going old school with our home security. There'll be another one up by the garage. I hired guards to man them twenty four hours a day. All ex-military. All armed."

Ian's proactive measures didn't surprise her at all and she nodded. "Good."

He set down his cup of coffee and reached for her, sliding his hand around her waist. "Are you freaking out about any of this?"

"We are not like other folks," she said, shaking her head. "As long as you don't try to keep any of it from me because you're afraid I can't handle it, I'll be fine."

Someone rang the gate, and when Kate looked at the screen, a car she didn't recognize waited to be buzzed in. Ian pushed the button and the gate opened. "Come on. I want to introduce you to Rob."

"Who is Rob?"

"He's the man who'll be accompanying you wherever you need to go when I'm not with you."

"You got me a bodyguard?"

"I like to think of him as a special companion who goes everywhere with you."

Kate wrinkled her nose. "That almost sounds weirder."

"Then yes, I got you a bodyguard. I know you still have social engineering assignments to complete and things you want to do outside the house. This way you don't have to feel as if your life has been totally disrupted, and I can feel confident about your safety." Ian had admitted how much it worried him that someone might try to follow her again—or worse yet—approach her. All they'd have to do is wait a few miles down the road and when she drove by they could tail her until she stopped somewhere, which would leave her wide open and vulnerable.

"By the way, he thinks you're being stalked by a jealous ex-lover and that we're taking the situation very seriously. He also knows discretion is important, so he's not going to ask questions outside of what he needs to know to do his job. If someone with questionable motives tries to get near you, they'll have to get past Rob first, and that's not going to happen."

The doorbell rang, and when Ian opened the front door, Kate understood immediately what Ian had meant when he said no one would get past Rob; he was the tallest and broadest man she'd ever seen. Not fat, just a solid wall of muscle that stretched almost seven feet into the air. It was the first time she'd ever seen Ian look up to speak to someone. He was a good ten years older than Kate and soft-spoken, and his gentle handshake surprised her when Ian made the introductions. She listened as Ian went over a few general instructions with him. His hours would be eight to six every day, Monday through Friday, and they would provide him with a vehicle.

"So we'll see you tomorrow," Ian said.

He nodded and looked at Kate. "I'm looking forward to it."

There was something about Rob's warm smile and calm demeanor that instantly put her at ease, and she decided that having a special companion might not be so weird after all.

Later that afternoon, several employees from a local auto dealership delivered a Range Rover with heavily tinted windows that Rob would drive and a Lexus SUV with equally dark windows that Ian would use as his personal vehicle.

"There's always a chance they'll just follow the new cars home again, but I'll be damned if I'm going to make it easy for them to know for sure who's inside them," Ian said.

Kate and Ian drove their old cars down to the barn—if you could call vehicles that had less than ten thousand miles on them old. The large, open building had room for the Spyder,

Tahoe, and Navigator, with plenty left over for Rob and the security guards' personal vehicles.

"We'll just tell people we confused horses with horsepower," Kate joked.

He slung an arm over her shoulder. "I do love your ability to roll with the punches, sweetness."

Kate laughed because it seemed they'd figured out what to use the barn for after all.

CHAPTER TWENTY-FIVE

ROB PULLED UP IN FRONT of the house, walked around to the passenger door, and opened it for Kate. She'd told him he didn't need to do that, but he'd insisted. He *had* conceded on the matter of letting her sit in front, but only because she'd argued he was her security detail and not her chauffeur. She'd adjusted quickly to the protocol Ian put in place, and it no longer seemed strange to text Rob when she needed to go somewhere.

"Good afternoon, Diane."

"Hi, Rob. How are you?"

"Can't complain. Where are we off to today?"

"I'm meeting a friend at Tuscarora Mill in Leesburg." Jade was working on a design job in the area and had asked Kate if she wanted to meet for lunch.

"That's one of my favorites. I'll have you there in half an hour, give or take."

"Great." That would give Kate plenty of time to come up with an excuse for Jade about why she hadn't driven herself.

She still hadn't thought of anything by the time they pulled into the parking lot, but Kate needn't have worried because Jade was already inside the restaurant, sitting at a table and sipping a glass of wine. They hugged, and Kate ordered a glass of chardonnay and opened her menu.

"I hope you haven't been waiting long," she said.

"Nope. I just got here five minutes ago."

"How have you been?" Kate asked.

"Good. This job is keeping me really busy. You should see this home. It's almost as beautiful as yours." Jade stifled a yawn with the back of her hand. "Sorry about that. I went on a date last night with someone I met online, and I was up later than usual."

Kate smiled. "It must have gone well."

"It started off great. We're the same age and he's a widower, so I figured we'd have a lot in common, and we did. At dinner there were no awkward lulls in the conversation. We went to a movie afterward and I felt like we'd been seeing movies together for years. But toward the end of the evening, he started asking these weird questions about whether I'd ever consider dying my hair red and if I liked to wear dresses. I finally realized he was looking for someone to fill the shoes of his late wife in a rather literal way, and it creeped me out."

Kate grimaced and took a drink of her wine. "I know it works for a lot of people, but I didn't have the best luck with online dating either. Luckily I met Ian shortly after my foray into the world of 'everyone's lying and the rest of you are just hiding your crazy.'"

"Who's Ian?"

Yeah, Kate. Who's Ian?

"Oh, I meant Will. His middle name is Ian. I call him that sometimes. My middle name is Kate, so sometimes we do this whole Kate and Ian thing." *Oh my God, shut up.*

"Okay." Her skeptical expression contradicted her words, and Kate hoped Jade didn't think she was hiding some crazy of her own.

"Tell me the kind of man you're looking for. What are some of the qualifications you listed on your dating profile?"

"I want someone who's kind and will treat me well. I don't mean that he has to be wealthy or anything. I just want him to be respectful. It doesn't matter if he's been married before, but I think maybe a widower isn't such a great fit after all. Why, do you know someone?"

"I might. I'll let you know if it pans out."

Jade insisted on picking up the check for lunch, and as they put on their jackets and prepared to leave the restaurant, Kate started to panic. She'd forgotten about coming up with a reason for why Rob was waiting for her in the parking lot and really should have been thinking about it sooner. Her body temperature rose as they made their way toward the door.

For the life of her, she could not come up with anything to explain the presence of Rob that would even remotely make sense, at least not in the next sixty seconds. She could claim she'd hired a car service because she knew she'd be drinking alcohol, but she'd only had one glass of wine—hardly enough to justify a designated driver. She could say she'd let her license expire, but the obvious solution would be to go to the DMV and renew it, not hire someone to drive you around. She could say her car was having some work done, but how many repair shops gave you a rental and threw in someone to drive it for you?

Kate's hand was on the door and she was about to push it open when Jade stopped suddenly. "I need to visit the ladies' room before I head back to work. I'm so happy you could meet me for lunch. I really appreciate your driving all this way."

Relief washed over Kate. "It was no problem at all." She and Jade hugged and Kate said, "Let's do it again soon."

"I have a fantastic idea," Kate said over dinner that night.

"All of your ideas are fantastic," Ian said.

"I think we should set Jade and Charlie up on a date."

His expression seemed to convey that Kate's idea was not, in fact, all that fantastic. "Really? Jade and Charlie?"

"Why not? I thought you'd be all over this. They're fairly close in age. They're both single. I bet Charlie's not nearly the player he wants everyone to think he is. We could invite them over for dinner and to watch a movie afterward or play some pool."

"What if they don't hit it off?"

"Then we don't do it again."

"Maybe we should give it some more thought," he said. "And trust me, Charlie is *definitely* a player."

"What are you not telling me? And when did we start keeping things from each other?"

Ian took a drink and wiped his mouth with a napkin. "I don't know if I want Charlie to come here."

"You don't know if you want to invite your friend and fellow task force member to our home?"

"I don't know if I'm comfortable with it."

Kate laid down her fork. "Oh my God," she said, sounding stunned. "You think it's Charlie."

"You told him where you were meeting Jade for dinner, and that very night someone follows you home. At the charity event, you said Charlie looked at you as if he knew you. The only agents who knew what you looked like were the ones from the field office in Minneapolis who were watching over you. I suppose any member of the task force could have googled you out of curiosity before I erased your images, but I doubt they would have taken the time."

"But Charlie knew the FBI staged the crash. He knew everything about the situation, including the fact that you were still very much alive."

"Yes, but Charlie could have been the one to give my name and location to the carders in exchange for money. Maybe he knew what they were planning to do after they doxed me, maybe he didn't. Either way, he got paid. When the carders found out I was dead, they were probably furious with him, but technically he'd held up his end of the bargain, so he stuck to the story. It's not his fault I died before they could act. That's why they sent Zach Nielsen into the food pantry to see if you were acting like someone who'd just lost her boyfriend."

"Okay. Say you're right about everything. Why would Charlie follow me home? Why would he hack our security system?"

"To verify the address and make sure it was really us. He's seen my car. One look inside our garage would confirm it. Maybe he grabbed a still photo or two off the garage camera as proof. Think about it. He now has information that might once again fetch a pretty good price if he were to offer it to the right people."

"Does he know about your money?"

"It came up once a long time ago. He made an offhand comment about my lifestyle not matching that of someone who was still trying to get a struggling business off the ground. He doesn't know all the details, but he knows I did some programming work and was compensated for it. He's smart. He would have read between the lines and figured it out."

"I'm running out of objections."

"I did too when I was going through it in my head."

Kate pushed her plate away because her stomach was now in knots. "I think you're wrong about Charlie."

"It's just a gut feeling I can't shake, and believe me, I've tried."

"I don't want it to be him."

"Neither do I."

"I like him."

"I know you do. I like him too."

"It isn't him."

"I hope you're right. But until I know for sure who it is, I can't have him here."

Ian was right, and there was no way she would ever argue for something that might jeopardize their safety, no matter how crazy she thought the theory seemed.

CHAPTER TWENTY-SIX

KATE AND ROB MADE SMALL talk as he drove her to her latest social engineering assignment. At first she'd felt a little silly bringing a bodyguard to work, but it wasn't long before she discovered that having someone idling in the parking lot sure came in handy when she needed to make a quick getaway.

When he wasn't with her, Rob hung out in the guard shack by the garage, which Ian had decided to expand into an outbuilding with enough room to install additional surveillance equipment and give the guards someplace to take a break. He'd equipped it with a fridge and microwave and put a couch and TV in the corner. There was still some interior work to be done, but it was coming along nicely.

"Can you please park over there?" Kate asked when they reached their destination, pointing toward a visitor spot near the front of the building. She would have preferred that Rob park in the back of the lot, but she'd learned he considered it one of the most unsafe things a person could do and insisted on parking as close to the door as he could. She leafed through her notes after he brought the car to a stop. Because the task force had been taking up increasingly large amounts of his time, Ian had agreed to let Kate complete all the pretexting for their current assignment. He would be responsible for hacking into the network, but he'd put her in charge of all nontechnical penetration as well as physical entry.

"I won't be long, probably less than five minutes," she told Rob.

She'd tucked her hair up under a baseball cap, and she wore a polo shirt that bore the logo of the waste-removal company that was scheduled to empty the dumpsters the next day the way they did every Thursday. Pen in hand and carrying her clipboard, she approached a guard shack similar to the one at their front gate.

The man stationed inside looked up. "Can I help you?"

"Hi. My manager received a call that you've got a problem with one of the dumpsters you use for your paper recycling. He sent me to take a look at it so we can get it fixed before tomorrow's pickup."

"I don't know about any problem."

"So you're not Mr."—she looked down at her clipboard, thankful he wasn't wearing a name tag—"Brady?"

Upon hearing the name of his boss, the guard seemed to relax. "No. He must have forgotten to mention that he called."

"No problem. It'll only take a minute. It sounds like the hinge might be broken. I can have a replacement sent right away if necessary."

He shoved a badge through the narrow opening at the bottom of the shack's window. "You'll need this to access the dumpster area." He pointed to another shack fifty yards away, situated next to a tall chain-link fence with a closed gate. "Bring it back to me when you're done."

"Thank you." She had to force herself to answer him cheerfully because there was something about him she didn't like. Probably because he looked at her as if he didn't quite believe her.

Kate got back into the Range Rover. "Can you pull around back?"

"Sure." Rob started the car, and when they reached the guard shack, Kate gave him her temporary badge so he could hand it over. The guard took a cursory look at it, came out of the shack, and unlocked the gate, waving them through and closing it behind them.

"What are you doing here?" Rob asked, scanning the area. He was used to dropping her off at the front door and watching her walk safely inside. This was the first time one of Kate's assignments would be conducted outdoors, and it clearly made him uncomfortable.

"See those dumpsters? I'm checking them to make sure the company is disposing of their sensitive documents correctly." Rob knew Ian's company provided security auditing, but neither she nor Ian had provided many details regarding the methods they used for collecting the data. "It's okay, really. I shouldn't need more than fifteen minutes or so."

Kate headed for the dumpsters toward the back of the lot where she was less likely to be observed. She'd transferred the contents of her purse into a cross-body bag and was glad she'd worn jeans and tennis shoes because she had to climb up the side of the dumpster and lower herself into it.

Everything in it should have been cross-shredded, yet it all appeared completely intact. She found a pile of company directories, their covers dusty and torn. They'd likely been cleaned out of wherever they'd been kept since the company transitioned to storing the information online. Interspersed with the directories were org charts dated eighteen months ago. The information wasn't particularly earth-shattering, but a hacker would now have enough ammunition to impersonate lots of different employees in order to plan and carry out other, more damaging social engineering exploits. She tucked the org chart and one of the directories into her bag so she'd have proof to show the client.

"What are you doing?" a voice asked.

Kate looked up and her heart skipped a beat when she realized it was the guard who'd issued her the badge. She pulled the org chart and the rolled-up directory from her bag. "I noticed someone had put these in the dumpster when I was examining the hinge. I thought I'd grab them so I could show Mr. Brady. He probably wouldn't want them to be recycled without shredding them first."

Kate started to climb out of the dumpster, but it was a lot harder to climb out of than it was to climb into. The man reached down, and she had no choice but to take his hand and let him help her out. When her feet were firmly back on the ground, he didn't let go and she pulled her hand from his grasp.

"There's nothing wrong with the hinge on this dumpster."

"I probably checked the wrong one."

"I don't think there's anything wrong with the hinges on any of these dumpsters."

Though she hated getting caught, it didn't make sense to try to talk her way out of it. She'd already convinced him to issue her a badge by pretending to have Mr. Brady's permission, and the org chart and directories were another infraction Ian could include in his report. The guard was getting way too worked up, and she didn't like the way he was looking at her. It would be in her best interest to come clean.

"Listen, I'm actually here because I'm doing a security audit. I have a letter that states my right to be on the premises. It's signed by your CIO." She withdrew it from her bag and handed it to him, but he crumpled it up and slipped it into his pocket without reading it. Then he took off her hat, and her hair tumbled out from under it. He eyed her appraisingly, and the expression on his face raised the hair on the back of her neck. She started to walk away, but he took two steps to the right and blocked her path.

"Get out of my way."

"Why so quick to leave? Maybe we can work something out."

She reached into her bag for her pepper spray, taking a step back and holding it up where he could see it. "Do not even think about it."

He chuckled as if she was no threat to him at all. "Bet you're too scared to use it."

Kate flicked off the safety. "Trust me, I'm not."

"You think that's gonna do anything?"

Her heart galloped in her chest. "I'm sure it will."

He advanced and she took another step backward. There were three dumpsters standing behind him and the open area where Rob had parked the car. She was lighter and hopefully faster than the guard, but to escape she would have to get around him. If he cut her off again, she risked being tackled to the ground where her chances of being seen by someone were very low. He looked quickly over each shoulder and rose on his toes slightly as if preparing to pounce. She raised her arm and pointed the pepper spray at him. If he charged her, she would spray him, and as soon as she'd disabled him, she would run.

"Get away from her right now," Rob said. The formerly-soft-spoken Rob had undergone a metamorphosis that would have frightened her had he not been coming to her aid. His voice had risen in volume, and the steely edge of it cut through the silence. Gone were the laugh lines at his eyes and the corners of his mouth. He seemed as if he would enjoy tearing the guard limb from limb and was simply waiting for one wrong move so he could do it.

"I caught her going through the dumpster," the guard said.

"I'm not going to say it again. Get away from her right now."

The guard held up his hands, smirked, and sauntered away as if he hadn't done anything wrong, and Rob clenched and unclenched his fists in barely contained anger. Kate lowered the pepper spray, and she and Rob walked silently toward the car.

The guard who'd waved them through the gate earlier was berating the other guard. "What the hell were you doing back there? Your station was unmanned and there were people roaming around."

Kate started shaking once they were back in the car, and Rob reached into the backseat and handed her the hoodie she'd left there a few days ago.

"Are you okay?"

"Yeah. I'm just a little shook up." What if this had happened before they got hacked and she'd come here alone? "How did you know?"

"It's all in the walk. You moved with purpose, as if you didn't care who saw you. His walk told me he hoped no one would notice him. I'm sorry I didn't get there sooner."

It had seemed like forever, but the encounter with the guard had probably only lasted a minute, maybe a minute and a half, tops.

"I take full responsibility," Rob said. "I should have known better than to let you out of my sight."

"It wasn't your fault. You shouldn't have to worry about an employee of the company accosting me while I'm on the job."

"Even so, I'll let Mr. Smith know what happened before I leave for the day."

He put the car in gear, and when Kate could no longer see the company in the passenger-side mirror, she exhaled as the tension that had been coiled as tight as a snake ready to strike left her body. She pressed her cheek against the cool glass of the window and closed her eyes.

No matter how bad Rob felt, Kate knew it was nothing compared to how Ian would take the news.

"How did it go?" Ian asked when Kate walked into his office.

She bent down to kiss him and then pulled some papers from her bag and handed them to him.

He flipped through the pages and looked up. It said a lot about how lax the company's security was if Kate had been able to score org charts and a company directory. "Where did you find this?"

"In the dumpster."

"You went dumpster diving?"

"Just in the one that holds paper. When I visited the company during my pretexting, I noticed they had a bunch of them at the back of the property. It made me wonder if they were being as careful about what went into them as they should." She told Ian how she'd convinced the guard to issue her a badge and then unzipped her hoodie. "I copied the image of the waste removal company logo off their website and used it on one of those online T-shirt design sites. Then I waltzed right in." She pretended her fingers were legs walking along. "Pretty resourceful, huh?"

Hell yes it was. He'd never had the patience for that much involvement. "Very impressive, sweetness."

She sat down on the couch. "There's something I have to tell you."

"What is it?"

"You're not going to like it, and it's going to make you angry."

Her tone and the look on her face sent a jolt of anxiety through him. "Kate, just tell me."

"The security guard that issued me the badge figured out what I was doing. I didn't like the way he was looking at me so I gave him my letter, but he crumpled it up. So then I got out my pepper spray, and he didn't care, and then Rob came around the corner, and nothing happened, and I'm fine."

He sat there for a moment, stunned. Jesus Christ, what had he been thinking when he'd agreed to let her do this? Steve would come *unglued* if he ever found out, and rightly so. What if Rob hadn't been with her? He held up a finger. "One second, sweetness."

He picked up his phone and dialed. "Hi. Will Smith here. One of my employees checked in with your security guard earlier today, and he later refused to acknowledge the letter stating she had the right to be on the premises. That employee also happens to be my wife. We have an agreement when you sign our contract that no harm will come to anyone who is working for me. Either that security guard is gone by the end of the day, or I escalate this."

He hung up the phone. Exhaling, he took off his glasses, laid them on the desk, and rubbed his eyes, suddenly feeling very tired. "What kind of cake would you like?"

She looked at him like he'd lost his mind. "Cake? What are you *talking* about?"

"For your retirement party."

"I didn't retire."

"I just retired you."

"I didn't think you'd make me quit."

"Because you wouldn't have told me if you did?"

"I would never keep something like that from you," she said and burst into tears.

He was on his feet immediately, coming around from behind the desk to sit down beside her and gather her in his arms. "Kate, I'm sorry. I know you wouldn't."

His apology only made her cry harder, and he rubbed her back as she sobbed.

"I don't know why I can't stop crying," she said.

It wasn't like her to get upset like that, but the tears were probably a delayed reaction. She could downplay it all she wanted, but the security guard's actions had undoubtedly scared her more than she was letting on.

"I've got you," he said, holding her tightly in his arms until she quieted.

When her sobs finally tapered off, she lifted her head from his chest and he looked into her eyes.

"Listen to me. There's brave and there's dumb. And you don't do dumb, sweetness. You never have. So can this not be about bravery or equality or any of the other things you're thinking it's about? Can this just be about me not wanting any harm to come to the person I love most in this world?"

"Okay," she said softly as he wiped her tears. "Please don't be upset with Rob. I know he blames himself, but it wasn't his fault. I went where he couldn't see me."

"I'm not upset with Rob. I'm glad he was there."

"I'll be right back."

When she hadn't returned after ten minutes, he went looking for her. Maybe they could compromise so she wouldn't have to quit entirely. The bathroom door was half-open, and

Kate was standing in front of the sink, looking down with her back to him.

"There are plenty of things you can still do from home. E-mail is just as effective for getting malware onto a target network. There's phishing and spoofing, not to mention all the things you can do over the phone. And there may be other assignments we can do together. I'd be okay with that as long as I was with you."

She turned around, and there were tears on her cheeks again. Had she gone to the bathroom because she wasn't done crying but didn't want him to see? He was afraid she'd taken the news of her retirement even harder than he'd thought until she grabbed his hand and placed something in his palm. It was a pregnancy test, and there was no mistaking the result.

"A baby?" he said.

"I thought my shirt seemed a little tight in the chest when I put it on this morning, and I seem to be in the midst of some sort of hormonal shit storm, because I cannot stop crying to save my life. So I started thinking maybe I should pee on a stick while I was in here."

"A baby," he said again. *Kate was going to have a baby*. His baby. Their baby.

She appeared to be laughing *and* crying when she said, "I guess you knew how to make them after all."

CHAPTER TWENTY-SEVEN

IAN WENT INTO HIS OFFICE after breakfast. Charlie had been privy to an almost endless stream of the hacktivists' online chats, but they'd failed to yield enough specific information to shed light on their agenda. They would assume the FBI was listening in and would therefore be cautious about the types of things they shared. Charlie felt certain that high-level members of the group were chatting on another channel, but so far he hadn't been able to wrangle an invitation to join them. The task force had spent hours in their meetings analyzing the conversations in their possession, but whatever the hacktivists were planning remained just beyond their reach. They knew something was heading their way, but what?

They'd theorized that the words *dark* and *darkness* that appeared in the first transcript Charlie shared with the group referenced a future denial of service attack. And while there had been a series of additional attacks on various websites, none of them had been particularly damaging. But lately Ian had been pondering a different outcome because when he combined dark and darkness with another word from the transcript, he thought they might be looking at a more literal interpretation.

Dark and darkness and *power.*

Dark and darkness and the power *grid.*

At first he'd dismissed his hunch because he considered it too unlikely to be taken seriously, but he hadn't put it out of his mind entirely and told himself there was no harm in gathering enough data to explore it further. He'd tracked down the person in charge of monitoring and collecting information regarding attacks on the power grid. The information was compiled daily and reports were issued quarterly. The last report, covering October through December, showed only slightly higher than normal activity, which seemed to disprove his theory. However, Ian didn't want to wait another month for the next report at the end of March; he wanted to see if there had been any recent changes. He could have asked Phillip to approve a request to run the report a few weeks early, but that would take time and Ian had never been known for his patience.

There were three major sectors of the power grid—the Eastern, Western, and Texas Interconnections, and they could be compromised in many different ways. The most alarming scenario would be an electromagnetic pulse, which would be the most devastating because it was one of the only things that could take down all three interconnections simultaneously.

The grid was also vulnerable to physical threats like the sniper attack that had occurred on a substation in California, which had left parts of Silicon Valley in the dark. The unsolved case had been the most noteworthy attack on the grid by domestic terrorists to date.

Lastly was the threat of a cyberattack. The power grid had been on the Cyber Action Team's radar for years because it was probed hundreds of times per day by hackers around the globe in an attempt to unearth its vulnerabilities. However, large-scale attacks were thought to be unlikely because the power grid's biggest vulnerabilities were also its strengths. Most regional utility companies were independently owned and weren't required to use the same hardware or software, so sending the entire nation into darkness with one exploit would be nearly impossible. Hackers would need a multitude of custom hacks to connect the various networks, and not many would be willing to attempt such a massive undertaking. China and Russia had the patience and the financial capability, but even then they'd have to get past the numerous high-voltage interconnects whose specific purpose was to prevent widespread outages.

Ian spent the next four hours hacking his way into the networks of some of the biggest power plants on the Eastern Interconnection. The number of probes left behind by hackers—tools whose sole purpose was to seek out vulnerabilities in the system—had skyrocketed in the past four weeks. At first Ian doubted his findings, but then he reached for his glasses and double-checked the numbers, comparing them to the last report. The spike in activity confirmed that his hunch might not have been so far-fetched after all.

Still, it didn't make sense that a group who resided primarily in the United States would do anything to jeopardize the power they themselves depended on.

Unless the hacktivists wanted to cripple segmented parts of the infrastructure in order to make a point.

Especially the areas of the grid that provided DC with its power.

Ian picked up the phone and called Phillip.

CHAPTER TWENTY-EIGHT

THE TASK FORCE ASSEMBLED QUICKLY, and once everyone had filed into the conference room, Phillip explained the reason for the impromptu meeting. "I'm sorry to call you in on such short notice, but Ian has uncovered some information that points to a possible cyberattack on specific sections of the power grid."

Ian ran through what he'd found. "In the past thirty days, there was a significant increase in the number of remote probes on the grid. All of them had malware attached and were found in a concentrated area stretching from South Carolina to Maryland. I think they're trying to take down all or part of the Eastern Interconnection, but so far they haven't been able to compromise the grid on a large enough scale to do any damage."

"So they take down part of the grid and it stays down until we can bring systems back online?" Pete said.

A look of unease appeared on their faces. The nation's capital had experienced a fluke storm called a super derecho a few years back. The hurricane-force winds had knocked out power to five states along the Eastern Seaboard, and four days later, the area's utility companies had managed to restore power to only two-thirds of its customers. Thousands of businesses were closed, 911 call centers could not respond to emergencies, and gas stations were unable to pump fuel. Many federal agencies in DC had no choice but to shut down temporarily. A targeted cyberattack had the ability to keep them in the dark for an indeterminable amount of time, with catastrophic consequences. Not only would there be devastating financial losses, but the safety of the population would be at risk almost immediately due to large-scale looting and crime.

"Why would a group located in the US plan a potential domestic terrorist attack just to make a point? They'd be subjected to the same repercussions everyone else would encounter," Tom asked, articulating what everyone was probably thinking. "That's like setting off a giant bomb in the building you live in."

"Because if they're the ones who cause the outage, there's nothing preventing them from relocating to an area that won't be losing power," Ian said. He shut his laptop. "It's the ultimate act of civil disobedience and retaliation. We took away Joshua Morrison's power. Now the members of his group are going to take away ours."

"Well, at least we know their agenda now," Charlie said.

"I've already notified the appropriate personnel and departments, and we'll be convening immediately to determine a strategy and discuss disaster-recovery protocol. Once I know how we plan to proceed, I'll let you know your roles."

Ian and Charlie left the building together.

"What's Kate up to today?"

"She's just hanging out at home." The only thing Kate had been doing much of in the past few weeks was kneeling in front of the toilet and throwing up every single thing she tried to put in her stomach. She couldn't handle anything sweet and subsisted mostly on saltine crackers. Kate loved her morning coffee, but even the smell of it brewing was enough to make her gag. Though she'd told him it wasn't necessary, he'd given it up for the time being. She rarely complained, and the only evidence she needed more rest than usual was her desire for an earlier bedtime. She was about ten weeks along, which meant the baby had likely been conceived when they were in Costa Rica. Before he'd left the house to drive to headquarters, he'd gone looking for her and found her curled up on her side on the cold, hard tile of the bathroom floor, looking about as miserable as a person could look.

"This is certainly one way to guarantee my retirement," she said, lifting her arms weakly in the air to make quotes around the word retirement. "I'm too sick to leave the house."

"Can I tuck you back into bed?"

"Sadly, I don't think I'm done. Karma is paying me back for that time I pretended to have morning sickness. She is such a *bitch*."

He sat down next to her and stroked her head gently.

"When are you leaving for headquarters?" she asked.

"In a few minutes. Will you be okay while I'm gone?"

"I'll be fine. I'll probably still be right here on this floor when you get back."

Ian stopped walking when he and Charlie reached the parking lot. He'd likely only been making small talk when he asked about Kate, but Ian didn't want to share anything about her with Charlie, and his suspicions prevented him from telling him their happy news, even though he would have liked to.

"Someone hacked our security system."

"You sure it was hacked?"

"Positive. I modified the existing system with additional safeguards when we moved into the house. Only a hacker would be able to penetrate it." Ian let the words hang.

Realization dawned on Charlie's face. "Hold on a minute. You think it was me?"

He kept his expression neutral. "I didn't say that."

Charlie's face fell. "Yeah, you did."

"She's my wife."

"I know. You say that a lot. I haven't forgotten what it's like to have one, you know." After Charlie's wife cheated on him, he hadn't wanted to talk about it much—with Ian or anyone else.

Charlie walked toward his car without a backward glance. Ian could have gone after him. He could have apologized and assured Charlie he didn't think it was him. But he stood his ground. He had to. He knew better than anyone that manipulation was all part of the game. If Charlie had to lie to reach his goal, he'd look Ian right in the eye while saying the words. Ian would do the same, and for that matter, so would Kate.

It didn't stop him from feeling bad, and at that moment all he wanted was to get home and put his arms around his wife.

CHAPTER TWENTY-NINE

IAN'S PHONE BUZZED ON THE nightstand, rousing him from sleep. At first he thought it might be Phillip or Charlie and that the hacktivists had been successful in attacking the power grid, but when he glanced at the screen he realized the call had come from Kyle, one of the guards working the overnight shift, and he shot out of bed.

"What?" he said by way of greeting, keeping his voice low so he wouldn't wake Kate.

"You better come out here. The camera picked up someone on the grounds. Rich came up from the gate, and we apprehended the guy and called the police. They're on their way."

He threw on some clothes, and fifteen seconds later he flew through the door of the outbuilding. A man whose expression was somewhere between calculating and furious sat in a folding chair, making no attempt to get up. When Ian looked closer, he realized Kyle and Rich had zip-tied his wrists to the arms of the metal chair. The man had short brown hair, and Ian guessed his age as early thirties. He withdrew his phone and snapped several pictures of the intruder's face.

"What's his name?" Ian asked Kyle.

"He won't say, and there's no ID on him."

"Who are you?" Ian asked. The man remained silent, and rage like Ian had never felt before burst forth from him. "Who are you!" He kicked the leg of the chair hard enough to move it several inches. Still the man said nothing, and it was clear he wouldn't be changing his mind anytime soon.

Ian paced until the police arrived, gritting his teeth so hard it would take two days before his jaw stopped aching. Before they led the man away in handcuffs, Ian pulled the officer aside.

"I want to know who he is, and I want him charged with anything you can charge him with."

The officer nodded. "Someone will be assigned to your case, and they'll be in touch as soon as possible."

But Ian knew it could be twenty-four hours or more before they had any information for him, and he had no intention of waiting that long. Ian stared at the metal arms of the folding chair after they left. "I don't suppose you know how to lift fingerprints?" he said to Kyle.

"No. But I've got a friend who's a retired detective. He owes me a favor. He can lift them for you, but he won't be able to run anything through the database. He doesn't have access anymore."

"If you get me the print, I can take it from there." The FBI maintained the database, so access wouldn't be a problem. Once Ian had the man's name, there were places he could go to find out all kinds of information.

"I want you and Rich to search the grounds in case there were two of them. Take turns patrolling the exterior of the house. Let me know when you have the print."

Kyle pulled out his phone. "I'll call him right now and see if I can get him out here first thing in the morning."

CHAPTER THIRTY

IAN WENT BACK INTO THE house. The pounding in his head had reached a fever pitch, so he stopped in the kitchen and rummaged in the drawer next to the sink for some Tylenol. He shook the pills into his hand and scooped up water from the faucet to wash them down. There was no denying a confrontation loomed on the horizon, perhaps in the not-so-distant future. In a way, he welcomed it because it meant taking a stand.

A confrontation meant an outcome.

It meant resolution.

No more looking over their shoulders or waiting for the other shoe to drop.

Because this time he would find out what they wanted.

Anything would be better than waiting and wondering if next time the intruder would somehow get past the guards and make it all the way into their home. Maybe when he wasn't there and Kate was standing in the kitchen or taking a shower. The visual sucker punched him, and he had to take a few deep breaths to get his head on straight. The guilt weighed on him like a brick pressing down on his chest. He'd already stripped her of her autonomy in an effort to protect her. She couldn't drive herself or go anywhere alone. He'd practically made her a prisoner in her own home, and now even that wasn't secure.

All because of him.

"Ian?"

He spun around because he was wound tighter than a spring and her voice had startled him.

"What's going on?" Sleepy-eyed with tousled hair, she wore only the shirt of her pajamas and it was unbuttoned all the way, exposing a sliver of each breast. He quickly crossed the room and started buttoning her up. There were just so many windows in the kitchen, and not all of them were covered by shades.

She laid her hands on his arms. "Why are you up? Why are all the lights on?"

"The guards caught someone on the property." Saying the words out loud made their situation real, and there was no going back now that he'd uttered them. If it wasn't already, the gravity of what they were facing would be that much clearer to Kate.

Fear clouded her expression. "Where?"

"Near the basement sliding door. It was a man. Early thirties. We think he was alone. Kyle and Rich detained him, and the police arrested him and took him away." He dug his phone out of his front pocket and held it up to Kate. "Is this the hacker who came into the food pantry? The one who said his name was Zach Nielsen?"

She shook her head. "That's not him. I've never seen that man before."

None of her past bravado had been false. But any bravery she'd once felt crumbled away as tears filled her eyes. He put his arms around her and felt her tremble under his touch. He used to think letting Kate believe he was dead was the harshest thing he'd done to her, but involving her in this mess was worse.

"Let's get you back to bed." He took her hand and led her to their bedroom, tucking her underneath the covers. "I'll be right back. I want to make sure everything's locked down tight."

The bedroom door closed with a soft click, and he stood in the hallway for a moment to get his bearings. His headache had dissipated slightly, but the pressure remained, making it feel as if his head were being squeezed in a vise. Silently he made the rounds of the house, checking every door, every window.

When he returned to their bedroom and slid underneath the covers, he put his arms around her and pulled her close.

"I'm scared," she said.

"I won't let anything happen to you." He stroked her head until he felt her body relax.

He would have been able to sleep if he had only himself to think about. If the repercussions of his decisions only affected him. But he'd dragged the woman he loved more than anything in the world along with him.

And that was why, when the sun came up the next morning, he was still lying there thinking about it.

CHAPTER THIRTY-ONE

"I WANT YOU TO go home to Indiana for a while." They were sitting at the breakfast table, both of them picking at their food. Phillip had put the task force on standby because early that morning, South Carolina Electric and Gas reported that one of their substations in North Charleston was having trouble accessing its systems, almost as if they'd been locked out of them. Between the intruder and the heightened risk of an impending blackout, Ian could think of no place he'd rather Kate be than with her family in Indiana. As soon as they dealt with the cyberattack, he would join her and they'd figure out what to do about the rest.

One problem at a time.

"Okay." There were dark circles under her eyes.

He'd expected her to argue, to remind him again that this was her home, but the fact that she didn't told him how scared she was, and if he had to guess, he would say the baby had changed everything. Kate was a fighter, but there was another person's safety at stake, and the best way to protect their child was for her to remove herself from the source of the danger, even if that also meant removing herself from him. He would send her away, but how long could he expect her to stay hidden? And would Indiana be the next place they'd look?

His phone rang, and Kyle's name showed on the display. "I've got that print," he said when Ian answered the call.

"I'll be right out."

"Who was that?" Kate asked.

"Kyle. He knows someone who agreed to lift the finger-prints. I want to see what I can find online."

"Won't the police run them to see if there's a match?"

"Yes, but they won't be looking in the same places I'm looking."

Kyle handed him the white card his friend had transferred the print onto with special tape.

"Thanks," Ian said.

In his office, he scanned and uploaded the print, and when he ran it through the main database, it returned the name Ted Lawson. He used a query and response protocol and then set about writing a program specifically designed to cross-reference the IP information to the search criteria he specified, including the IP address associated with the hacking of their security system.

It took two hours for the program to sift through the in-formation, but in the end it returned nothing that would indicate the man had even a tenuous connection to any kind of cybercrime. He was either incredibly lucky or as skilled at hiding his identity as Ian.

Ian scanned the data a second time to ensure he hadn't missed anything. Then he mentally braced himself, picked up the phone, and called Kate's dad.

Steve didn't take the news of the intruder well at all.

"You look tired," Kate said when Ian walked into their bedroom.

He sat down on the bed and rubbed his eyes. "I am."

"Heard anything more from Phillip?"

"The utility company in North Charleston is still trying to get their systems back online. Charlie's taking a look at it right now. He'll call me if he finds anything."

"Do you think my dad believed you? About the supplies?"

"Yes." Ian told Kate that when he talked to Steve, he'd also told him about the possible attack on the power grid and urged him to buy bottled water, batteries, and canned food. Kate's dad was at the opposite end of the spectrum from those who practiced doomsday prepping—so was Ian, for that matter. But neither man could deny that the time had come to take the risk seriously. Indiana was on the same Eastern Interconnection grid as DC.

"Are you ready to get in the shower?" she asked.

"Yes." Ian was still in the sweats and T-shirt he'd pulled on when he got out of bed, and Kate had never made it out of her robe.

He turned on the water, waiting until the shower stall filled with steam. Kate hung her robe on a hook and stepped under the spray. He followed her in, and when her hair was wet, he reached for the shampoo and washed it. He loved the way she closed her eyes as he massaged her head. He'd give anything not to have to send her away, but it was the right decision. If whoever had found them again didn't make another move soon, Ian would have to find a way to draw them out and get to the heart of their demands. Because they wanted something. He had no doubt about that.

He rinsed out the shampoo, and the suds ran down her chest. His palm followed, skimming along her slick, wet skin. His hand drifted lower, and he stopped suddenly when it reached her stomach. It would probably be another month or two before the pregnancy would really start to show, but the previously flat expanse of skin now had an almost imperceptible rise to it that he could have sworn hadn't been there yesterday, and it was only because he knew her body so well that he'd noticed it at all. "When did this happen?" he asked, resting his hand on her belly.

She placed her hand over his and looked up at him. "I don't know. I feel like it almost popped out overnight."

"Why haven't I felt it?"

A smile played at the corner of her mouth. "Your hands have been quite occupied with my pregnancy breasts."

"I had no idea." Kneeling down in front of her, he ran his palms over the slight swell. "This is so wild."

She rested her hands on his head. "I know."

When he stood, she pulled his mouth down to hers. He had never felt more loving toward or more connected to Kate than he did at that moment, and the gentle kiss they shared spoke volumes. No one would take his wife and child from him. He would lay down his life for theirs without question.

When the kiss ended, he reached for her body wash, intending to continue on with their shower. But she pulled his mouth to hers again as if she needed to stockpile his kisses so there would be a well of affection to draw from in his absence.

Nearly all their mornings began with one of them touching the other, and by the time they made it into the shower, they'd usually already made love. He adored washing Kate, and he adored *being* washed by her. It was a habit they'd started back in Minneapolis, and while it was playful and sexy—and sometimes led to them quickly drying off and returning to bed for another round—it was mostly an affectionate routine they both enjoyed. This morning, after tossing and turning most of the night, he'd slipped from bed before she awakened because he had too much on his mind to lie there one minute longer.

Kate showed no sign of wanting to stop, and when she rubbed her breasts against his chest, slick with leftover suds from the shampoo, he was a goner. She was right; he *had* been paying extra attention to them. How could he not?

He cupped them in his hands, feeling the softness of their weight and the changes in their size and shape. Further evidence of the transformation her body was undergoing. The thought made him sad. Her safety depended on their separation, but how many of these subtle changes would he miss while she was gone?

Though they didn't have much time, he backed her up until she was pressed firmly against the back wall of the shower. He didn't know how long they would be apart, and he suddenly felt a need to stockpile a few things of his own. She lifted her leg and he hitched it higher on his waist, and in one fluid motion he entered her. The water rained down on them as they found their rhythm, and she held him tight, kissing him as he moved inside her. Her movements grew frantic, and there was something so primal about her need, so sustaining. There were times she expressed her desire toward him in this way and it made him feel like a king to be wanted so desperately. Wildly, she clutched at him, pulling him deeper into her until she cried out. Her body gradually relaxed, and he found his own release, as tender as hers had been wild.

They washed each other, and when they got out of the shower, as Ian was rubbing her gently with a towel, she looked up at him and said, "I don't want to go, but I will. I can get through this now."

He finished drying her and wrapped her in the towel. "I know you can."

Unfortunately, he wasn't at all certain that *he* could.

CHAPTER THIRTY-TWO

"WHEN ARE YOU LEAVING?" Diane asked. Though her mother was trying her best to hide it, Kate could hear the worry in her voice.

"As soon as I finish packing. Ian said the plane should be ready to take off by four." She rifled through drawers and carried stacks of clothes to her suitcase.

"I'm so glad you're coming home," Diane said.

"I am too."

When Ian had called her dad to say he was sending Kate home and to warn him about the possibility of a major power outage in DC, her mother's worry had kicked into overdrive, and the only thing that had calmed her down was the assurance that she'd have her daughter back home by that evening.

Kate had such a bad feeling about everything. A problem with the power grid coming so close on the heels of their intruder lent an especially ominous feel to the situation. Ian already had enough to deal with, and the stress of both situations had stretched him thin. She'd awakened around four a.m. to go to the bathroom, and even though his eyes were closed, Kate knew by the way he'd tossed and turned all night that sleep hadn't come easy for him, if at all. At six, when she woke up for the day, his side of the bed was already cold and empty.

Kate put the last of her things in the suitcase, closed the lid, and zipped it. "I have to go, Mom. I'll call you when we're in the air. I love you and I'll see you soon."

Ian backed his SUV out of the garage and left it idling out front while he went inside to get Kate's suitcase. His phone rang, and Charlie's name flashed on the screen. To his credit, he'd done a good job of keeping how he felt about Ian's accusation from affecting their work relationship.

"Where are you?" Charlie asked.

"Home. I'm leaving now to take Kate to the airport."

"If what's going on in North Charleston can be confirmed as a cyberattack—and everything we know seems to be pointing to it—Homeland is going to ground all planes. Phillip also said they'll deploy the Cyber Action Team."

Ian's stress level kicked up a notch because the last thing he needed at that moment was an unexpected roadblock. But if the grounding was imminent, Kate could get stuck on the runway, or worse yet, be up in the air when the alert came. They'd have to reroute her, and who knew where she'd end up. And once the Cyber Action Team had been deployed, Ian's presence would be needed at headquarters immediately.

"How much time do I have?" He'd already given Rob the time off after explaining that Kate was going to be visiting her folks and therefore his services wouldn't be needed for a few weeks. If he wanted to get Kate safely out of town—and he wanted that more than anything—he'd have to drive her himself.

"How much do you need?"

"Enough to meet Kate's dad halfway between here and Indiana."

"I doubt you have that long."

"I'm gonna try anyway. Call me if anything changes," Ian said.

Kate was standing in the open front door next to her abandoned suitcase when Ian roared up from the barn in the Spyder. He threw open the door, and when he reached Kate, he grabbed her suitcase with one hand and her by the other and led her to the car.

"Why are we taking the Spyder?"

"Because we're in a really big hurry." The hybrid vehicle was not only fast, it also didn't require stopping as often for gas. "I just got off the phone with Charlie, and there's a good chance all planes are about to be grounded." He shut her door and ran around to the driver's side.

Next he called Steve. "I can't put Kate on a plane, and I'm going to be needed at headquarters very soon." As he spoke, he typed Zionsville into the navigation system and chose a route. "If we both hustle, we can meet somewhere in the middle and as soon as Kate's with you, I'll turn around and head back."

She was perfectly capable of driving herself, but she understood Ian's reasoning. And once he knew she was with her dad, he could concentrate on his job without worrying about her.

Ian hung up the phone. "Okay. Let's do this." He left a spray of gravel behind in the circle drive and headed for the gate.

They had already put DC in their rearview mirror, traveling a brisk fifteen to twenty miles per hour over the speed limit, when Charlie called again. Ian pressed the hands-free button on the steering wheel. "What's the latest?"

"A little over one hundred thousand customers in North Charleston just lost power," Charlie said, his voice filling the car. "Their system is crippled. Forensics is trying to determine the exact cause."

"Ian, they need you," Kate said.

He didn't respond immediately, mentally weighing his options. "Let me call you back," he told Charlie and disconnected the call.

"I can drive myself." He started to protest, but before he could get the words out she said, "Pregnant women drive cars all the time." Her morning sickness had finally begun to taper off as she neared the end of the first trimester, but she still couldn't stomach the thought of coffee, and even the smell of it continued to send her running for the bathroom. Other than that, she only felt slightly nauseated, and that was mostly first thing in the morning.

He reached for her hand and gave it a squeeze. "I know they do."

"Would you rather I dropped you off at headquarters and went back home to wait this out?"

What he wanted was for Kate to be safely tucked away with her family, even if Indiana ultimately lost power. If the unthinkable happened and the whole Eastern Interconnection went dark, he and Charlie and the rest of the task force would have to work nonstop until they figured out how to solve the crisis and the danger had passed. He didn't want to think about how long that could be, and the last thing he wanted was for Kate to be at home.

In a blackout.

Even with access to generator power that would keep a few of their home's lights on, and with the security guards watching over her, he could not fathom it.

"No. I definitely don't want you there."

"If you turn around right now, I can drop you off at headquarters and in less than twenty minutes I can be on my way again. Then you'll be free to focus on what seems to be shaping up as a major crisis. I know you won't be able to talk, but I'll text you every time I stop for gas. The longer we debate this, the more time we're wasting."

"You're sure you can make the drive?"

"Of course I can."

He called Charlie back. "I'll be there in fifteen," Ian said. He disconnected the call, got off at the next exit, and headed back toward headquarters.

Kate called her dad and advised him of the change in plans. "The task force needs Ian, so we're heading back to headquarters to drop him off."

"I'm already in the car, and I brought Chad. You can get in with me, and Chad can follow behind in your car. Get back on the road as soon as you can, okay? Your mother isn't going to stop calling me until you're home."

"I will. As soon as we arrive at headquarters, I'll say good-bye to Ian and be on my way."

In the parking lot of FBI headquarters, Ian exited the car after grabbing his laptop case from the backseat. Kate walked around the front of the car, and he put his arms around her.

"I know why I have to go, but I hate leaving you behind," she said. She pictured the city in darkness, or worse, lit up from the fires the looters would surely set if DC were to lose power.

The wail of police sirens. Gunshots. Breaking glass. If the Eastern Interconnection went dark, Indiana would face the same fate, but at least she'd be with her family. She only wished Ian could be with them too.

"I'll be fine at headquarters. Phillip's not going to let any of us leave if he thinks it isn't safe."

"You have to promise you'll join me as soon as you can. As soon as things are under control, tell Phillip and the others you have to go." She took his spot in the driver's seat, and Ian crouched down beside her.

"I'll leave for Indiana as soon as I'm able. Be careful. You won't have to stop as often with a hybrid engine, but I want you to keep the gas topped off. Don't drop below half a tank." He glanced at his watch. "You've got about another hour of daylight. Your dad and Chad should reach you by nine thirty. If the power goes out along the way, keep driving until you run out of gas. Sit tight with the doors locked until your dad and Chad reach you. Hopefully they'll have enough gas to make it to the next city." He leaned into the car and kissed Kate tenderly on her forehead. "I love you. Now go."

"I love you too."

CHAPTER THIRTY-THREE

A CRISIS OF THIS MAGNITUDE required all hands on deck, and an off-site location was not an option. The task force and the FBI Cyber Action Team—whose sole objective was to provide rapid incident assistance—were at that moment pouring into headquarters. Ian was no longer worried about running into whoever had doxed him. As he walked down the hall, he decided that if whoever had tracked him and Kate was somewhere in this building, he'd welcome the opportunity to confront them. But his instincts told him whoever had breached their alarm and trespassed on their property probably wasn't the type of person who'd be willing to run defense against whoever was behind the cyberattack on the grid. It just didn't add up.

Unless of course the person who'd doxed him was Charlie.

Ian burst through the door of the makeshift war room. This wasn't the first time he'd ridden out a crisis here, and it wouldn't be the last. There were twenty long tables, upon which sat rows of laptops. Cell phones, coffee cups, and legal pads covered the remaining surface. Someone had hung an electronic map of the Eastern Interconnection on the wall, which when lit up would resemble a scoreboard. Agents milled around, some huddled together in groups of two or three and some sitting alone, eyes focused on the screen in front of them. The task force was seated at its own table at the front of the room, and Phillip was standing next to it. He held a clipboard and appeared to be coordinating activities. Ian sat down next to Charlie and pulled his laptop from its case.

"Get Kate back on the road?" Charlie asked. His tone wasn't unkind, but it held more than a hint of the reserve that showed itself every time they spoke, which told Ian he still resented the implication he had anything to do with Ian's doxing.

"Yeah. Her dad and brother are meeting her halfway."

"She'll be fine. North Charleston is the only outage."

"For now."

Disabling the Eastern Interconnection wouldn't require bringing down every substation; compromising one out of every three would place a crippling load on those that were still functioning until they too succumbed and fell like dominoes as their systems strained and faltered under the increased weight.

When the task force figured out what the hacktivists were planning, the FBI had appointed teams who'd been dispatched to assist the utility companies in preparing for an attack. The protocol they put in place specified that if a substation were to fail, its power load would be split between several others so as not to overpower it and start a cascading outage. This had worked exactly the way they'd hoped it would when North Charleston fell, but the task force could not afford a false victory, so they remained vigilant even as they breathed a sigh of relief over clearing their first hurdle.

"Do we know what they used for the attack?" Ian asked. Most of the prior attempts to attack the power grid were attributed to a specific malware called BlackEnergy.

"We should know soon. Forensics is working on it now," Charlie said.

Fifteen minutes later, Phillip motioned to the task force and they gathered around him in a loose huddle.

"One of the forensic analysts has identified the malware. It's not BlackEnergy, although we're probably all going to wish it was."

"What is it?" Ian asked.

"It's custom. Something they've designed for their own use. They've used an open-source programming language that isn't especially sophisticated as far as technology goes, but it's working well enough to get the job done."

"Why wasn't the malware uncovered during the scans?" Tom asked.

"Maybe they hadn't deployed it yet," Ian said. "They could have sent phishing e-mails that appeared to be from businesses and organizations the utilities regularly corresponded with. There would be no reason to fear clicking on the link or opening the attachment because they'd probably been sent long before we warned them of the possibility of an attack. Then the infected computers sent the access data to a server, which kept the channel open until they needed it. Now they're sending the payload with a wiper utility that's destroying parts of the system's hard drive and causing the actual loss of power. The malware not only stops certain processes from running, it also erases the stored information. Then a backdoor opens, which gives them all the remote access they need."

"That's why the utility company in North Charleston first reported being unable to access their systems. Now that they're dark, they've got a backdoor, which means they can't control them at all," Phillip said.

"They're building a botnet," Charlie said.

The revelation surprised no one. Ian hated to admit it, but the hacktivists had come up with an ingenious way to link together an aging infrastructure that often seemed connected by paper clips and string.

"Do you realize how long it would take to make sure enough substations were compromised to allow for a widespread outage?" Tom asked.

"Months," Charlie said. "Maybe longer."

"That means we wasted our time telling the utilities to patch all their holes," Brian said.

"So what city's next?" Tom asked.

"My vote is for Columbia. I imagine they'll keep linking their way north until they reach DC," Charlie said.

Phillip asked the agent running the electronic map to mark North Charleston with a pinpoint of red light and the remaining cities between North Charleston and DC in white. It was easy to see the path the attack might take as the string of white lights crawled to the north.

Half an hour later, the noise level rose and the chatter intensified as an agent announced that approximately 130,000 residents in Columbia, South Carolina, no longer had power.

"Sometimes it sucks to be right," Charlie said.

Everyone in the room looked toward the electronic map on the wall and watched as the light representing Columbia, South Carolina, changed from white to red.

CHAPTER THIRTY-FOUR

AN HOUR AND A HALF into her drive, Kate stopped just outside Hagerstown, Maryland, to use the bathroom and fill her gas tank. Ian had sent a brief text.

Ian: *Major outages reported in North Charleston and Columbia. Don't worry. Just keep driving. Love you.*

Kate: *Just stopped for gas. Will get back on the road ASAP. Love you too.*

Fingers of dread worked their way up her spine. Did that mean more cities in South Carolina would follow? Then North Carolina and Virginia? Would the outages nip at her heels until she met up with her dad and brother? What if they traveled faster than she could?

She pictured what driving in a blackout would be like and was grateful she'd just filled her tank.

Her brother called as she was placing the nozzle back on the pump.

"Hey, Chad," she said as she screwed the gas cap on and got back in the car.

"Are you listening to the news?"

"It's already on the news?" Before she'd pulled into the gas station, she'd been listening to music.

"You know about it?"

"Ian sent a text. I'm at a gas station. I thought they'd try to keep it out of the news."

"Good luck with that. Pretty hard to ignore an outage that big. It probably didn't take long for the media to get on it."

"Did they say what caused it?"

"They said the utility companies are working on it, but they didn't provide any details. It looks like we'll reach each other in a little under three hours. We're at three-quarters of a tank, but we're going to top off as soon as we pass the next gas station. Make sure you do the same in another hundred miles or so."

"I will." She started the car and pulled out of the parking lot. "See you soon."

As she drove west on I-70, Kate switched to a news station and listened to an update on the power outage. Chad had been right when he'd said that details were scant. They were probably being withheld so as not to plunge the country into panic mode. If people knew the loss of their power was imminent, would they try to lay in supplies, causing a panicked run on grocery stores, or would they flee, creating a gridlock in an attempt to escape the blackout? She thought of Susan. Phillip had likely taken just as many precautions as Ian, but it still bothered Kate to think Susan would have no one with her if the power in DC and the surrounding areas went out. And who knew how long it would be before Phillip made it home?

Kate adjusted the cruise control, raising her speed from seventy to seventy-five after deciding a speeding ticket would be a small price to pay for reaching her dad and Chad sooner.

Forty-five minutes later on US 40 right outside Cumberland, Maryland, the Porsche began to lose speed. At first she thought she'd accidentally tapped the button and disengaged the cruise control, but when she pressed down on the gas, the car continued to slow. When it became apparent she might be stranded in the middle of the highway, she had no choice but to pull to the shoulder. There had to be something wrong with the car because she hadn't been going fast enough to trigger Ian's speed alarm, and besides, he had his hands full and likely wouldn't be able to do anything about it even if he wanted to.

She tried to start the car, but she couldn't get the engine to turn over, and her repeated attempts had probably flooded the engine. She'd wait ten minutes and try again, and if the car still wouldn't start, she would call her dad and Chad and wait for them to come get her.

A car pulled off the highway, slowed to a crawl, and came to rest right behind her bumper. She could make out the faint glow of lights floating like a halo above the next town a mile or two down the road, but the fairly desolate stretch of road she was on was dark with only a few cars passing by. She heard the slam of a car door and took a few deep breaths. Probably just a concerned motorist making sure she was okay.

She double-checked that the doors were locked and reached for her phone, her finger hovering over the keypad. If they asked her if she needed assistance, she would tell them she'd already called for a tow truck and refuse any invitation to get out of the car.

Right before the person came into view, when they were still slightly to the rear of her driver's side window, her seat belt unclicked and the Spyder's locks popped up. And when the door opened and the interior light came on, she screamed as Zach Nielsen shoved his hands underneath her and propelled her over the console and into the passenger seat as if she were nothing more than a rag doll.

CHAPTER THIRTY-FIVE

FOR A FEW SECONDS, she forgot how breathing worked. Her shallow, panicked inhale failed to inflate her lungs to their full capacity because when she exhaled there didn't seem to be enough air to blow out.

Zach typed something into his phone, and the door locks clicked into place again. The engine turned over with ease, and the voice of the news reporter burst forth from the stereo, the volume seeming too loud in the small space. He jabbed at the dial to silence it. The illumination of the dashboard lights allowed Kate to see him better. Gone were the warehouse-worker clothes he'd been wearing when he'd visited the food pantry. Instead he wore a button-down shirt and dark jeans, and his short hair looked freshly trimmed. To anyone else, it might have appeared as if they were going on a date or heading to a gathering with friends. Kate reached toward the floor for her purse, thinking by some miracle she might be able to grab her pepper spray, but Zach blocked her wrist before she could get to it.

"I don't know what you're reaching for in there, but don't try it again." He took the purse and set it on the floor of the driver's side. "I don't want you to be afraid, Kate. I don't mean any harm, and I promise this will go smoothly, but only if you cooperate."

"Ian will give you whatever you want." She spoke quietly, trying to keep it together and not give him the satisfaction of hearing the tremble in her voice.

"Of course he will. I have his wife. Now give me your phone."

She pulled it from the front pocket of her jeans, unlocked it, and set it on the console. Arguing or resisting would be futile—if she didn't hand it over willingly, he'd take it anyway. They sat in awkward silence as he turned off her location devices. Then he put the phone in his pocket, buckled his seat belt, and pulled back onto the highway. She wanted to ask where they were going, but all of the potential responses terrified her, so she said nothing. A beeping sound filled the interior.

"You need to put your seat belt on," he said, and she obeyed. "Maybe it's because of your work at the food pantry, but you strike me as someone who would never ignore a safety rule. I really do admire you for helping all those people back in Minneapolis. It tells me what kind of person you are."

Kate's mind raced as she tried to piece together what had happened. Maybe Ian had been right about Charlie. Maybe he and Zach had been working together, and the reason they'd accessed footage of the garage camera wasn't to see what cars they drove, but to hack the cars' networks and set up some kind of remote alarm that would let Zach know which car was in use. It had probably infuriated them when they'd switched out the cars and Rob started accompanying Kate everywhere she went. Charlie had been the one to call and summon Ian back to headquarters, and what better time to apprehend Kate than when he'd be totally immersed in his work with the task force? Ian had probably mentioned that Steve planned to meet

Kate halfway between DC and Indiana, otherwise how else would Charlie know Kate would be alone on this very stretch of road? Once Zach hacked into the Porsche's network, he'd have access to her exact route and all the tools he would need to take control of the car the same way Ian had.

"So this is how it's gonna go down," Zach said. "Like you said, Ian will give me whatever I want, and what I want is money. Your husband has a lot of it, so it only makes sense. When we get to the airport, I'll use your phone to call him and give him an amount. He'll wire me the money, and approximately 2.5 seconds after I receive it, it'll be gone again. If he tries to put me off or delay payment because he wants to set up some kind of bullshit FBI rescue, you'll get on the plane with me and we'll fly to another location. I don't think he'll like that at all."

"You can't fly," she said, the words rushing out before she could stop them.

"Why the hell not?"

And then Kate *knew*.

It wasn't Charlie after all.

It wasn't anyone working for the FBI.

The airports that relied on the Eastern Interconnection had surely been briefed and were standing by, waiting for the signal to ground all flights whether their airport still had power or not. It was doubtful the general public would know anything about the warning. But if Zach and Charlie were working together, their plan would not include any kind of air travel, at least not in the immediate future.

"I just meant flights can be delayed."

"We're not flying commercial. The pilot will take off when I tell him to."

Kate didn't know which airport Zach planned to use or what he would do when he discovered the plane couldn't take off.

Or what would happen if it could.

Her elation that Charlie was not involved was short-lived, because no matter how happy it made her to know he had nothing to do with it, she still had a frightening problem to solve.

"Are you the one who doxed Ian?" Her right hip had caught the edge of the console when he shoved her, and it throbbed.

"Do you even need to ask? I thought you were brighter than that. I was poking around in a network trying to get past a firewall one night when I encountered another hacker. I wasn't that surprised actually. We figured the feds were on to us. They're always hiding behind their aliases, trying to catch us doing something we shouldn't, and this hacker seemed to know this was someplace he might find one of us."

Kate remembered when Ian's laptop alarm had gone off in the middle of the night and she'd been so worried he'd have to leave.

"So we're battling it out, and I got curious and decided that instead of trying to get past the firewall, maybe I should try to determine who this guy is and where he's located. I figured the information could be valuable. So naturally he's hidden his IP address, but I've got this amazing tool—it's like a little cell phone tower—that intercepts Wi-Fi signals and shows me their locations. I bought it off a guy at a hacking convention, and let me tell you, it wasn't cheap but it sure has come in handy. There's some triangulation involved, which is a giant pain in the ass, and he must have pulled the battery on his phone because I lost him literally seconds after I homed in on his location, which was your street. I still had some work to do, but once you get that far, it's really just a matter of legwork and patience."

Kate remained silent. She would not give him the satisfaction of asking for more information. It didn't matter though, because he kept on talking.

"There are places where we store facts about our FBI friends. Screen names, aliases, pictures. That sort of thing. I copied all the images on file and I studied them. Once I relocated to your city, I stationed myself outside the apartment buildings on your street, and I observed the people coming and going. Even though the picture's pretty old, there was no mistaking the man who walked out the front door of yours one morning. By the end of the week, I knew where he lived, the name of his pretty girlfriend, and her job at the food pantry. But would you believe I still didn't know *his* name?"

Yes, Kate could absolutely believe it.

"It took me a few weeks to figure it out. I had to be careful not to draw attention to myself from the other carders, because that was the kind of thing a lot of people would be interested in. Eventually, I learned the picture of him had come from an old MIT yearbook. One of the forum members who went to college with him had heard from a friend of a friend that he'd been forced to work for the FBI after getting busted hacking something big."

With the FBI, Kate thought. *Not for.*

"That's when I tracked down that yearbook, found the picture, and learned his name was actually Ian Bradshaw. Not that I can find his real name anywhere online. I mean, the guy has more aliases than anyone I've ever known. But after a few more conversations with his college buddy, I discovered Ian Brad-shaw had once done some programming for a certain start-up venture. It was all very hush-hush apparently, but where there are contracts and lawyers, there are also records if you're willing to dig and know where to look. As a former attorney, you probably know all about that. I already wanted to dox him because we knew the feds were starting to close in, and I'm not a big fan of jail. That's when I realized extortion is a much faster and more efficient way to acquire wealth than stealing credit card numbers, and his lovely girlfriend would make an excellent bargaining chip. My own little distributed denial of service attack. But then Mother Nature had to come along and fuck everything up with a storm, and the message board blew up with all this chatter about an undercover hacker named Ian Merrick whose car had plunged into the Mississippi. When someone posted that yearbook photo and I realized Ian Mer-rick and Ian Bradshaw were the same person, you cannot even imagine the extent of my rage."

He sounded a little unhinged, and Kate knew he would not let anything stand in the way of his goal.

"It seemed a little too coincidental. I mean, he's not the first hacker who's faked his death, but dying so soon after I doxed him and hacked his girlfriend made me wonder, you know? I admire the steps he was willing to take. That's the thing that separates people like Ian and me from all the others. We're willing to put in the work, to do what it takes."

"Ian is nothing like you."

Zach ignored her comment. "I thought about dropping the whole thing after that, but there was just so much money on the line. I have to hand it to you, you're a phenomenal actress. I never once saw you break cover to smile or laugh.

And the tears and the red eyes. No offense, but you really looked like shit."

"How did you find us?" she asked, hating his smug arrogance and herself even more for asking after she told herself she wouldn't. But she had to know.

"I know a few hackers who live in Minnesota and don't ask questions if the price is right. They'd already helped me out by watching the lobby of Ian's apartment building after the accident and nosing around at the auto storage facility. I decided to send one of them into the food pantry last summer, and that's when I learned you'd quit. I found that information very interesting, so I asked my friend to become a regular client of the food pantry. The woman who took your place treated him with kindness and compassion, but he told me Helena was his favorite. He said he even considered her a friend. Can you believe that, Kate?"

Six months ago, she wouldn't have. But now that she used the same manipulative and deceptive tactics to get people to do her bidding and tell her what she needed to know, she absolutely could. Ian had been right; it didn't matter how secure a network was. People were the biggest vulnerability in every system.

"You'd be proud of Helena. She wouldn't say a word about where you'd gone, no matter how many times my friend tried to trick it out of her. I knew you were from Indiana, but I didn't think that's where you would go. I sent someone to make sure, of course. But strangely, you were never seen dropping by your parents' house. So without knowing which way you'd gone, I was pretty much dead in the water. And then one day a picture appeared on Helena's desk. Did you know Bert bought her a photo printer for Christmas? She's got photos of her grandchildren all over that desk. She also has one of you. In it, you and a woman who looks like an older version of you are enjoying a glass of wine at a table outdoors. It took another couple of visits for my friend to snap a picture of the picture. Once he sent it to me, I made it bigger and clearer. There was a wine bottle on the table, and I could see the crest of a Virginia vineyard on it. I thought to myself, 'Now why would Kate and her mother be at a vineyard in Virginia? Were they visiting our nation's capital? Or did Kate's boyfriend—the dead hacker—relocate to DC for his job, taking the lovely Kate with him?'"

"This isn't Scooby-Doo. I don't need to hear how you pulled it off. I just wanted to know how you knew where to look."

"Scooby-Doo. That's clever. I used to love that show." He took one hand off the steering wheel and jabbed it in the air to punctuate his words. "I would have gotten away with it if it weren't for you meddling kids."

Kate didn't want to hear anymore, but Zach was really on a roll now, and she could tell he wanted her to know exactly how he'd done it.

"I think you'll really appreciate the amount of time and dedication I put into this. A new city meant I had to start from scratch. The vineyard was in Leesburg, but that was a dead end because that wasn't where you lived. It took me a while to make my way through the surrounding cities, and I'd almost given up by the time Middleburg came up on my list. And can you even imagine how many Realtors' sales pitches I had to sit through? I bet I've thrown away ten burner phones because they wouldn't stop calling me. I was almost ready to give up when I found Linda. I told her repeatedly that privacy was very important to me, and finally one day she mentioned that I reminded her of a couple who'd recently bought a home in the area. Privacy had been very important to them too. It seemed I was getting a little warmer, so I persevered and I strung her along for so long I nearly had to buy a goddamn house. She insisted on giving me all kinds of referrals I never asked for: contractors, decorators, painters. That's how I found Jade. Following her around almost became a full-time job. I must have tailed her to the home of every client she had. But there was one house with a gate, and I had a hunch about who might live behind it. I couldn't be sure though, and it drove me nuts. Then one night I followed Jade from a client's house to a restaurant. I was hungry anyway, so I decided I might as well get a table. And then you walked in the door and hugged Jade and sat down at the bar with her. Can you even imagine what that was like for me? I made sure you never saw me, and I followed you to the home with the gate. Don't tell me you can't appreciate dedication like that at least a little bit."

They would never be able to hide from him. If Ian gave him the money—and Kate knew he would—Zach would be back for more. Maybe not right away, but eventually. All he would have to do is be patient. Talk to the right people. Bide his time.

Maybe his next target would be their child.

The only way to ensure they'd never have to worry about Zach Nielsen again was if he spent the rest of his life behind bars. And the only way to accomplish that was to somehow let Ian know she was in trouble so he could send help.

Her only hope was that he would call before they reached the airport, because Kate had an uneasy feeling that despite what Zach had said, he planned to take her with him anyway.

CHAPTER THIRTY-SIX

As THE MALWARE MOVED THROUGH each system, the wiper utility destroyed parts of it before linking it with the next. Myrtle Beach, South Carolina, went dark twenty minutes after Columbia, and Raleigh, North Carolina, followed moments later. If the outages continued, Virginia would soon be affected. Once the hacktivists finished taking control of the utilities' networks, they wouldn't be linked to each other but rather the botnet, which would leave them holding the key. It would be the largest denial of service attack in history, and if they wanted to, they could hold the grid captive indefinitely. The attackers would make their demands, and the United States would have little choice but to give in to them. Freeing Joshua Morrison from prison would surely be at the top of the list.

The mood of the war room turned frantic. Voices rose and fingers flew across keyboards as members of the Cyber Action Team worked to stay one step ahead of the attacks.

Ian had an idea, but he didn't think Phillip would approve it.

The Pentagon most *certainly* wouldn't.

The president wouldn't be too keen on it either.

The Department of Homeland Security would probably have *plenty* to say about it.

But no one could deny the United States was woefully un-prepared for an attack on the power grid. Until it actually happened, there was no way to put an exact protocol in place for how they would defend themselves. Currently a team of specially trained cyber experts were working frantically to deploy botnet-removal programs to scrub the infected systems and bring them back online, but that could take hours, maybe days, and the reactive solution did nothing to thwart additional outages. All they were doing at this point was playing catch-up.

Ian shared his idea with Charlie. "We don't know exactly which substation or utility they'll attack next, but we know where every single substation, utility, and power cooperative is located, right? And we have access to those systems?"

"Yes."

"We need to take them offline ourselves. As soon as possible."

"You think we should take the *grid* offline?"

"Not the whole Eastern Interconnection. Just everything between here and DC. If *they* take the system down, the malware stops certain processes from running and annihilates parts of the hard drive, which means we'll have a mess when we try to bring them back online. But if the utility owners can power off their own systems at least there won't be any damage left behind. If they're already locked out, we'll have to hack in and take them down ourselves."

Charlie nodded. "That would stop the botnet from growing and give us time to catch up and scrub everything."

"We'll still be dark, but the overall outage will be smaller and more contained. And we'll be in control of it."

"Think Phillip will go for it?" Charlie asked.

"I don't know. Let's go find out."

Phillip pondered the suggestion. "How many hours would we be down?"

"At least forty-eight. Maybe even seventy-two. We'll have to remove the botnet and all the malware. Some of the older systems will undoubtedly have difficulty coming back online. If we get started as soon as possible, we might be able to reduce that."

"I'd have to get approval," Phillip said. "From… so many people."

Ian cocked his head toward Charlie, and they opened their laptops. "We'll just get started while you're doing that." If there was anything Phillip should know by now, it was how bad his two best hackers were when it came to following the rules and how hard it would be to rein them in.

Phillip sighed, the stress and exhaustion of the past twenty-four hours etched clearly on his face. "Shut these assholes down. I'll worry about the rest."

"That's the spirit," Ian said.

For the next hour, everyone in the room worked without stopping. The agent running the map of the grid used blue lights to show the cities that were dark as the result of their defensive measures. Ian could no longer hear the din of the war room and was only marginally aware of the spike in noise level as substations in Norfolk, Richmond, and Alexandria went dark. But this time the lights were blue and the agents cheered.

Ian smiled and breathed a sigh of relief because he had more than one reason to celebrate. Kate should be somewhere in West Virginia by now, far away from the danger of a blackout and within an hour of connecting with her dad. As soon as they got things under control in Washington, he would go to his wife.

He pulled out his phone to confirm her location and stared at the app for a moment, forcing himself not to panic but trying to think of a single reason why it would say she was offline.

And no matter how hard he tried to come up with a good one, he couldn't.

CHAPTER THIRTY-SEVEN

"I BET THIS CAR can really haul," Zach said, as if they were two friends taking a road trip. He revved the engine a bit, and Kate would have bet money he was wishing he could see what the car could do. She stole a glance at the speedometer as it hovered at eighty and then rose to eighty-five. *Higher*, she thought. *Trip that alarm.*

Kate scoffed. "I've driven much faster than you're going."

"That's quite clever of you, appealing to my competitive nature. Banking on the fact that I wouldn't want to be shown up by a woman. If I drive too fast and get pulled over, there goes my plan. I can't say I'm surprised, because I know you're smart. Those sob stories you gave me back at the food pantry and those tears you manufactured on command were pretty convincing. You even had me fooled for a while."

Though he reduced his speed, the minutes passed and the miles flew by quickly in the darkness. He hadn't changed direction or veered from her route, so Kate assumed he'd booked the charter at an airstrip far enough ahead to give him time to catch up with her. She worried they might reach it soon.

The phone rang and Kate's heart leapt, but it wasn't Ian's number that flashed onto the screen; it was Chad's. "That's my brother. If I don't answer, he'll just call back."

That seemed to throw him. He scrubbed his hand over his face as the ringing filled the car, the sound echoing off the walls. "Make it short and tell him you have to go."

He pushed the button to answer the call, and Kate said, "Hey Chad. I just stopped to go to the bathroom. I'll call you right back, okay?"

"Sure, Kate—"

Zach disconnected the call before Chad could say anything else. Kate had been monitoring their route on the navigation screen, and by her rough calculations, she figured Chad and her dad were somewhere in Ohio by now. If Zach stayed on course, they would soon be less than half an hour away from each other.

Kate tensed when the phone rang again less than a minute later, but her heart filled with joy when she realized who was calling. "That's Ian."

"Keep it short and don't say anything that will cause a complication for me. Trust me when I say my way is better for all of us. If you freak out and start screaming, things will become much more difficult for you. But if you do what I tell you, nothing bad will happen."

But Kate didn't believe him. Anyone willing to put this much time and planning into achieving his goal would stop at nothing to attain it. If he was pushed into a corner, Kate would see exactly what Zach Nielsen would resort to, and she knew it would be far more violent than his calm demeanor illustrated. Money had a way of turning people into monsters.

Zach answered the call and jabbed his finger at Kate.

"Hey, sweetness," Ian said. She could hear the fatigue in his voice, but she heard wariness too. Had he noticed the tracking on her phone had been turned off?

"Hey!" She forced herself to sound cheerful and upbeat, praying that Ian—the most observant man she knew—would pick up on the slight tremble in her voice. Before he could utter another word she yawned loudly and said, "Sorry about that. I need a cup of coffee." The sentence wouldn't seem strange to Zach. She'd been driving awhile and it was late, so coffee would be an obvious choice for anyone in her situation and should not arouse suspicion.

"Coffee, huh?" There had been a pause that seemed a bit long before he said the words, but Zach hadn't seemed to notice, so maybe it only seemed long to her.

"Yes. I stopped at Starbucks on my way out of town and got one of those silly Frappuccinos Charlie's always talking about, and I could use another." Kate almost gagged. Coffee itself was bad enough, but it was especially nausea-inducing when she thought of it combined with a sickly-sweet flavoring. She swallowed hard and kept talking. "You said I wouldn't like it because it would be too sugary, but Charlie was right when he said they put just the right amount of syrup in. I told you he always has my best interests at heart. I was right about him and you were wrong."

Zach twirled his finger in the air: wrap it up. She didn't want to stop talking. She needed to hear Ian's voice because it was the only thing grounding her at the moment.

"Sounds like I *was* wrong about him. Hey, sweetness. Let me call you right back, okay? Somebody needs me real quick."

"Okay—" She barely got the word out before Zach disconnected the call and her heart sank. Ian was the smartest person she knew, and Kate clung to the belief that the real reason he'd hung up was because he'd understood. He would need a few minutes to gather his thoughts and determine the best way to move their conversation forward in a way that would not arouse Zach's suspicion.

"That was good, Kate. Somehow I thought your conversations would be a bit less boring, but that's marriage for you, I guess. When he calls back, make sure you stick to some more of that uninteresting Frappuccino conversation. And keep it short."

She turned her head away from Zach and stared out at the darkness as tears filled her eyes. At that moment, she would have given anything to be enjoying one of those marriage moments he found so dull. *Oh, Ian. I need you.* But there was no time to feel sorry for herself, because they still had work to do.

Kate did take comfort in one thing. When it came to her and Ian, Zach Nielsen had no idea how smart they were and just how well they worked together.

CHAPTER THIRTY-EIGHT

IAN SET THE PHONE DOWN on the desk. The hum of the room faded away, and he no longer heard the sound of celebratory voices or fingers typing on keyboards. He'd heard what Kate said, had picked up on the slight difference in the cadence of her words. She was scared but trying to hide it.

There was no way she would stop for coffee considering her aversion to it, and the only reason she'd said that was to get his attention. It was the second part of the story she'd really wanted him to understand.

I was right about Charlie and you were wrong.

Charlie hadn't been the one who'd doxed him. But the only way she could know that for sure is if the person who had was in the car *with* her, and that was the part he was having trouble wrapping his brain around.

The next thing he did was send a text to Chad and Steve.

Ian: *Don't call or text Kate. I'll explain in a minute.*

Chad: *What's going on? I tried to call her and she practically hung up on me. She said she'd call me back but hasn't. We're worried.*

Ian: *Give me ten minutes.*

Whoever had hacked them hadn't used the garage camera to find out the kind of cars they drove. He'd used it to hack the cars, none of which had been driven since.

Until today.

He didn't have time to sit around and beat himself up for the mistake, because Kate needed his help. He took a deep breath and called her back.

"That was quick," she said.

"Sorry about that. I can't talk long. Pretty busy right now."

"That's okay. I understand."

"How's everything going?" He held his breath as he waited for her answer. Would she remember the signals from their social engineering assignment?

He wanted to hear the word "great," but what she said was, "Couldn't be better," and with three little words, she confirmed she was in trouble. But she sounded so cheerful that for a split second, he questioned whether he'd mixed up what the responses meant. *Is this really happening?* But he knew he hadn't.

"Okay, cupcake. I hear you."

"I'll let you go. I'm sure you have lots of work to do. I love you." Her voice cracked a little, and it broke his heart.

"Don't worry, I'm sure I can get it all done. I love you too." It killed him to disconnect the call.

Ian looked around for Charlie and spotted him a few rows over, typing and focusing on his screen, securely in the zone. He rushed to his side.

"I need your help."

"Little busy trying to figure these lights out, Smith. Maybe you can ask someone you trust for help."

Ian felt horrible. How could he think Charlie would ever betray him? "Yeah, I'm an asshole. I know that. I will apologize every day for the rest of my life, but Kate's in trouble."

Charlie took his eyes off the computer screen. "What are you talking about?"

"Someone's in the car with her."

"What? How?"

"They must have put a tracking device on the Porsche. No one's driven it since I swapped out our vehicles after we got hacked. It probably triggered an alarm the minute I drove it up from the barn."

"And you think they're in the car with her now?"

"I'm positive. We worked out some signals on a social engineering assignment we did together a few months back. She just gave me the response for 'things are not okay' because they can hear our conversation."

"What do you need me to do?"

Ian handed Charlie his cell phone. "He disabled her tracking device. I told myself I was being paranoid, but when I designed the app, I added a feature that would trigger a backup locator if something like this ever happened."

"I'd be thoroughly disappointed if you hadn't."

"She's still on the original route. Open the unnamed white app, get an update on her location, and drop a pin. Tell Phillip I need him. I'll be in your office."

The first thing Ian did once he reached Charlie's office was try to access the Porsche's network, only to discover he'd been locked out of it. He took a deep breath because even though he'd expected the roadblock, taking control of the car would require a few more steps.

Phillip burst into the room, Charlie hot on his heels. "What's going on?"

"Someone's intercepted Kate in the Spyder."

"What do you need me to do?"

"Use my phone to call Steve. Tell him what's going on, and then keep him on the line. His and Chad's phones can both track Kate, and they should be coming up on her fairly soon. I want to know when they can see her. I'm sorry. I know you've got other things to worry about right now." The blackouts were no longer only the task force's problem. By now the affected cities would be following disaster-recovery protocols, and emergency management would have been dispatched to keep things under control until they could get the power back on.

Phillip squeezed Ian's shoulder, and at that moment, he had never seemed more like a father figure. "It's okay. We've got plenty of people out there working on it."

"Charlie. Can you get law enforcement on the phone? Give them Kate's location and tell them to send whoever's closest to pull the car over. Tell them to hurry."

"On it."

Ian turned his attention back to his laptop. If someone thought they could keep him out of a network, especially one that belonged to him, he couldn't wait to show them just how wrong they'd been.

CHAPTER THIRTY-NINE

THE PHONE RANG AGAIN, but this time it was Zach's and the muffled ringing grew louder when he pulled it from his pocket. "Yeah." He listened for a minute. "What do you mean you can't take off? What the hell is this shit? I paid you. You were supposed to be waiting on the runway with your fucking engines idling." His voice had taken on an icy edge that absolutely terrified her, and she knew that at this point he wouldn't let anything stand in the way of his goal. He simply had too much invested. He listened for another thirty seconds and then disconnected the call without responding.

Without warning, he yanked hard on the steering wheel, drove through the grassy median, and merged aggressively into the eastbound lanes of the interstate to a chorus of honking horns and squealing, skidding tires as they narrowly avoided being mowed over by a passing semi. Kate curled into a ball, bracing herself for impact, but Zach remained calm and seemingly unaffected.

She had no idea where they were headed. Would he go somewhere to wait out the ban on air travel? Or was he driving her to wherever he'd planned to fly? She'd assumed his final destination was somewhere outside the United States, but maybe it wasn't.

She didn't dare ask him. Mostly because she was too scared to hear the answer.

Ian scanned the Porsche's network, looking for the Remote Access Trojan, or RAT, which was not unlike following an actual rat into a maze. There were dead ends and plenty of backtracking as he hit one virtual wall after another. He'd scanned the network three times and hadn't found the RAT yet, which told him whoever had done this possessed a decent level of technical skill.

"Thought you'd be in by now," Charlie said.

"It's a little different when it's your wife and child."

"Wait. Kate's pregnant?"

"Yes."

Charlie watched him struggle. "Come on. This is child's play for you."

Kate had to be terrified, but she'd done what she needed to do to get her message to him.

Turn off your emotions, he told himself. *Use your brain to help her.*

Ian might identify as a hacker, but in reality it was his programming abilities that made him so good at what he did. His skills were far superior, but he'd allowed anxiety and fear to invade his normally calm state and had wasted time using an automated program that should have easily found and eliminated the Trojan but hadn't. He switched to a custom tool he'd designed himself and launched it. He would find the Trojan and destroy it, and then he would take back control of what was his.

They needed Phillip back in the war room, so Charlie now held a phone to each ear. Chad had stayed on the line to let Charlie know when he and Steve reached Kate, and Charlie was using Ian's phone to relay Kate's location to the dispatch officer.

"He just turned around," Charlie shouted into the phone. "He's heading east on I-68. Tell the officers he's going in the opposite direction."

"What?" Ian said without taking his eyes off the computer screen or his fingers off the keyboard. "Why would he do that?"

"I don't know. The officers haven't reached Kate yet."

"What's his speed?"

Charlie ignored his question, which told Ian it was fast enough that it would only bother him to know. "Are you in?"

"Almost."

He heard Charlie tell Chad and Steve they were now behind Kate instead of heading toward her. "Let me know when you catch up to her. You'll have to drive faster."

A few more clicks of his mouse, and the RAT was history. Ian accessed the Porsche's network, and this time the door might as well have been wide open as easily as he was able to get in. He was so focused on the task at hand that he didn't hear Charlie saying his name until he yelled it.

"Ian!"

"What," Ian said without looking at him.

The most profound feeling of relief washed over him when Charlie said, "The police can see her."

Kate's head rested on the glass of her window, which meant she was looking right into the passenger-side mirror when a row of flashing red lights appeared in the inky darkness of its reflection. She lifted her head as a feeling of sheer joy washed over her. Her celebration was short-lived when Zach shoved her head against the window where it connected with a dull thud.

"You bitch!"

She brought her arms up to shield herself from another blow, but he'd turned his attention back to the road and punched the gas pedal. She stole another look in the mirror. The police cars were closing in, and there seemed to be an awful lot of them. Zach's driving became more erratic as he attempted to elude them, and he clipped the guard rail and sent a shower of sparks into the night as the speedometer inched up past 150 miles per hour. At 180 miles per hour, the steering wheel started to vibrate.

Kate watched with near-hysterical fear as the needle continued to rise until the speedometer maxed out at 210.

The first thing Ian did now that he had control of the network was cut the engine, and the second was apply the brakes. The car was traveling at an incredibly high rate of speed, and it wasn't going to stop on a dime. Operating the brakes remotely wouldn't give him quite the immediate control he'd have if he were pushing the actual brake pedal with his foot, but the speedometer reading began to fall.

With the police closing in, whoever was driving the car would be feeling the pressure, possibly starting to panic, and the likelihood of them losing control was high. He tightened Kate's seat belt. Then he disconnected the driver's side air bag and seat belt.

"What are you doing?" Charlie asked.

"Ending this."

There were too many sirens for her to notice the sound of the engine cutting out, but the car jolted violently and Kate knew immediately that the brakes had been engaged and who had done it. Her seat belt tightened and it felt like a hug. *Hold on, sweetness. I've got you now.*

The speedometer reading had fallen to seventy-nine miles per hour by then, and the police car directly behind them was almost touching the Porsche's bumper. Zach had nowhere else to go. But it appeared he had some sort of last-ditch, Hail Mary pass up his sleeve because there was a bridge up ahead, and though his speed continued to fall, Zach aimed the car at one of the concrete pillars that supported it.

In Charlie's office, he and Ian waited.

"What's happening?" Ian asked, pointing at the phones Charlie still held in each hand.

"I don't know. Dispatch hung up on me as soon as the police had her in their sights." Charlie paused, then asked Chad and Steve, who were still on the line, "Can you see her?" He looked at Ian and shook his head.

It was a blessing, really, because it meant none of them would know about the bridge.

Seventy-eight, seventy-seven, seventy-six.

Zach veered suddenly to the left, bumping the patrol car that had figured out what he was about to do and was trying to box him in.

Seventy, sixty-nine, sixty-eight.

Kate felt the bump when the tires left the pavement and bounced along the grassy area toward the pillar.

She screamed and covered her head with her arms. *Still too fast*, she thought.

Too fast, too fast, too fast.

CHAPTER FORTY

SHE FELT LIKE SHE WAS floating. *I must be dreaming,* Kate thought. Ian was with her, but when she tried to speak to him, no words would come out. Zach was there too, his expression full of fury, and Kate squeezed her eyes shut and plunged into the safety of the darkness until there was only black. The dreams kept coming. Sometimes she heard voices and people softly saying her name. Sometimes there were shadowy images near her face that seemed familiar.

The next day, when the fog of sedation finally dissipated and she awakened fully, Ian was there beside the bed, holding her hand. There were tears in his eyes.

"Did I lose the baby?" she asked. That had to be the reason he looked so sad.

He stroked her forehead lightly "The baby's just fine. Heartbeat's strong." His hand was resting lightly on her stomach, and it was only then that she felt the strap of the heart rate monitor under his palm and noticed the machine next to the bed recording every beat of their child's heart. "Are you in pain? Your ankle was badly broken."

Kate shook her head. They must have her on some pretty powerful medication because she couldn't feel anything at all, at least not right now. "It was my fault. It was the picture I sent to Helena. That's how Zach found us."

"None of this is your fault," he said.

"I wasn't fearless. I was scared."

"I'm so sorry, sweetness."

She started to cry in earnest then, and he leaned over the bed and put his arms around her until she calmed down, her sobs tapering off and her eyelids growing heavy again.

"Hey, sis," Chad said appearing at the other side of the bed. He smiled at her and laid his hand on her shoulder. "Dad left to get Mom. She's freaking out a little. They should be back soon."

"Chad." She was so happy to see him, but she struggled to get the word out.

"You go to sleep, okay? We'll be right here when you wake up."

She tried to answer him, but the darkness swallowed her again.

Ian watched as the nurses shuffled in and out, checking Kate's vital signs and assuring him that rest was the best thing for her. The doctor had come in earlier to explain the possible risks to the baby if Kate were to have surgery to set her ankle, but after hearing them, she wouldn't even consider it. Instead, they put her in a splint while they waited for the swelling to go down and would switch her to a cast in a couple of weeks. In addition to her broken ankle, she had numerous cuts and bruises, including a rather vicious one on her hip. She'd lost consciousness for a brief period of time right after the crash, but the doctors said she'd escaped any measurable head trauma and in time, all her injuries would heal.

She had still been strapped into the passenger seat awaiting the paramedics who would safely extricate her from the vehicle and load her into the ambulance when Steve and Chad reached the scene. They crossed the median and screeched to a halt, parking their car haphazardly in the sea of flashing lights and police cars amid the bits of rubber and pieces of metal scattered in a wide swath under the bridge. Steve rode with Kate in the back of the ambulance to a hospital ten miles down the road, just across the border between West Virginia and Ohio. When the second ambulance arrived at the hospital thirty minutes later, it arrived without lights or sirens and with considerably less urgency. Zach Nielsen had gone through the windshield at the moment of impact, and Chad had watched as they zipped his battered remains into the bag that lay open on the grass.

Unless Kate could shed some light on it, they would never know if he'd hit the bridge pillar because he'd lost control or if his actions had been intentional.

In the days that followed, the cities affected by the blackout gradually came back online. It took almost seventy-two hours to restore power to all the residents, but the repercussions were much less severe than they could have been, and miraculously, there were no lives lost. Spring was only a few weeks away, so they did not have to battle extreme heat or cold, and there were numerous reports of communities coming together to help those in need.

Diane and Steve returned to their hotel at night to sleep, but Ian wouldn't leave Kate's side during the three days she spent in the hospital. He slept only when she slept, in a chair pulled up next to the bed. Sometimes he would dream he'd gotten it all wrong and Kate had been behind the wheel of the Spyder, not Zach, and that it had been her seat belt and air bag he'd disabled.

On the second night, when her pain medication didn't seem to be working as well as it had been and the guilt threatened to swallow him if he didn't let it out, he said, "I should have let you go. I should have let you have a normal life."

"That's not what I wanted. I can handle whatever life throws at us, but I can't handle hearing you say something like that."

"I don't deserve you."

"That's not how we measure love," she said, reaching for his hand.

He squeezed it gently, and when the hospital discharged her, he chartered a plane and flew home with her to Indiana.

CHAPTER FORTY-ONE

CODA

ONE MONTH AFTER THE CYBERATTACK on the Eastern Inter-connection, in a medium-security federal prison in Oklahoma, a cell door opened on its own, as if an invisible man held a remote control. This should have sounded an alarm, but no noise rang out in the quiet hallway. The video surveillance feed should have picked up on it, but the image on the screen in front of the security guard responsible for monitoring this particular area showed an exterior shot. Then—although there was no fire—the sprinkler system went off and everyone's focus shifted to stopping the water before they had a mess on their hands.

And Joshua Morrison, the man Ian Bradshaw had once sent to prison, a black hat hacker in every sense of the word, waltzed right out the door and into a waiting car.

CHAPTER FORTY-TWO

EPILOGUE

THE SOUND OF A YOUNG child singing, her voice pure and clear, floated on the breeze. Ian drew closer so he could listen to his daughter's song and stopped just short of the hammock stretched between the two pillars that supported the deck's overhang. It was Shelby's favorite spot, and he could often find her here because she liked to pretend the monkeys that lived in the trees were her audience. Not that she lacked admirers, because at four years old she already possessed the kind of voice that made strangers in the village stop what they were doing to seek out its source.

"Hey, sweet girl. Want to go fishin'?"

"Is Grandpa coming?"

"Yep. And Uncle Chad."

"Okay." She reached for him and he swung her up in his arms.

"I like the song you were singing. Is that a new one?"

She beamed. "Yes. I made it up for Grandma Ellen."

That hit him right in his heart, but it was a good feeling. "Something tells me she's going to love it."

Once they'd boarded the twenty-four-foot Panga fishing boat, Ian slathered Shelby's exposed skin liberally with sunscreen and pulled the straps tight on her life jacket. He fired up the Yamaha outboard motor and pointed the boat in the direction of the fishing grounds of Cabo Blanco. Steve liked to troll along the surface using live bait, but Chad and Ian preferred casting their lures close to the rock formations where the tuna and snapper were most plentiful.

Shelby scanned the water. "Look, Daddy! I spy with my little eye a dolphin."

"Way to go, Shelby. Let's see if you can spy a turtle."

The fish were biting, which was a good thing because Kate wanted to serve the fresh catch to their party guests that evening. "What if we come back empty-handed?" he'd asked, coming up behind her to nuzzle her neck.

She laughed. "Then I'll send you back out again."

Steve pulled in a giant snapper, and Shelby squealed as it flopped around on the floor of the boat until Chad put it on ice.

"Kate will be happy to see that one," Ian said.

"I'll be happy to eat it as long as you're the one who's going to clean it," Steve said good-naturedly.

"That's me: boat driver and fish cleaner."

After the accident, it had been hard for Ian to be in the same room as Steve because he hadn't been angry the way he'd been after Ian had faked his death. Ian would have welcomed the anger because the silence was worse. Steve hadn't spoken to him at all for a while, which had bothered Kate and Diane immensely, but he understood. Steve needed time to process what had happened, and nothing he could have said or done would even begin to touch the anguish and remorse Ian carried around in his head and his heart for a good long time. Eventually, both of them learned to let go of the negative emotions associated with the crash, and their relationship knitted itself back together in the way it often did with men.

Ian never returned to the task force after the blackout.

"What do you think Mommy's doing?" Ian asked when they got home two hours later, hungry, hot, and ready for lunch.

"Probably feeding the baby. She's always feeding him."

He tugged gently on one of Shelby's long brown braids. "Maybe we should feed you."

"I'm starving for ice cream."

Diane came outside. "Oh, you're back. Are you hungry, Shelby?"

"She's starving," Ian said.

"For ice cream," Shelby added.

"Your mommy and I made lunch while you were gone. You wanna come eat with Aunt Kristin and Cousin Molly?" Chad and Kristin had a three-year-old daughter and a son on the way.

Shelby took her hand. "Okay, Grandma."

"You can have ice cream for dessert. Maybe we'll eat that first."

He walked down the hallway to the master bedroom. Shelby was right. Kate was attempting to nurse their son, which she'd said was like trying to hit a bull's-eye on a constantly moving target, especially since he'd started walking a month ago. He watched them for a moment, thinking he must have done something awfully right to end up here.

When Spyder spotted him in the doorway, he lurched off Kate's lap and ran toward Ian. Kate laughed. "I give up."

Ian crouched down. "How's my birthday boy? You ready to party?" Dressed in nothing but a diaper, his spiky bedhead stuck up in all directions as he grinned and drooled.

When Chad and Kristin had come to visit Kate in the hospital, her brother said, "Hey, Spyder," when Ian placed their son in his arms.

"Chad!" Kate admonished from her hospital bed.

"What? Isn't that what you guys do? Name your kids after your cars?"

"His name is William, after Ian's dad. We're going to call him Will."

But at his three-month checkup, he was seventy-five percent for weight but completely off the chart for height.

"He's all limbs," the nurse said. She smiled at Ian. "Probably going to be tall like his father."

Ian scrutinized his son. "You know his body does have a certain—"

"Don't say it."

"Spiderlike quality."

Kate laughed. "And you said it. I was actually thinking the exact same thing a few weeks ago when I was changing his diaper."

Maybe Kate wouldn't want to be reminded of the Spyder. When Ian asked her if the nickname would bother her, she assured him it didn't. "I will always remember how excited you were when you gave me that car. That's what I think of when I hear the word Spyder. I'll be sure to let Chad know it was our son's arms and legs that inspired the nickname and not my car. I don't want him to think he was right."

There had been no more cars, and a golf cart was the fastest vehicle either of them drove these days.

"What time does the plane land?" Kate asked.

"Rob's picking everyone up at five. You excited?"

"I can't wait," she said as she kissed Ian and scooped up twenty pounds of squirming, laughing towheaded baby and headed for the door. "I'll be right back. I promised Susan she could give Spyder his bath."

She was dressed for the tropical weather in a thin-strapped tank top and knee-length skirt, and her long legs looked tan and strong. Because she'd opted to delay surgery, her ankle had not healed well, and when Shelby arrived six days after her due date—healthy and perfect—Kate had been terrified that her leg would give out and she would drop her. Diane had stayed with them for the first month, and either she or Ian would bring Shelby to Kate when it was time to feed her. At night, when Shelby would stir, Ian would carefully lift his daughter from her bassinet in their bedroom and would whisper to her in the darkness as he placed her in Kate's arms. Afterward, he would change her diaper and put her back in the bassinet. When Shelby was three months old, the doctor rebroke Kate's ankle so he could set it properly. It had taken almost a year for the limp to disappear completely, and sometimes when she was really tired, he could still see an almost imperceptible difference in her gait.

And it would always be a painful reminder of how close he'd come to losing her.

He'd brought Kate and Shelby to Costa Rica when Shelby was six months old and it had become apparent to everyone that something was wrong with Kate. She'd lost weight, and she was having trouble sleeping. Though she tried her best to hide it, she seemed listless and sad, as if the light had gone out of her. Whether it was a lingering postpartum effect, too many traumatic memories, or the problems she'd had with her leg, he wasn't sure. But he needed to find a way to help her, and Costa Rica had been a shot in the dark when nothing else seemed to be working. They'd flown down for a week's visit, and the change in Kate had been almost instantaneous as the weight of what she'd been carrying lifted and she came alive again before his eyes.

"Can we stay?" she'd asked him one morning after sleeping through the night for the first time in a long while.

He was spooning her the way he always had and the way he always would. "Would you like that?"

"Yes," she'd whispered.

And so they'd stayed, because he would have given her anything she asked for. Kate never set foot in the Middleburg house again, and Ian sent the movers to box up the contents and send everything to them.

Costa Rica had been good for him too, and he'd done his own share of healing here.

He imagined they would stay forever.

They bought property in Malpais, a remote cattle-farming and fishing village with white-sand beaches, lush jungles teeming with wildlife and birds, and breathtaking views that had become one of Costa Rica's hidden jewels and drew adventure travelers from around the world.

They'd purchased land on the coast with a long stretch of private shoreline. They built a large, one-level home, and when that was complete they added several small guesthouses accessible by well-lit stone paths to ensure there would always be room for visitors. Renee had agreed to come with them now that her own children had moved to opposite sides of the country, and she had her own private bungalow.

Ian was reasonably certain the hacktivists believed he was dead, and with Zach Nielsen no longer proving a threat to his family, he could breathe easy for the first time in years. But he wasn't taking any chances, and he'd convinced Rob to come with them too. He did all the driving, ferrying Kate and the kids down the pothole-filled dirt roads to the airport or into town.

Ian finally bought a plane of his own and kept a pilot on standby, and Indiana was by far the most frequent destination.

They would always be cautious about who they shared their personal information with, but there were a few people Ian felt it was safe for Kate to get in contact with, and he encouraged her to make the calls. The first were Paige and Audrey, and to say the revelation stunned her friends was an understatement.

"I'm almost positive they thought they were being punked," Kate told him. It wasn't until Ian flew them and their families down to see Kate that they'd finally believed her.

Next, Kate told Helena. "I married a man and we live in Costa Rica. I would love for you and Bert to come for a visit. We'll fly you down. We have plenty of room."

"I would love to see you if you're sure it's not too much trouble," Helena said.

"It's no trouble at all."

Kate worried the news might be too much for Helena. Before they went inside the house, she turned to her and Bert. "I have something I need to tell you."

"I hope it's nothing bad," Helena said, looking worried.

Kate's eyes filled with tears and she reached for Helena's hands, squeezing them tight. "It's something wonderful. I feel horrible that I've been keeping this from you for so long, but Ian is waiting for us inside."

Helena's eyes grew wide as saucers, and the news rendered her and Bert speechless. They looked more than a little apprehensive, and Bert finally said, "What do you mean by that, Kate?"

"I mean that he didn't die when his car went into the river. He wasn't even in it." Kate explained about Ian's work with the task force and the doxing, and by the time she'd finished, Helena couldn't wait to get inside the house. When she threw her arms around Ian, she burst into tears and so did Kate. Shelby was a year old then, and when Kate fetched her from her crib where she'd been napping, Helena lost it. No matter how hard she tried to compose herself, she cried spontaneous and intermittent tears of joy for the next twenty-four hours.

They showed Helena the picture Ian took of Ted Lawson, the man they'd found on their property, and asked if she'd ever seen him.

"That's Ronnie. Why do you have a picture of him? Is he okay?"

"We think he might have been looking for us."

Helena's face fell. "I never told anybody where you'd gone. I remembered what you said before you left, Kate, so I was extra careful."

Kate reached for Helena's hands. "I know you didn't. You did exactly what I asked."

The only thing the police had been able to charge Ted Lawson with was trespassing, and after they released him, he likely hadn't stuck around. They would never know whether he had any knowledge of Zach Nielsen's larger plan or if he'd been paid handsomely not to ask questions. Zach Nielsen was actually a man named Mike Nelson, and his body had been claimed by his next of kin after the hospital unraveled his identity based on information they found in his wallet. Ian had many regrets about everything that had happened that day, but what he'd done to Zach's seat belt and air bag would never be one of them.

He was sitting on the deck watching Shelby and Molly play when their guests arrived and started making their way outside after stopping in the house to greet Kate. His mother was first.

Ian went to her and she hugged him tight. "How was the flight?"

"It was so smooth. Your plane is lovely, and there was room for all of us."

Shelby spotted her grandmother. "Grandma Ellen! Grandma Ellen!" His mom's face lit up when Shelby threw herself into her grandmother's arms. "I have a new song to sing for you!"

She hugged Shelby and kissed her cheek. "I can't wait to hear it."

His daughter knew nothing of the rocky past between her father and grandmother, and she never would. All that mattered was that she knew there were many people who loved her.

He had Kate to thank for the reconciliation. She'd insisted on mailing a birth announcement, and no one had been more surprised than him when his mother called. He'd often wondered if she still had his number.

She wanted to know if he could come home. "Just for a short visit. I'm sure you're very busy."

At Kate's urging, he'd agreed. "You won't truly find peace unless you can forgive her. But tell her how you feel. Don't keep anything in."

He'd flown to Amarillo, rented a nondescript, midsize car, and met his mother at an IHOP off I-40. She fidgeted in the booth, spinning a gold wedding ring on her finger.

He gestured to her left hand. "What's he like?" He knew so little about her current life and nothing about the man she'd married after he left home.

"His name was Walter. He was a wonderful man, but he died last year. Heart attack."

"I'm sorry. Do you have someone in your life now?" He needed to know if the real reason she'd reached out to him was because there was no one left.

"Yes. I can't bury another husband, and boyfriend sounds silly at my age. But he's a good companion, and I'm grateful for his company."

"Then I'm happy for you."

"Did you bring some pictures of the baby?" she asked, and there was such yearning in her voice.

He reached into an envelope and withdrew several photos in a variety of sizes. "We had these taken about a week after Shelby was born."

She looked as if he'd presented her with a precious gift. When she'd had her fill, she slid them back to him.

"They're for you to keep, Mom." He handed her his phone. "There's a whole bunch more if you want to page through them."

"She's beautiful. So is your wife. She looks very kind," his mom said when she handed the phone back to him.

"Kate is many things. Kind and beautiful are just two of them."

As they sat in the corner of the restaurant sharing a meal for the first time since he'd left home, his mother began to reminisce about how happy his own birth had made her. "We were quite young, but we were so eager to become parents. I remember how proud I was the day we brought you home from the hospital. Your dad told anyone who would listen that his son was going to do amazing things someday."

Ian smiled because his dad had said those words to him many times.

"There was a small theater company in downtown Amarillo. It's long gone now, but from the time I was fifteen years old, there was never a production I wasn't a part of. Sometimes I had the lead, sometimes I was the understudy. A few times I had small parts, and once I volunteered to help with the sets so I could still be involved. I loved it all, but musicals were where I really shined. All my life people had been telling me how special my voice was and that someday I'd go far with it."

Ian remembered coming across an old scrapbook in the basement once. In it were playbills and pictures of his mother wearing different costumes. He hadn't paid much attention to it back then because no one ever talked about it with him.

"Six months after you were born, your dad encouraged me to return to the theater so I could get out of the house in the evening, and I got the role of Velma in *Chicago*. News spread quickly that a Hollywood scout would be in the audience on opening night, and after the show the theater director pulled me aside and introduced us. He filled my head with all kinds of things and wanted me to move to California for a few months so I could go on auditions and have a screen test, but I told him I had a baby. He said I should leave it at home. Your dad was already working long hours to support us, and I didn't have anyone I trusted enough to take good care of you while I was gone. It didn't matter, because I couldn't bear the thought of being separated from you. My understudy flew out instead, and she never came back. I still see her face in magazines sometimes."

He knew in his heart she'd tried to stop it. But once the seeds of resentment had been sown, they'd likely grown stronger and flourished with each passing year away from the spotlight.

"I never stopped loving you, Ian."

"I reached out to you so many times. And every time you turned me away."

"I didn't think I deserved to be in your life after the way I treated you."

Ian remembered Kate's words. "That's not how we measure love."

"I'm sorry. Missing out on all this time with you is my life's biggest regret."

Before they got into their respective cars in the parking lot, Ian said, "I'd like for you to visit us. Get to know Kate. Spend time with Shelby."

His mother had started crying then, and she'd been coming to visit ever since.

Shelby led his mother away so she could listen to her song. Phillip and Susan appeared next. They'd no doubt spent some time inside with Steve and Diane, whom they'd gotten to know quite well in the past few years. Phillip had retired at fifty-seven—mandatory for the FBI—and he and Susan enjoyed frequent visits to Costa Rica. Shelby called them Nana and Papa and liked to tell people she had extra grandparents.

Charlie appeared on the deck last. He shook Ian's hand, plopped down in the empty chair next to him, and handed him a beer. "You sure have a lot of women in your house. They gave me these beers and told me I was in their way. Better keep 'em coming all weekend, Smith. You still owe me."

"It's Bradshaw and you know it."

"I always forget which one I'm supposed to use."

"That's the only one you need now." Ian took a drink of his beer. "Where's your better half? I'm surprised she hasn't made it out here to say hello to me yet."

"Are you kidding? I'm sure there's a bottle of wine being passed around the kitchen table as we speak. They're probably on their second by now."

It turned out that Kate was right: Charlie wasn't such a player after all, and he'd married Jade two years ago in a sunset ceremony on Kate and Ian's very own white-sand beach. Charlie did have some reservations about settling down, but they had nothing to do with how he felt about Jade.

Shortly after Joshua Morrison walked out of prison, Charlie had been sitting in his office at FBI headquarters on an otherwise normal Tuesday when a message popped up on his computer screen: WE KNOW WHO YOU ARE. Charlie had known immediately who'd sent it, and before he started dating

Jade, it hadn't bothered him much. "My badge came with a gun," he'd told Ian. "I'm not concerned."

But even after he'd fallen in love with Jade, he kept her at arm's length because he worried about putting her at risk. She set him straight one day and told him that after she lost her husband, she vowed not to worry about things that might never happen. She lived her life in the moment, and Charlie decided that sounded like a good plan for him too.

They ate dinner on the lawn with a breathtaking view of the ocean. Adults and children alike gathered at a long rectangular table and dined on blackened snapper and marinated tuna caught fresh that morning. There was shrimp and steak and crab, and so many side dishes that Kate reminded everyone to save room for birthday cake.

They brought it out after dinner—a large sheet cake for the guests and a small single-layer cake for the birthday boy. Kate stuck a candle in the shape of the number one into the center of it, and after she lit it, they all crowded around Spyder to sing. On the third stanza, everyone but Ian's mother sang, "Happy Birthday, dear *Spyder*," because Ellen had never been able to call her grandson anything but William.

Kate stripped him down to his diaper when they finished singing and set the small cake on the tray of his high chair. He grabbed fistfuls of cake and smeared frosting in his hair, and when all that was left of it was a smashed pile of sticky crumbs, they took him swimming because a dip in the ocean would always be infinitely more fun than the bathtub.

The sun sank lower on the horizon, and the sky filled with streaks of pink and orange. The excitement of the day had finally caught up with Spyder, and he'd fallen asleep facedown on Ian's chest, still wrapped in his beach towel. Kate, Kristin, and Jade were watching as Shelby and Molly dipped wands into a bucket of soap suds and ran across the grass, their giant bubbles trailing behind them. Diane, Susan, and his mother joined them.

"You were right," Ian said. "There are a lot of women here."

"Quite a few men too. Must be hard for a loner like you."

Ian laughed and took a drink of his beer. "My wife may have convinced me life is more enjoyable when you're surrounded by family and friends, but you can be replaced."

"I'm not gonna lose sleep over it, Bradshaw. We both know I'm the only one who can put up with you."

"You're not the only one," he said, because if he had to choose the person responsible for turning him into the man he was today, Kate would win in a landslide.

"How are things going with the company?" Charlie asked.

"We've got more work than we can handle." He and Kate had grown the business at a steady rate, but they took on only the clients that interested them, and if the assignment couldn't be done from their home office, they passed. They put in no more than three to four hours per day; less if they didn't feel like it. And when Ian needed legal services, he need not look farther than across the breakfast table. He quite liked having his own in-house attorney.

Shelby took Grandma Ellen's hand and attempted to pull her away from the group on the lawn, no doubt because she wanted to sing another song and knew her grandmother would always listen. His mother said a few words to Kate who smiled and nodded her head. He'd noticed that she always deferred to her, as if she wasn't sure of her place, but Kate never once made it seem as if she didn't have every right to be there. Maybe she came by it naturally; the Wattses were remarkable when it came to forgiveness.

"Do you miss it?" Charlie asked, and Ian didn't have to ask him what he meant.

"Sometimes. But if you live your life convinced you're missing out on something, that's exactly what will happen."

"What are my two favorite hackers up to?" Kate asked when she joined them on the deck.

Ian shifted Spyder so there was room on his lap for her.

"You don't even want to know," Charlie said.

"Don't believe him," Ian said. "He's all talk."

Shelby spotted them and ran to join the rest of her family. She plunked down on Kate's lap, and Ian wrapped his arms tightly around all of them.

"Looks like your lap is pretty full there, Bradshaw," Charlie said.

Ian smiled at Kate. "Nah. I've got the perfect amount of room."

Later, Kate's parents, his mom, and Phillip and Susan lingered at the kitchen table drinking coffee. From across the room, Ian caught Kate's eye and beckoned her with the crook of his finger. When she reached him, he put his arms around her.

"Our beach?" he whispered in her ear.

"Yes," she said.

Shelby and Spyder were fast asleep with no shortage of adults in the house available to do their bidding should they awaken and need anything.

The full moon cast its glow on the water as Ian drove the golf cart past the security building and Rob's bungalow. Their destination was half a mile farther, tucked inside a small cove. It was private, and they were the only ones who were allowed there.

Kate spread a blanket out on the sand and Ian popped the cork on the bottle of champagne he'd brought to surprise her.

"There are no strawberries," he said as he filled their glasses.

"You're slipping, Bradshaw."

"I brought birthday cake instead." He unwrapped it and fed Kate a bite from his fingers.

"Who needs strawberries?" she said as she licked the frosting from his thumb. "Cake is so much better."

They shared the cake, stopping occasionally to take a drink of champagne and exchange sugary kisses. "I'm as sticky as Spyder," Ian said when they were done.

"Then it's straight into the ocean with you."

"Only if you join me."

"I wouldn't miss it for the world." She took his empty champagne glass and laid it on the blanket next to hers. "Take off all your clothes."

He shook his head slowly, as if he couldn't believe her request. "It's always the same with you, Katie. 'Take off your clothes, Ian. Turn around in a circle, Ian.' I'm starting to feel objectified."

She grinned. "I'm waiting."

He stood and stripped off his shirt. Unbuttoned his shorts and let them fall.

"Keep going."

He put his fingers in the waistband of his boxer briefs and they landed on the sand. He gave her a lengthy, three-hundred-and-sixty-degree view of his body. "Stunning, isn't it?"

"Humble as ever."

"Come here."

She went to him and he stripped her of her clothes. Her skin glowed in the moonlight, and he knew it would feel every bit as soft as it looked. With his finger, he traced a path that started just below her ear and ended at the curve of her hip. He took her by the hand and led her into the water.

"Are you happy?" he asked as they floated on their backs in the warm water, their fingers interlocked. He didn't mean only at that moment.

She squeezed his hand. "It's everything I'd ever hoped for."

Nothing was more important than what they'd built together. It hadn't been without its ups and downs, but he felt certain Kate would agree that the love they shared and the life they'd created had been their biggest adventure of all.

THE END

AUTHOR'S NOTE

The amount of research required to write a book with a story line about hacking often felt daunting during the eighteen months it took me to write *Heart-Shaped Hack* and *White-Hot Hack*. By the time I was done, I'd read fourteen books on the subject and filled two binders with information I found online. Not all of this information made it into the book, but it was instrumental in helping me determine how much the reader would need to know.

I was thrilled to discover last summer via an article in *Wired* magazine that hackers had successfully taken over the controls of a Jeep Cherokee while it was being driven. I had already planned for the hacking of Kate's Spyder to play a big part in the book, but it was wonderful to have a resource for exactly how it could be done.

Though I tried to educate myself as well as I could on how various hacks and social engineering assignments could be carried out, I have taken liberties in the name of creative license and/or clarity.

All mistakes are my own.

ACKNOWLEDGMENTS

I am deeply grateful for the contributions, assistance, and support of the following individuals:

My husband, David, because his encouragement means more to me than he'll ever know.

My children, Matthew and Lauren. Thank you for being patient—again!—while Mom spent all that time with her laptop. I love you both.

Elisa Abner-Taschwer, Stacy Elliott Alvarez, Hillary Faber, Peggy Hildebrandt, Erika Stone Gebhardt, and Tammara Webber. Thank you for every bit of your beta feedback, for your encouragement, and for helping me to see what I could not. Special thanks to Dr. Trish Kallemeier and flight paramedic Rick Kallemeier for their medical expertise regarding broken bones and surgical procedures during pregnancy.

Sarah Hansen at Okay Creations. Your talent is immeasurable. The covers for this series are truly my favorites, and I've spent a ridiculous amount of time just staring at them.

Anne Victory of Victory Editing. Thank you for your eagle eye and your words of encouragement. You helped me in more ways than one.

Jane Dystel, Miriam Goderich, and Lauren Abramo. You are truly the trifecta of literary-agent awesomeness.

Special thanks to the book bloggers who have been so instrumental in my ability to reach readers. You work tirelessly every day to spread the word about books, and the writing community is a better place because of you.

I want to express my sincere appreciation to the booksellers who hand-sell my books and the librarians who put them on their shelves.

My heartfelt gratitude goes out to all of you for helping to make *White-Hot Hack* the book I hoped it would be. Words cannot express how truly blessed I am to have such wonderful and enthusiastic people in my life.

And last, but certainly not least, my readers. Without you, none of this would be possible.

ABOUT THE AUTHOR

Tracey Garvis Graves is a *New York Times, USA Today,* and *Wall Street Journal* best-selling author. She lives in a suburb of Des Moines, Iowa, with her husband and two children.

She can be found on:

Facebook at www.facebook.com/tgarvisgraves and

Twitter at https://twitter.com/tgarvisgraves, or

you can sign up for her newsletter at http://traceygarvisgraves.com to receive her latest updates.

OTHER BOOKS BY TRACEY GARVIS GRAVES

ON THE ISLAND
UNCHARTED (ON THE ISLAND, 1.5)
COVET
EVERY TIME I THINK OF YOU
CHERISH (COVET, 1.5)
HEART-SHAPED HACK (KATE AND IAN #1)

CPSIA information can be obtained
at www.ICGtesting.com
Printed in the USA
LVHW030140200422
716645LV00005B/172